To [illegible]

T[illegible]

your support

Enjoy!

Cordelia Hare

Alyda's Bluff

Cordelia Hare

iUniverse, Inc.
Bloomington

ALYDA'S BLUFF

iUniverse books may be ordered through booksellers or by contacting:

iUniverse
1663 Liberty Drive
Bloomington, IN 47403
www.iuniverse.com
1-800-Authors (1-800-288-4677)

Cover landscape photography by Cordelia Hare

ISBN: 978-1-4759-6881-1 (sc)
ISBN: 978-1-4759-6882-8 (dj)
ISBN: 978-1-4759-6883-5 (e)

Library of Congress Control Number: 2012924032

Printed in the United States of America

iUniverse rev. date: 3/11/2013

For Joe

August 9, 1950–July 8, 2001

Always my love,
always my muse

The day which we fear as our last is but the birthday of eternity.

—*Lucius Annaeus Seneca*

Someday, after we have mastered the winds, the waves, the tides and gravity, we shall harness for God the energies of love. Then, for the second time in the history of the world, humankind will have discovered fire.

—*Pierre Teilhard de Chardin*

Acknowledgements

Family and friends mean the world to me, and they are the people who have assisted me and encouraged me throughout the creation of this story.

My parents, Franz and Elisabeth Gehmacher, my sisters and their families, my daughters and their spouses, and the extended family of my late husband, Joseph Hare, have all provided me with safe and happy havens during my life's journey.

Deep gratitude is extended to these ideal readers for their insights: Diane Ablett, Jillian Barteaux, Arlene Gehmacher, Evelyn Gehmacher, Doris Gunnell, Courtney Hare, Crystal Hare, Sherri Hare, Marissa Maitland Hare, Anita Molzahn and Sherry Pulles. Special thanks to Arlene, Courtney, Crystal, Doris, Evelyn, Marissa, and Sherri for allowing me to impose upon them numerous times.

The following people provided me with research information, or accompanied me on graveyard jaunts: Jillian Barteaux, Tom Chillman, Anne and Andrew Clinch, Sharon Guitard, Angeline Hare, Crystal Hare, Bet and Ger Hughes, Twila Robar-deCoste, Nigel Scott, Leighton Watkins, and Audrey Wellwood. I am indebted to them for their support. If I have neglected to mention anyone who merits recognition, I apologize.

A number of books were helpful resources as well as enjoyable reads: *Life How Short, Eternity How Long* by the Nova Scotia Museum and Deborah Trask; *Over The Mountain and Down To The Bay,* a history by the Margaretsville Women's Institute; *Seashores of the Maritimes* by Merritt Gibson and Twila Robar-DeCoste; and *Yester Years at Port George, Port George, Annapolis County* by Sherilyn M. Fritz.

One individual remains to be acknowledged: my beloved first grandchild, Caleb Joseph Maitland. The Caleb of my story was conceived in 2007, and my grandson was born on January 13, 2011. For a time I considered changing the name of my protagonist, but ultimately found that I could not do so. His name was truly etched in stone.

Prologue

November 1885
Southampton, England

I am his child
Do not forsake him
Let not wind or water take him

A MEMORY RISES, luminous as the moon, and asserts itself.

Granmama's hand descends to my shoulder. Head bowed, I lower myself to the floor and grind my knees into the hooked wool of the rug. Shiver as the sateen of her skirt brushes my arm. She seats herself on the edge of my bed and elicits the prayer from me, again and yet again.

"I am his child . . ." It's a simple verse that she has invented, one that possesses the cadence of a witch's chant. But then this night is truly one for the witches, an unholy night of fierce winds and churning waters, and my father's ship has still not entered the harbour.

"Again, Alyda."

"I am his child . . ." I make straight my spine and re-steeple my fingers. I must be strong. Yes, I am his child, and I'll raise my voice to give contest to the elements. It may be a vain notion, the prayer, but I will recite it until my throat rasps for mercy and my knees can take no more; until my father throws his laughter to me from the bedrock of our shore.

CHAPTER 1

June 10, 1972
Fundy Shore, Nova Scotia

Slowly fading, languishing, dying
Like the leaf he passed away
Heeding not our tears of anguish
Heaven has claimed its own today

CURIOSITIES. MR. SWEENEY'S office may be choked to the rafters with them, but only two of them command my attention.

First, there's Mr. Owen Sweeney himself: historian, museum curator, guardian of the old burying ground in our village of Port Carlyle on Nova Scotia's Bay of Fundy. I've known the old man for many years, but can't resist an urge to gawk at him. He's gaunt—a study in angles. Skin glossy and white at the joints; fingers knotted. His eyes, pale grey, are deeply set into a tight-lipped, lantern-jawed head. A few coarse, grey hairs are anchored to the balding skull.

And then there's the book that has claimed the surface of Mr. Sweeney's old oak desk. Large and rectangular, in the shape of an accountant's ledger, it is an artifact of a different era. An odour rises from it, one reminiscent of mud flats in a tidal river basin.

The front cover of the book is missing, but the projection of the back cover gives a glimpse of brown alligator-like skin. The corners are blunted by time, the gilt-edged pages rippling from an infusion of moisture. Within a wreath of faded ivy leaves on the first page, float the alphabetic ghosts of a name that starts with the letter A.

"Alyda," Mr. Sweeney confirms. "The book is damaged beyond repair, but if you insist on doing your first graveyard profile on Alyda Teasdale, it might give you some insight into her character." Amber-stained fingers gesture to the book. "Turn the page."

I don a pair of white cotton gloves to follow his instruction. The die-cut illustration of an angel greets me; it takes up almost all the page. The colours are faded, but it's possible to distinguish that the female angel is clothed in a fur-lined cape and holds a flaming candle in one hand.

"It's a scrapbook," he says. "They were popular in Victorian times."

On the next page, another angel makes her appearance. Clad in a diaphanous gown, she rides a sled of flowers that is drawn by two enormous moths. She is smaller than the first angel and is situated in the bottom right hand corner of the page.

The rest of the page is blanketed in a tidy, slanted script, which has faded to pale shades of promise. Not every word is discernible; by my estimation, sixty to seventy percent of the script can be read at first or second glance. A clause from one of the sentences immediately piques my curiosity: *three forerunners of death made claim to me.*

"How was it damaged?" I ask.

Mr. Sweeney explains that he found the scrapbook, wrapped in a sheath of oilskin, in the rafters of a shed that was once attached to the back of the Whitfield house. Hairline cracks had evidently breached the oilskin over time, and with the development of leaks in the roof of the shed, moisture had seeped in and compromised the sections written in ink. "It's a stroke of good fortune that I found it," he says. "As you know, the house will be torn down soon."

An imposing Victorian two-storey, the Whitfield house has endured more than a hundred years of wood-warping seasons by the Bay of Fundy. It's just a mile up the road from my grandparents' home on the

North Mountain, the northern ridge of Nova Scotia's Annapolis Valley. The house serves as a touchstone for me, a repository of happy memories from my childhood. It's true, however, that its bones are now brittle, fit only for the kindling bin. My stepfather, Jack Tavener, plans to build an inn on the property, and his insurance company won't let him break ground for it until the abandoned house is destroyed.

I glance up at Mr. Sweeney. "Why was the book found on the Whitfield property? Didn't Alyda live right in the village?"

"She did. But the house once belonged to her uncle, a Dr. Joseph Teasdale, and she spent a great deal of time there."

I contemplate the faded script again. "The writing's not about the angel."

"No, it's not. It's her personal diary."

Dismay. I stare at the entry—its idealized angel and the echoes of its orderly script. And as I consider the significance of the loss, a notion begins to take shape in my mind. The surviving words and sentences become beacons in a wasteland. They demand recognition, issue a challenge. "Do you know what this entry is about, Mr. Sweeney?"

"I do." As soon as those words escape him, tension floods his face; he looks stricken by this admission. "I have a source," he finally says. "But I can't reveal the source to you."

That doesn't matter. He knows what the entry is about.

I caress the edge of the scrapbook with a long sweep of my thumb.

Perhaps Alyda's voice has not yet been stilled.

CHAPTER 2

This lovely babe so young, so fair
Called hence by early doom
Just came to show how sweet a flower
In paradise would bloom

OWEN SWEENEY HAS hired me as his assistant while he oversees projects for Port Carlyle's bicentenary in 1973. He's well-regarded as a provincial historian, and work experience under his guidance will enhance my résumé. I had written to him from Toronto early in the spring, pleading with him to create such a position for me: *It's true I left the mountain a long time ago, but my roots there are strong and I'd like to give the village its due.* He had finally consented, citing the gift of a provincial government grant that would cover my modest wages.

The man has never married, and has spent almost his entire life with his mother, Alma, in the house next to his old schoolhouse museum on the Port Carlyle Road. He operates the museum in controlled fashion: interested visitors are required to make an appointment, and numbers can go no higher than ten. He never allows exceptions to the rules.

He has no formal background as a curator, but he completed both undergraduate and postgraduate studies in history at Acadia University. In three consecutive summers during my teen years, he taught me how to catalogue items, set up exhibits, and clean and restore artifacts. And despite our history of working together, he has always insisted on addressing me as *Miss Tavener* and not just *Rianne.*

Yes, the old man is a bit of an oddball, but I've learned to respect his eccentricities.

The Alyda project grew out of my proposal to include graveyard tours in next year's summer-long celebrations. They would take place at dusk, with participants carrying old-fashioned kerosene lanterns. Bony Mr. Sweeney, garbed in the black top hat and sweeping cloak of a Victorian-era undertaker, would inspire awe as a guide. I also plan to provide short biographies of some of the more interesting denizens of the graveyard.

Young Alyda Teasdale will be the first subject of such a profile, provided Mr. Sweeney holds to his consent. Once I'd declared my intention to reconstruct her journal entries, he displayed reluctance in assisting me in this task. He'd be happy to give me details for a conventional biography, he told me; surely no one would expect or need more. He hadn't reckoned with my obstinacy. We batted suggestions and objections back and forth to the point where he could no longer support his own arguments.

"Choose Henrietta Mortimer," he had said, referring to a tombstone with an angel—a white angel with a massive wingspan, playing a broken flute. "That will capture everyone's interest."

It wasn't about the tombstone, I had pointed out. Visitors would gravitate automatically to the more striking ones. What lies beneath is what interests me.

He finally admitted that he had only meant for Alyda's scrapbook to act as inspiration. "We'll have a go at it," he said, "but—" He hadn't finished the sentence; he didn't need to. That last word and its delivery were a caveat. He'll help me with this project, but he'll also manage it to the ultimate degree.

The graveyard tours will take place in Port Carlyle's old burying ground of Ocean's Edge, eleven acres on the western boundary of the village, overlooking the Bay of Fundy. It's not technically a graveyard—that term is reserved for a burying ground situated by a church—but I prefer the word "graveyard" to "cemetery." It possesses heft and an old world cachet.

Put your hand to the latch of the black iron lichgate; listen to it groan as it resists the intrusion. A haphazard tableau meets your eyes: thick gravestones, skinny ones, lurching, leaning, crumbling ones. Stones of soaring elegance or quiet humble footnotes. Works of art, all of them. History placed into context.

In the northwestern corner, like losing chess players pushed to the boundaries of the board, a small cluster of more modern granite stones has staked its territory. Most of these are simple headstones that bear the names of the deceased, the dates on which they were born and died, and short epitaphs. *Forever in our hearts* is a popular one. Your eyes, however, will first be drawn to the Celtic cross of my grandfather's first wife, Adelaide Harris Montgomery—a soaring, eight-foot-high exception to this rule.

In true Christian fashion, all the graveyard's markers face the rising sun in the east, in readiness for the summons on Judgement Day. There are also heathen influences here, most notably the obelisks with their Egyptian origins. Some of the obelisks are true heliographs, their pyramidal points redirecting the rays of the sun. All of them attest to Port Carlyle's prosperity as an important shipbuilding centre in the previous century.

Many of the tombstones exhibit one-line or four-line epitaphs with a religious theme common to the eighteenth and nineteenth centuries: a certainty of departure from this earthly vale of tears to a glorious eternity in paradise. *Her ailing soul has winged its way to one pure bright eternal day.* And depending upon the time period in which they were sculpted, they display symbolic carvings of willow trees or flowers, urns, doves, clasping hands, and trumpeting angels. We even have the carving of a death head from 1773—a skull with enormous wings and a toothy grin.

My first visit to the graveyard took place in the company of my maternal grandparents. I was six years old at the time. Ivory-knuckled, holding onto the crossbar of the lichgate with a death grip, I refused to go inside. I finally admitted I was afraid—afraid of ghosts.

Gramps crouched down beside me. "See those tombstones?" he said. "They're good and heavy and they'll weigh a ghost down, Rianne. You don't ever have to worry about ghosts creeping out." Not too long ago I learned that my grandfather's theory was a belief held by our ancestors.

My initial fear banished, I would join my grandparents at times on twilight strolls among the tombstones. Nan brought flowers from her gardens to garnish the graves of family members. Gramps would perform roll calls of ear-pleasing names in his baritone voice: *Hepsibah Crumie, Euphemia Merryfield, Obadiah Sevens.* How could one ever forget those names?

We were usually alone during our visits, but sometimes Owen Sweeney would be there, seated on a stone bench beneath one of the towering spruces on the western boundary of the graveyard. One leg extended and propped on an old log, a wince birthing at the corners of his lips. He rarely spoke to us, but always inclined his head politely. "Joshua," he would say. "Rachel." During those early years he never acknowledged me.

Mr. Sweeney is one of the promoters of our local legend of the paralysing stone, the recumbent tombstone that marks Alyda Teasdale's eternal resting place. It's a false tomb—a slab large enough to accommodate a body, but one that simply covers the ground beneath which the body is buried. And it has the reputed power to induce numbness in the limbs of anyone who touches it. "Power of suggestion," the sceptics have scoffed. "Too dangerous to take any chances," the advocates have always shot back. In 1955, they planted a hedge of wild roses around the tombstone to protect it from believers and non-believers alike.

Three years after the rose bushes were planted, the sceptics were finally silenced. A villager by the name of Morrie Piper breached the natural fence and bore the consequences. Piper was an eccentric, who always sported a tam and did odd jobs for the people in the village. He had a routine of drinking with his buddies in the village every night and then using the cemetery as a short cut to reach his cabin in the woods. One night, after a particularly boisterous evening of revels, he didn't make it all the way to the cabin. He stomped his way through the young rose bushes and passed out on the slab. In the early morning, when he came to, he found that he couldn't move a muscle in his legs. Two fishermen, checking the weir by the old wharf below the graveyard, heard him bellowing like a wounded ox and scrambled up the hill to his assistance. A mystifying return of the polio he'd had as a child—that was the verdict of the medical community. Everyone else knew better. The stone had finally presumed to show the extent of its powers.

Alyda Faith Teasdale, beloved daughter of Elias and Verity Teasdale, departed this realm on June 3, 1897, aged seventeen years, four months, and eighteen days. Buried with her is a baby, born only a few days before her death and not identified by name or gender. A young Victorian-era mother and a child born out of wedlock: *Both not lost but gone before.*

Her tombstone defeats Mr. Sweeney's argument that I choose a more imposing or interesting marker for my first profile. It may be a simple slab that lacks eye-catching adornments, but its owner invokes pathos and the stone itself plays to village lore. Why would the man be reluctant to showcase it?

To that question and a host of others I'm determined to find the answers.

Chapter 3

My flesh shall slumber in the ground
Til the last trumpet's joyful sound
Shall bid my sleeping dust arise
To meet my Maker in the skies

I THINK OF the Whitfield house and its significance to Alyda as I walk home from Mr. Sweeney's office. And as I enter the side road leading to my grandparents' home, I see a figure in the distance that also represents a connection to the abandoned house.

Tall body resisting a stiff breeze from the bay, Ben Allenby leans against the rural mailbox at the end of his parents' driveway. I feel a sudden rush of pleasure, a slight twinge of apprehension. We were close friends during childhood and throughout most of my teen years, after I had moved to Halifax. The last eight years—my years of going to school and working in Toronto—have brought about a distance that geography alone can't claim.

He'll only be on the mountain for a week, I remind myself. He still represents everything that is good about home.

Ben leans down, skims my shoulders in a brotherly hug when I reach him. I like the scent of him, wet grass clippings and Timberline aftershave. He's tied back his long, raven-black hair with a narrow strip of leather, and he's sporting his signature red *Che* T-shirt and frayed jeans. "I hear you're back for the summer," he says.

"I might even stay into the fall."

Nine years ago, I left Nova Scotia to pursue undergraduate and Master's degrees in English literature in Toronto. I started a career as an editorial assistant in a small publishing firm, and I've since worked for two other companies in the same industry. Like many of my colleagues, I harbour a dream of becoming a writer. That dream has yet to be realized, but it will be nurtured and kept in the forefront as I work with Owen Sweeney.

I haven't seen Ben or spoken with him in almost a year. When I last visited my family during the Christmas holidays, he was in Mexico with a group of university friends, vacationing and studying sea life off the Baja Peninsula. We'll have one week together before he heads to Sable Island to do field work for his doctorate in marine biology.

Ben's heard about the fate that awaits the Whitfield house; he too can't imagine our patch of the mountain without it. We often explored it when we were children and filled it with competitive echoes. I want to pay my respects to the house and conduct one last search through it, and he agrees to accompany me. He understands my love for it, but he's also always willing to play devil's advocate. He points out that we tore it apart over the years, that we never did find anything interesting.

"What about the spyglass?" I challenge him. The brass telescope was an early find, high up on the top of a kitchen cupboard. Ben had laced the fingers of both hands and boosted me up to take a look.

"*One* item of interest in seven or eight years of exploration."

"That's not why I want to go. I like the atmosphere. You know I like imagining things."

"A dead guy decked out in the parlour—"

"Perfect! Pennies on his eyelids—"

"His skull crushed by a crate being hoisted aboard a ship—"

"His broken body lovingly washed and put into its Sunday best by the womenfolk—"

"Who performed indignities on it because he was an evil, abusive old bastard."

"You're warped."

"Oh?" Ben tries to raise his right eyebrow, but it catches at an arrowhead of a scar. The remnant of a wound that I forged with a chip of gravel, cradled by a snowball, a long time ago. "You're going to dictate how *I* imagine events?"

If I insist on bringing the house to life through imagination, I must admit that Ben's version is superior to mine.

"Owen Sweeney knows a lot about that house," I say. "Maybe he'll have some interesting stories for us."

And Alyda Teasdale lived in that house. Its history will soon be revealed to me.

The Whitfield house stands at the end of a dirt-and-gravel side road that runs parallel to the bay and perpendicular to the Port Carlyle Road, the road which links the seaside village to the larger town of Danton in the valley. Only two other houses share this isolated side road: the Gothic Revival farmhouses of Nan and Gramps, and Ben's parents, Kaye and Warren Allenby. The Whitfield house sits in seclusion at the end of the road, close to the edge of the bluff that extends above the bay.

Ben and I begin our walk to the house around seven o'clock in the evening, flashlights and rain gear in hand. It's been unseasonably hot for two weeks, and the blackflies are vicious. Dark clouds will soon amass over the bay. The air is almost palpable, heavy with a ripening storm.

Ben's malamute-coyote mix, Lucy, noses through the ditches as she follows us up the road, fur knotted and matted, mud pearling on her tail. She sports a garland of twisted, winter-defeated grass that coils itself around her muzzle and up behind one ear. Lucy will sit guard outside once we reach the house. We've barred all dogs from the house since the day that Lucy's mother discovered a family of raccoons on the second floor and snapped the neck of the mother. Ben and I managed to scoop up the babies and find them a home in a local private zoo.

Ben's silent as he takes his customary long strides; I work hard to keep up to him. He swats at the blackflies at times, kicks stones into the ditch. I glance at his profile, at the strong outlines of his nose and cheekbones, but cannot read his expression. I ache to talk to him, am almost afraid to talk to him. It hadn't been difficult to establish a rhythm to our conversation a few hours ago. Is he feeling inexplicably shy now, as I am?

The house looms, commands our attention. It is marooned in a sea of wild grasses, naked, its paint long stolen by salt-laden winds. The bay windows of the first level are boarded; the glass panes of the second storey are coated with pollen and grime. The roof sags in the centre, the defeated back of an old nag. A good number of its shingles are missing. They've lifted and flown into the hearts of numerous storms, taking their cargo of mosses and lichens with them. Tonight, a multitude of others will join them.

Lucy flushes a cock pheasant from its hiding place beneath the veranda steps as we reach the back of the house. The bird bursts into the air in a drum roll of frantic feathers, and she pursues it into the surrounding fields.

Ben and I drape our rain gear over the railing. Jack has given me a key to this door, but I can't get it to turn in the lock. Ben tries as well but can do no better. He sends me a conspiratorial grin, leaps to the bottom of the steps, and kneels to the ground. A few seconds later he holds aloft the crowbar that we'd stashed beneath the steps a long time ago.

A hideous eye patch of plywood covers the small window by the back entrance. It's stained and splintered, as if it once provided leverage for a mud-mired vehicle. When Ben pries it back with the crowbar, it groans and then separates from the frame. The house sighs and exhales a fusion of dust and mould. It drifts past us into the weight of the evening air. Ben briefly cups his hand to his nose then slips inside to the mudroom. I follow.

Ben leads the way from the mudroom into the library, with its floor-to-ceiling shelves and built-in ladders. The only object in the room now is a 1958 Danton Motors calendar. It lies on the floor, studded with the imprint of a boot tread, opened to the month of May and its accompanying photo of a turquoise Ford Edsel.

What kind of books did those shelves once hold? Did Alyda enjoy reading, as I do? Did she sit here for hours on end, curled up in a comfortable chair with a favourite book?

We move into the parlour with its high ceiling and elaborate mouldings. I know immediately—sense that he does too—that something has shifted in this room. Our lights train at the same time on a gaping wound in the wall where the fireplace mantelpiece once stood. I remember the elegant white marble structure, fluted jambs on its sides and a simple frieze with a scallop shell in the centre.

"Did Jack have the mantelpiece removed?" I ask, glancing toward Ben. His eyes are dark and recessed, his neck covered in smears from the blackflies he cuffed on our walk to the house.

"Don't know," he says. "He didn't say anything to me."

"The dead guy we talked about—the one decked out in this parlour. If anything terrible had happened in this house, there'd be ghosts. And we've never come across a ghost here."

"Not everyone can see ghosts or sense them."

"Maybe they've been avoiding us."

"Thoughtful ghosts. Live and let live."

Ben sweeps his light to one corner of the room, where a gouge ploughs through the green and white stripes of tattered wallpaper. Five names are barely visible in the boundaries of the gash: Ted MacLeod, Dick Cranston, Gary Upshall, Ben's and mine. Ghosts of signatures. These are the members of the club that Ben and I founded during the summer of '56. We met in the old house twice a week and bickered about everything from our secret password to our agenda. Indulged in antics like *Nicky nicky nine doors,* which I loathed. We disbanded the club at the end of the summer, before we could even settle on a name for it.

At the top of a long rectangular window to the left of the fireplace, jagged strips of lace hang from a rusted metal rod. I ask Ben if I can borrow his Swiss army knife, explain to him that I want to cut off a piece of the old curtain.

"I'll do it," he says. "You won't be able to reach." As I aim my light at a strip on the left, he bends his knees slightly and springs into the air. The knife blade flashes as it tears free a segment of the old curtain. I sneeze as Ben lands beside me and rouses a cloud of dust. The small patch of material that he hands me is soft and ivory-coloured, slightly sticky with grime. I tuck it into the pocket of my jeans.

"I'll get you a bigger piece," he says. Before I can tell him that I'm happy with my sample, he leaps into the air again. He achieves greater height this time, and comes down with accelerated force on the floorboards. I hear a bone-jarring crack, a metallic thud. The skittering of the knife across the uneven floor.

My stomach twists. "Are you okay?"

Ben groans. He's pitched forward, body hunched to the window, his right leg buried beneath a floorboard. The board has split in half with the impact, the edges forming a collar around his jeans. I kneel down and pull back the two halves of the board, twist them free of their moorings. Directing the beam of my light, I see that his left foot is twisted to one side, resting against an angulated pipe on a rusty, metallic surface.

"Put your arm around my shoulders," I tell him. I bend my knees and brace myself. He has a good four inches on me and is packed with muscle from his part-time construction jobs of the past years. I feel him tense up beside me—gearing up the necessary energy, anticipating the pain. To minimize my involvement, he distributes his weight between his good leg and the arm braced against the window sill. Then he hoists himself upward, gasping as the injured leg pulls free. Somehow we both manage to keep our balance. And almost lose it as a broad beam of light slides over our shoulders.

A bolt of fear as the light pins us to the walls, and then the wash of relief as I recognize the cadaverous angles of Mr. Sweeney's face.

Ben, slumping against me, raises his head with effort. "Thank God you're here," he says to the old man. "Rianne needs help."

The wind moans softly around the corners of the Allenby house—a shy mourner inviting us to share in its grief. I feel anticipation in my gut, a familiar tingling throughout my limbs. A storm on the mountain is a welcome event.

It's ten o'clock at night, two hours since Mr. Sweeney surprised us in the house. He didn't ask us what we were doing there, nor did he explain his presence. He had immediately offered to stay with Ben while I ran for help. Lucy, returning from the pheasant hunt, had refused to accompany me. She had stayed in front of the house, stiff-pawed and stubborn. Howling to make one's blood sing while I had sprinted to fetch Gramps and Warren.

It was Kaye, on shift as a nurse at the out-patient department of the Danton Hospital, who brought us the news that Ben had fractured his ankle. "Well, Ben, you've gone and done it," she'd said, showing us the break on the x-rays. Kaye is short and plump, always crackling with energy. She sounded cheerful, almost congratulatory, as if he'd finally achieved an injury worthy of years of exploits.

Ben now rests in an old recliner at his house, on the veranda that looks out to the bay. His casted foot is supported on a matching footstool. Lucy, still distressed by this change in her master, props her muzzle beside it.

Rain drums on the rooftop, rattles the metal gutters. I've stationed myself at the west corner of the house, with a view to a row of sugar maples planted decades ago as a windbreak. Limbs grotesque in the darkness, they gyrate to the commands of an invisible choreographer. A low, heavy branch from the lead maple snaps off and plunges to earth. A second branch quickly follows in its wake. And then another branch—long and slender, its corona thick with leaves—spirals across the yard toward the house. I step back with a start as it collides with the screen just inches from my face.

Ben laughs. "It's going to be a good one," he says.

Thunder growls in the distance as I retreat to the end of an old wicker sofa. Its cushions are damp with salt spray, but that doesn't matter to me. I have a perfect view to the bay, to the ribbon lightning dancing on the water. To the bolt of lightning that suddenly strikes the lookout tree, a huge spruce that Ben climbed as a child to view the bay and the countryside around him. Fire—a burning spear of fire—drives down the length of the trunk, splitting the tree into two halves that pulsate with flashing lights. It is over within seconds. Did it really happen? As soon as I turn to Ben and see the outline of an ear-to-ear grin, I know that it did.

The rolling thunder culminates in a jarring crack. I jerk like a marionette; Lucy leaps up, growls. Ben sweeps his hand over her head and along her spine; she settles to the floor of the veranda again. We all sit quietly then, surrender to the remaining explosions of thunder as the storm crests the house and starts to move inland.

"Your last job," Ben says to me. "Nan told me you were excited about it when you started a few months ago."

I grimace. "I was, at first. I liked my boss and my co-workers, but my work space was the size of a broom closet. And that title of editorial assistant—let's just say it was always open to interpretation."

"Did you let them know you weren't happy?"

"I didn't talk to them," I admit. "It was a small operation, probably on its last legs anyway. I can't see how they would have been able to change things to my liking."

"City the size of Toronto, there must be lots of other opportunities. I'm surprised you'd come back to live here for a while."

The wind tears a section of rain gutter from the top of the house and sends it clattering down the roof of the veranda and onto the lawn. It gives me time to work out a response. "I like it here," I finally say. "I loved living here when I was a kid and then coming back in the summers."

Ben shakes his head. Does he not believe me? "You'll feel isolated," he says.

"I can always escape if I need to, but I'll be busy doing my projects for Mr. Sweeney and spending lots of time with Gramps and Nan. And Jack's invited me to give him suggestions for the inn. That appeals to me."

"We can do some catching up as well."

Guilt flares. I've neglected our friendship during the past few years, stinted on letters and phone calls. Most of the time I've received news second-hand through Nan or Gramps. "Tell me about Sable Island," I say. "What's your team going to be doing there?"

"Collecting skin tissues from the carcasses of whales and dolphins." He pauses for a moment, as if he's gauging my level of interest. "Then we'll start doing molecular genetics studies with them."

"Explain that to me."

A long period of silence. "I will," he finally says, "but not tonight. Brain's fuzzy from the Demerol."

The lamplight in the room behind us flickers and dies. There is peace in the profound darkness, in the extinction of every light on the mountain.

Ben's the one to finally break the silence. "I'd say that was a nine out of ten."

"Agreed."

His silhouette begins to emerge from the darkness. "Hopefully we'll see more of those over the next few weeks."

My conscience, my skin—both prickle with anxiety. Ben will now be here for several weeks, if not for the entire summer.

How will I contend with that?

CHAPTER 4

In peaceful slumbers here we lie
Remote from care and vanity
Till the blest morning of the just
Reanimates our sleeping dust

I LOVE THE morning after a thunderstorm on the mountain. The world, no longer cowering from the storm's fury, has stabilized its footing, regained its rhythm.

Cool. Calm. Clean. Those are the words that define "after the storm" for me. I *feel* these words as I lie in bed, listening to birds initiating their morning activities, sensing the sun's patience behind the blinds.

A chainsaw starts in the distance, a sinister buzz that quickly heightens to the crescendo of an angry swarm of hornets. Soon another one joins the chorus. This one is closer to the house, and its sound is raw, nerve-jangling. There will be no peace after this storm. In a twist of anxiety I rocket from the bed, snap up the blind, and look down the road to the front of the Allenby property. I exhale in relief. Against all odds the lookout spruce is still standing, its trunk a charred but defiant spear to the heavens.

The sun streams into Nan's kitchen through half-opened blinds, paints bars on the burnished pots and pans that hang from the ceiling. A tea kettle hums on the stove, and the room brims with the scents of crushed berries and rising dough.

At one end of the butcher block table sits an abandoned plate with traces of congealed egg yolk and a few burnt hash browns. Gramps has no doubt gone to help Warren with the post-storm clean-up. As he always does, he has left me half a grapefruit, its segments all neatly excised from the pith. I clear away his dishes, sit down at the table, and dig in.

The tea kettle starts to whistle as Nan, morning newspaper tucked under one arm, strides into the kitchen. Barefoot, toenails painted in screaming red. She is a kaleidoscope of colours in a paisley blouse and a flowing, floral-patterned skirt. Today, her long, silver hair is constrained by a bandana.

She pitches the paper onto the table and whisks the shrieking tea kettle away from the stove, over to a large mug that features a motif of blood-red poppies. The mug suffers from a hairline crack near the handle, but she's stubbornly refused to retire it. She holds the kettle high and pours a continuous stream of boiling water onto an Earl Grey teabag. As always, I steel myself. Once again, the mug holds.

Nan finally joins me at the table as I'm chasing the last drops of grapefruit juice onto my spoon. Her facial skin glows with a Nivea sheen. She's a walking advertisement for the product: the wrinkles that fan out from nose to cheeks—like ripples from a stone dropped into a pond—are subtle.

Opening the newspaper to the obituary section, she quickly scans it. Her eyebrows arch then swoop down like two seagulls converging on the same morsel of fish. "Oh, my soul," she says, "Here's Robbie Ketchum's already. *Died tragically and unexpectedly.* I'll say! He downed two quarts of Jack Daniels and parked himself in one corner of the walk-in freezer in his father's butcher shop. Can you imagine coming across a scene like that? Everyone's saying he did away with himself, but come to think of it, what proof do they have that he did? Maybe he was disoriented and wandered into that freezer by mistake. Now, if he'd gulped down rat poison, the way Harold Early did when he came back from the war—"

"Nan? I'm at the door now, easing my feet into an old pair of running shoes. "I've got to go, okay?"

"Go?" She peers at me over her reading glasses. "Go where? What's the rush?"

"I'm off to see Owen Sweeney, to talk about next summer's graveyard tours."

"And you think Owen is going to allow strangers to march around his graveyard?" Nan's eyes narrow to a sceptical squint. "That graveyard is his baby. A couple of years ago he wouldn't even let the Scouts camp in the woods outside of the graveyard on Halloween night."

"Cubs, Nan. Young boys."

"My point, exactly. Have you forgotten those little monsters that burned the tool shed to a tidy crisp a few years ago? You just watch; those tours might not be like anything you imagined."

I hide a smile as I shrug into a light jacket. "There's lots of time yet. Right now I'm just interested in getting my story on Alyda Teasdale going."

Nan shoves the newspaper aside. "You know, I'm not sure I like your idea of poking around in that girl's past."

"Why wouldn't you? There may be an interesting story to go along with that legendary tombstone."

Nan pulls a face. "We're all entitled to our secrets," she says.

"Wait a minute. You just told me things about poor Robbie Ketchum that I'm sure he would never have wanted publicized."

"That's just *gossip*. God knows I've been the source of it in my day, and it's perfectly acceptable in our little circle up here on the mountain. But when you've been dead as long as Alyda Teasdale has been, you've earned your rest."

My grandmother's perspective compels me to stop and contemplate. Should Alyda be granted the secrets that she carried in her short life? Implicit in that notion is respect, and it's difficult not to heed that.

Nan interrupts my thoughts. "This is about your mother, isn't it?" Her voice has lost some of its edge.

"No." It's not something that had occurred to me, at least not at a conscious level. I'd be in a better position to test her theory if my mother were here. An ER physician with expertise in drug addictions, she recently flew to the Northwest Territories to help set up a new treatment centre in Yellowknife. She'd committed to this stint before learning about my plans to come home for the summer.

I consider offering Nan a counter-argument to her gossip theory, presenting a case of the importance of history and the lessons to be learned from it. I know she won't listen, however. Nan always considers her logic eminent, and she always stands her ground.

Today I'll stand mine as well. Perhaps it's now an instinctive response to Mr. Sweeney's resistance, this need to discover all I can about this young woman.

The graveyard lichgate is still gleaming with moisture as I approach it. Dead leaves, forced into flexibility by the storm, are woven into its wrought iron design. A bough from the spruce closest to the gate dangles, swings in the light breeze. I twist it free.

A note on the museum door brought me here; Mr. Sweeney is assessing the damage inflicted by the storm. I survey its effects—sodden newspapers draped over gravestones and collections of branches huddled together like beaver dams. A few of the downed branches from the apple orchard on the north boundary still look sleek and healthy in mocha-tinted puddles.

The tangled fence of rose bushes around Alyda's grave has escaped major damage. Extracting a wad of Kleenex from my jacket pocket, I crouch down to remove mud splatters from the brass plaque staked into the ground at the head of the grave. It bears the same epitaph that is etched into the surface of the slab, a six-line elegy that is difficult to read when the rose bushes are in full bloom:

Beneath this stone lies more than one
Who saw too soon life's setting sun
Alyda here is softly sleeping
Her brief pilgrimage is o'er
And she bade her young babe join her
Both not lost but gone before

"You're single-minded, Miss Tavener. I've got to hand that to you."

I turn to greet Owen Sweeney. He's wearing a black cable knit sweater with a chest pocket, fingering a pack of Export 'A's that rides the pocket's rim.

"She *bade* her young babe join her. Have you ever wondered what that means, Mr. Sweeney?"

He slots the cigarette pack back into its pocket, peers at the epitaph. "The word 'bade' bothers you, does it? It comes from 'bid,' which means 'to offer' or 'to invite.'" He steps back now and cocks his head as if to give himself a new and helpful perspective. "I can see the problem, because it implies that our baby here could make a choice."

"That's what I thought at first. And it doesn't make any sense, of course. But I took a medieval English course once and I remember learning that the word 'bid' can have a stronger, more literary connotation. It can mean 'to command' or 'to order.'"

"You're suggesting she was actively involved in her baby's death?"

"No." I'm taken aback by his question. "How could I? I don't know anything yet about the circumstances of her death." I look directly into those grey eyes. "But you do, don't you?"

"Sometimes it does no good to speculate."

What is he trying to tell me? Does he not know? Is he being coy?

He toes the ground at the base of the plaque. "It's this epitaph, then, that sold you on Miss Teasdale as a candidate for the tour?"

"Yes. I think people would be interested in the history implicit in it. Think about it, Mr. Sweeney. Here she lies for all eternity, a single mother from the late Victorian era, a time when illegitimate births were still scandalous. What led to the pregnancy? Who was the father of the baby? How did she cope with being a young, unwed mother in the fish-bowl of a village?"

"It sounds as if you're already rehearsing pitch lines for the tour."

"You might not have all the answers to those questions, but anyone who visits her grave would be thinking about them." I pause, hold his gaze. "Don't you agree?"

He's not convinced; that's immediately apparent. And I realize at the same time that Nan is right: this project does hold a personal element for me. Like Alyda, my own mother became pregnant at the age of sixteen. And she still hasn't given me the answers to all my questions.

"We'll see," Mr. Sweeney says. "And now, if you'll excuse me—" He removes the pack of Export 'A's from his pocket and shakes one of the cigarettes free.

"I'll help you with the clean-up."

"No need. The groundskeeper will be arriving soon."

"You can't use the extra hand?"

He pauses for a moment, then nods his thanks to me and consigns the cigarette to its pack again. In all the years I've known him, Mr. Sweeney has never smoked in front of me.

As I fall into step with him, I have one last question: "You don't believe in the legend of the stone, do you?"

It doesn't take long for him to respond. "Ah, legends," he says. "That's what makes life tolerable, isn't it? That there's always more than meets the eye."

Chapter 5

Father, farewell, thou art happier far
Than we who linger here
Thou art a bright and shining star
While we are mourners here

The old lookout spruce was magnificent until the lightning bolt attacked it. As a child, Ben used to scamper up and down it with the ease of a monkey, ignoring the pleas of his elders.

And then came the day when he insisted that I go to the top with him. I was thrilled that I'd been singled out for this honour and worried sick that I would lose Ben's respect by declining the invitation. I was terrified of heights.

"You first," I said, my mind scrambling for an excuse that wouldn't invoke scepticism.

Ben hoisted himself to the lowest branch and started his ascent. Branches sighed and bristled as he co-opted them into leverage. He was close to the top in what seemed like seconds. "C'mon up, Ree!" he whooped.

I placed my hand on the tree, listened to its heartbeat as I tried to ignore my own. Resin bled from the bark, imprinted sticky tattoos on the arc of my palm.

Ben called down, "I can see the keeper on the island! He's just walked out of the lighthouse." He was looking out to the Isle of Haute, ten miles from the mainland.

"Liar! There's no way you can see that far!"

A branch snapped. Ben laughed. I hunched over instinctively, but the branch came to a stop somewhere above me, snared by its kin.

"You did that on purpose!"

He laughed again, didn't deny it. "What's keeping you?" he shouted.

My legs weighed a hundred pounds apiece; they would never be able to draw me up. "Stop shaking the tree!" I pleaded, as a shower of needles flew by my upturned face.

The vibrations finally subsided. I peered up through the branches. A flash of yellow—Ben's T-shirt—taunted me. It was at least a mile away, maybe two. I raised one hand, clamped it on a lower branch.

"Ruby Ree! Don't chicken out on me!"

I swallowed. I started climbing.

I would do anything for Ben.

The tree looks intact from a distance, as if the spectacle of a week before was only an illusion. But when I enter the field and approach it from its south side, I see the effect of the lightning strike, the long and hideous scar where the bark has been blown away.

Ben sits at its base, his eyes closed, his back leaning into the trunk to one side of the split. His cast rests on one of the exposed roots. He's positioned himself for comfort, but his body radiates distress. The blackfly bites on his neck are starting to heal, but there are dark smudges beneath his eyes, and his skin is as pale as a moth trapped in moon glow.

He's beautiful, and I could stand there and look at him for an eternity.

Beautiful. It's not an assessment one would make of me. I'm the owner of pleasant blue eyes, a "ski-slope" nose that calls too much attention to it, and lips that could use a helping of generosity. Call me a tall, scrawny redhead (shade of claret wine) with feet at least one size too big for my body.

I don't understand what Ben once saw in me.

I'm surprised now that he hasn't sensed my presence. "Hey," I finally say, almost in a whisper. His eyes fly open. In the shadows below the branches, their steel-blue hue is subdued.

"Our tree survived," I say.

He shakes his head, straightens his body out of its slouch. "We don't know yet. With that deep gash it'll be exposed to insects and disease and be more vulnerable in the next storm."

"I'd hate to see it go."

I lower myself to the ground and support my back on the other half of the damaged trunk. It must be my imagination, but it still seems to emanate warmth from the fire.

"How's the foot?" I ask.

"Still hurts like hell at times. Go ahead, distract me."

The ground beside me is thick with ancient needles. I scoop up a palm's worth, watch them disintegrate as my fingers curl forward and crush them. Release them in a shower to the packed earth again. "I've finished the first Alyda passage," I say.

Ben leans to me, gently turns my right hand. Old bruises fan out from an anchoring blackfly bite in the centre of the wrist. They look like mirror-image pansies, royal blue fading to yellow. "What happened here?"

I shrug. "You know how it goes. You bump into something, but you're busy at the time and you don't remember doing it." It's the same account I gave to Nan.

He waits. He's angling for a different explanation, but he's not about to get one. "I'm going to run the passage by Mr. Sweeney this afternoon."

He relents, leans back against the trunk of the tree again. "I was wondering what you were up to in the last few days."

"I've been going down to the library in Danton as well, doing research on the late Victorian era. I don't want to do just an abbreviated biography of Alyda. I want to expand it to include descriptions of life in the village at that time. Customs, industry, political and cultural climate—"

Ben's eyes absorb more light. "Your first book," he says.

"Don't tell Mr. Sweeney."

"Is he being helpful? He didn't hold back, did he?"

"No, I don't think he did. He reconstructed the events for me and gave me some good insights into Alyda's character traits. I just want to make sure the passage is as close as possible to the original entry."

"Mr. Sweeney's source could probably help you with that. Let's try to find out who it is."

I shake my head. "If his source is a person, he would probably be even more protective of it."

"You're not curious?"

"Yes, of course, but right now I just want to focus on writing the passages. And things will get easier as we go along. The early entries suffered a lot of water damage, but the ones further away from the water source are almost intact. They give me a good sense of her writing style, and I'll be able to keep referring back to them."

Ben shifts his weight, leans to pull one of his crutches to him. "Let's go up to your place, then. I'd like to take a look at this scrapbook."

"Wait. It's at the museum, locked in one of the desk drawers in the main office." I laugh. "You know Mr. Sweeney. You don't think he'd trust anyone other than himself with it, do you?"

He settles back against the tree. "Maybe he will, over time."

"No, he's always one to exercise control. He won't even give me an overview of Alyda's life right now. He's decided that we're going to go through the whole scrapbook, entry by entry, in the order the journal entries were written."

"Why?"

"I have no idea. Just part of the whole control thing, I guess." I rise to my feet, dust needles from the seat of my pants. "I'm going to head over to the museum now to show him that first passage. Wish me luck."

"You won't need it. You never do."

Wind-driven shadows move across Ben's face. It strikes me again how tired he looks, almost woeful. "That wasn't much of a distraction," I say.

"Go."

"I'm sorry I wasn't around much this week. I just wanted to get this first passage under my belt."

He grabs one of his crutches, stabs it in my direction. "Go," he says. "I mean it."

"Read it to me."

"*Read* it to you?"

"Yes." Mr. Sweeney hands my notebook back to me. He hasn't even opened it.

I clear my throat. Quell a flutter in my belly. Clearly, I've decided that something is at stake here. Mr. Sweeney eases things for me by closing his eyes. I begin:

One thousand months: If we live to see them, we have achieved a grand old age. We are virtual ghosts then, our hair snow white and scant and our skin leached of colour. Our bodies float, withered and sere, on a sea of goose feathers. We may not hear the three loud knocks, may not see one of our weary loved ones break vigil to greet the caller, only to find that no one is at the door.

The forerunners of death do not present themselves to everyone. But yesterday, on a night of wind-driven snow and breath-snatching cold, a ship foundered off the western tip of Ile de Haute, and three forerunners of death made claim to me.

It was a quarter of an hour before midnight that the bells of St. Luke's came to life. They jolted me out of my sleep; ice fingers squeezed my heart. Sibley and I emerged from our rooms at the same moment, our whispers clouding into frost in the bitter air. We went into Mama's room; she was struggling to rise, but we urged her to remain in bed. She was still recovering from an infection of the lung, and it wouldn't do for her to breathe in the night air.

Shaking and shivering, Sibley and I forced our limbs into sealskin jackets, capes and boots. I gasped as I stepped outside and the frigid air stole my breath away. The wind-driven sleet pellets stung my cheeks. Sibley hunched her shoulders and drew her cape over her mouth.

Already several villagers were down at the shore, their lanterns delicate beacons in the driving snow. Sibley and I were not yet at the water's edge when a shout was taken up; the lanterns had pierced the darkness and they now revealed a small boat. The wind hurled it onto the shore, mere seconds before another skiff joined it.

"Laliah B! *They're from the* Laliah B!"

Sibley sounded a sharp cry and gripped my hand beneath my cloak. "It can't be, Allie," she said. The ship was not due home for another two days.

I heard them, scant seconds before I saw them: the clash of iron-shod hooves on the rocks of the shore and lungs pumping like the bellows of a blacksmith's fire. And when the three white horses rounded the curve of the bluff, they did not break pace. They soared over the survivors in the boats, over those wretched men glistening with ice frost. Then they disappeared into the night, scattering musk in the bone-chilling air, hoof-beats echoing. And when Sibley and I joined the villagers and helped to remove each one of the hollow-eyed crewmen of the bark, we could not find among them the one face that we sought.

Papa had not made it to shore.

Mr. Sweeney's pale grey eyes will not meet mine. He fixes them on an antique map of Nova Scotia on the wall behind me. His Adam's apple twitches once, twice.

The forerunners of death do not present themselves to everyone. I want to ask him if he's ever seen any, but I can't summon the nerve.

He still won't look at me. I've felt self-conscious of my effort from the start and now I'm filled with doubt. "Mr. Sweeney, tell me what's wrong."

"How could there be anything wrong, Miss Tavener?" He finally directs his gaze to me. "This is your project, and I trust that you'll continue to do a good job."

A good job. "What I want to know is whether it's true to Alyda."

"It's true," he says. "And it's good." Something lies deep in his eyes. An echo of pain? Of mourning?

"It's more than good," he concedes. "But this reworking of Alyda Teasdale's passages—it goes beyond what we first discussed. I've gone along with your idea of the graveyard tours and the mini-biographies of some of the villagers buried there. And I'll continue to supply you with the information you need about Alyda—on one condition. I'll have final say on whether any of the journal entries are included in the biography."

"That isn't fair." The protest slips out before I consider its potential for a negative impact. But how can I argue against this proviso when I haven't been completely honest with him? I'm determined to test my book-writing skills with Alyda's story, and the journal entries are critical components of that story. The biography would suffer without their inclusion.

Mr. Sweeney's lips have compressed, almost vanished.

"It's my condition," he states. "And I presume you accept."

CHAPTER 6

The voice at midnight came
He started up to hear
A mortal arrow pierced his frame
He fell but felt no pain

THE SKY IS a montage of tangerine and crimson as Jack and I leave the house at seven o'clock this morning, equipped with Thermoses of coffee and a bag filled with Nan's blueberry muffins. Our destination is Halifax. Jack has an appointment with the architecture firm contracted to do the plans for the inn; my mission is to research the sinking of Captain Elias Teasdale's barque the *Laliah B.* at the Maritime Museum of the Atlantic.

It's a two hour journey into the city, and I spend most of it dozing, chin tipped to my chest and feet propped on the dashboard. Slipping in and out of consciousness to the aroma of coffee and the murmurs of a talk show on the radio. I'm still in a fog when Jack's hand lightly brushes the top of my head. "Your stop," he says. He hands me my Thermos, and I take a few sips of tepid coffee before entering the Citadel branch of the museum.

A variety of resource materials are soon stacked in front of me, but I can't yet bring myself to look up the *Laliah B.* Nibbling one of Nan's muffins on the sly, I peruse statistics, newspaper articles, photos and illustrations of dozens of ships that were lost off the shores of Nova Scotia between 1859 and 1896.

A lithograph of the sinking of the *S.S. Atlantic* mesmerizes me. A passenger steamer, she struck the Golden Rule Rock off Mosher Island, near Halifax, at three o'clock in the morning on April Fool's day, 1873. There were 954 passengers on board; 562 of them perished in the biggest ocean liner disaster before the sinking of the *Titanic.*

The Currier & Ives print depicts the ship listing in a churning sea, its deck jammed with passengers. A rope, with several passengers clinging to its length, runs from the ship to land. About a dozen people, faces frozen in fear, struggle in the water close to shore. Some of them are women, being pulled onto the rocks by heroic rescuers. But here's a frightening fact: not a single woman survived the accident.

The cited "cause of event" was an error in judgement. Unfamiliar with the coastline of Nova Scotia, the *Atlantic's* captain and officers took few precautions in stormy waters in the dead of the night.

And Captain Teasdale? Did he play a role in the sinking of his ship? Finally, I give my attention to the *Laliah B.*

There is only one photograph of the three-masted barque, taken two days after the storm. I search the materials again, hoping to find a photograph or illustration that depicts the vessel in its prime—sails filled by the wind. But I'm left with only this: the *Laliah B.,* listing to the shore in the icy waters, already stripped of her sails and rigging. The ship is surrounded by several small boats. Legitimate salvagers? Or looters?

I read two newspaper accounts about the disaster and an excerpt in a book on provincial maritime history. The newspaper accounts refer to the ship as a *bark*—the same spelling that Alyda used—and the reference book, written almost forty years after the sinking, calls it a *barque.* In none of the accounts does Captain Teasdale's conduct come into question. An outage in the lighthouse beacon of Isle of Haute, however, contributed to the tragedy. The blizzard drove the barque onto the rocks of the island's western shoals, Quaco Ledge. Fourteen crewmen crowded into two small lifeboats and first tried to reach the island, but high winds coerced them to the mainland, ten miles away. There was only one fatality: Captain Elias Teasdale.

Can you see my father that night? He is the one standing at the helm of the Laliah B., *his hair and moustache lacquered with ice, his lungs rasping for air as he shouts orders to abandon ship. Gale's winds slam into the* Laliah B. *from above; they have just snapped her main-mast as easily as they would a matchstick, and now the rocks of Quaco Ledge attack from below, gouging grievous wounds into the hull. There is no recourse; my father must see to it that he and his crewmen gain the beach-head of Ile de Haute.*

As befits his rank and station, my father is the last man to leave the vessel, and as he descends on a rope to the lifeboat, he loses purchase and plunges into the water. He surfaces briefly, gasping for air; surely he must see all the anxious hands extended to assist him, feel briefly the clasp of his first mate, Myles Handley, but then a wave of mighty proportion sweeps him up and dashes him against the hull of his ship.

Do you judge it unseemly that I write of my father's death in such a way? Do you think I am a ghoul for indulging in these details? If so, you do not understand—I must be there with my father.

"I had him," Mr. Handley said. "I had him." His voice was hoarse, his words broken by a wracking cough that made me fear he would yet be a victim of the tragedy. Three days he had been out of the water, but he still smelled of brine, as if his skin were drenched in salt spray.

Aunt Helen took his hand and said to him, "You mustn't fret so, Mr. Handley. You did all that you could." Her voice was soothing, her words but a variation of those spoken earlier by Mama. Sibley, Mama, and I have all tried to comfort him, but he becomes more agitated in our presence and so we now maintain our distance.

"He feels he's failed you," Aunt Helen said. "He cannot bear to be reminded of it."

No one holds Myles Handley responsible for the outcome save Mr. Handley himself, but Aunt Helen is right: the poor man is devoured by guilt.

Can he not understand that the cold robbed his hands of agility, that the power of a wave generated by a winter storm exceeded any strength that his battered body could marshal?

Does the man subscribe to the notion of predestination? Does he believe that our Lord has already deemed him to be one of the saved or one of the damned? Such an infuriatingly simplistic notion it is, pre-ordaining not only that an unfortunate such as Mary Ann Nichols should stray into the path of Jack the Ripper but also that our Joshua Slocum should circumnavigate the globe in a vessel far more fragile than the Laliah B.

I cannot believe for one moment that God elected Myles Handley to fail my father. Nor that he chose my father as a sacrifice to that storm.

I cross the room and sit down beside Mr. Handley. I slip my hand into his.

Before we leave the city, Jack takes me to see the blueprints for the inn. The architectural firm is located in an old fieldstone building close to the harbour. The blueprints are displayed on a drafting table, in front of a huge window with a magnificent view to the water. There are different sheets: floor plans for each storey and an artist's sketches of the building's exteriors. Jack's head is bent to these, his tonsure reflecting the light of the afternoon sun. The tip of his tongue massages the lining of his right cheek as he pores over the documents. It's a habit that surfaces whenever he is excited. When I was younger, I always wanted to knuckle that cheek into submission. Now I find it endearing.

Jack has ensured that many of the features of the Whitfield house will be reflected in the inn: three-sided bay windows, a tower on the northwest corner, and a widow's walk with a wooden railing. He's hired designers to incorporate elements such as chimney pots and the intricate dentil trim around the eaves, and he's even commissioned a local artisan to create stained glass sidelights for the front entrance.

There will only be one working fireplace, Gramps having spelled out the impracticality of feeding and maintaining the three units of the initial design. The inn's mantelpiece was to have been original—the white marble one that had stood in the parlour of the Whitfield house. The gaping hole that Ben and I saw the night of his accident had been left by the thieves that had torn it from its moorings.

"Can you imagine how it would have livened up the front drawing room?" Jack says. "I felt sick when I found out it had been stolen."

He tells me that the thieves removed the boards from the bay window and set up a ramp to the sill. It would have taken considerable time and the right equipment to remove such a large and heavy fixture, and they escaped notice by choosing the day on which Nan and Gramps and the Allenbys had gone into Halifax to say goodbye to my mother. It galls to know that locals must have done this, people on the mountain who knew of the existence of the fireplace and were aware of the schedule of the two families that lived on the one road to the house.

"Somebody must have seen something," I say now. "Nobody noticed a strange van or truck pulling out onto the Port Carlyle Road?"

Jack shakes his head. "I got the police involved, but so far they've had no success. That mantelpiece is probably long gone from this province.

And these people are unscrupulous. They broke into two other houses on the mountain the same day, houses that were known to have antiques. In one case, an elderly widower was tied to his bed for hours as they took away everything of value."

I think of Owen and Alma Sweeney, experience a sense of relief that they were not victims of the home invasions. I tell Jack about Mr. Sweeney's connection to the Whitfield house—his knowledge about one of its former owners, Dr. Joseph Teasdale.

"Owen came to me about three weeks ago," he says, "and asked if he could have a key to the house. He must have wanted to have one last look around, just like you did."

"Did you go with him?"

"No. I offered, but he insisted on going alone."

"I wonder if he discovered Alyda's scrapbook that night. He told me he found it sometime ago in an old shed that was once attached to the house, but I wonder now if that's true."

"Why would he lie about that?"

"If he found it more recently, you could claim ownership."

Jack frowns. "I'm not about to ask Owen Sweeney if he's taken something from my property."

"No. I know you can't. It's a strange feeling, though, knowing that Alyda's scrapbook might belong to you. To *us*."

He shakes his head, smiles. "Owen Sweeney's a good historian and he loves his village. Look at it this way: the book is in good hands."

I am his child / Do not forsake him / Let not wind or water take him

An anguished child and a prayer repeated at least a dozen times. The winds abated, the ship limped into Southampton harbour with its crew in sound health, and my devout grandmother smiled a knowing smile. My father and I would see eleven more years together.

Dear Granmama. I do miss her terribly. She could be daunting at times and send my younger cousins scurrying to the skirts of their mothers, but I understood from a young age that she was but an actress, nourished by drama and invigorated by its excesses. She was grateful that I was never cowed by her presence. I always wear the gold locket that she gave me as a keepsake before we sailed for Nova Scotia. It now holds a folded piece of paper with Papa's signature upon it. I wish I had a twisted lock of his hair to accompany it.

I am his child . . . *The fate of the* Laliah B. *destroyed the prayer's hypnotic beauty and promise. If Granmama were here now, she might claim that the prayer didn't exercise its power because I didn't call upon it. I could not have known, however, that my father's ship was imperilled in the storm this week past.*

Would it have made a difference? I suspect it would not have. I am no longer a child, and the prayer has become an annoyance, a constant recitation that pokes my mind and refuses to come to a conclusion. Such are my nerves that they are frayed to the quick.

I cannot even calm myself to pray for peace of mind.

Alyda prayed to God to spare the life of her father.

For years, even though I'd not been brought up in a churchgoing household, I prayed to the Christian God of convention and asked that He send my father to me. I knew nothing about my father. Mom had made it clear to me he was off limits as a subject, and Nan and Gramps refused to give me answers they said were my mother's to give.

Head bowed at my bedside, hands clasped in entreaty, I gave my father a physical reality. I'd decided early on he had to be skinny and a redhead, and that's where Ginger Hebblethwaite came in. Ginger was a literary character, a protégé of flyer James Bigglesworth in the popular Royal Air Force adventure series to which Ben introduced me. He may not have been the main character, but he was highly intelligent, a runaway, and a scrapper—all qualities that appealed to me.

And so, on the day that Mom told me she was going to marry Jack and that she would finally tell me about my father, I almost turned her down. How could anyone, real or otherwise, compete with Ginger Hebblethwaite?

Mom chose Nan's garden as the place to tell me her story. We sat on the frayed webbing of two old lawn chairs, facing each other, beside an arbour of tea roses. She'd put on a pair of sunglasses to protect her eyes from the mid-day sun. A bumblebee droned in the roses.

"What was his name?" I asked.

"Greg."

"Greg? That's it?"

"I don't remember his last name," she said. "That's not important, is it?"

I was speechless, fury trapped in my throat. A blush stole across her face. She crossed her legs at the ankles, hugged her arms to her chest. Leaning forward, she launched into her story then. She told it at an almost breathless rate.

She had spent the summer of '45 with her mother's parents and other members of the Harris clan in Boston. Mom's cousin Margot, who was two years older than her, was working as a counsellor at a summer camp for physically disabled children. Mom sometimes volunteered at the camp, and that's where she met Greg. He was twenty years old and had just returned from the war. A rear gunner, he'd been shot down over France and had lost the lower half of one leg. "He was a volunteer as well," Mom said. "I guess he was there as inspiration for those kids." For the first time I detected some warmth in her voice.

"*That* night—" she continued. "Really, I don't know why it happened. I wasn't swept away, you know. Margot egged me on, I guess. And I was curious."

I held my breath, enthralled now by the story. It was as exciting as anything I'd read in my secret stash of *True Confessions.*

Mom shifted in her chair, removed a leaf from her shorts. Now irritation flashed across her face. "I don't know why you want to know all of this. He didn't mean a thing to me."

Gut-punched, I could only stare in disbelief. He didn't mean anything to her? Did I?

"I don't want to hear another word," I spat. I jumped up, stumbled against my lawn chair as I turned to run back to the house. I first kicked it aside, but then I booted it again, made it sail like a broken box kite and pitch onto Mom's lap. She didn't look at all upset when she batted the chair to the ground; the expression on her face was one of profound relief.

I resisted the introduction of Jack into my life. I was twelve years old by then, and that would have been expected of me. And I wanted to punish Mom. The truth, though, is that I liked Jack from the start. He was kind and attentive, and somehow I knew it wasn't a front. He cared about me.

Maybe I still had that desperate yearning for a father, but it was easy to love him.

Chapter 7

Asleep in Jesus blessed sleep
From which none ever wakes to weep
A calm and undisturbed repose
Unbroken by the last of foes

My hair—that strident red hair. I've come to appreciate its distinctiveness, but it has elicited comments over the years.

Such a shame it isn't auburn or chestnut. A great-aunt, never renowned for her tact.

There's not much you can match to that, is there now? A clerk in a department store in Halifax—not the adventurous type.

Some lucky girls are born red. Others catch up. A stranger at a cocktail party in Toronto, citing the Clairol slogan in a cowardly aside.

And then there was Ben's perspective as we celebrated two feet of freshly-fallen snow one winter's day. He was eight; I would have been six. Under a dazzling sun I threw myself on my back into the snow to sculpt an angel. My hat flew off, and he pointed at me, shouting, "You should see your hair, Ree! It's on fire!"

As I struggled to sit up, shuddering as clumps of snow slid down the back of my jacket, he continued, "Ruby Ree! Yeah, you're a Ruby Ree, Ree!" And then he stomped around me in circles, chanting: *"Ruby Ree, sittin' on a flea! Ruby Ree, buzzing like a bee! Ruby Ree's got a Band-Aid on her knee!"*

Ruby Ree hung around for a few years. I don't remember the complete rhymes anymore, but I do know that no two endings were ever the same. And when Ben started taking guitar lessons, he expanded his repertoire beyond the nursery school-like rhymes: *Ruby Ree, don't you turn on me!* Or *Ruby Ree, ya gotta set me free!* Strumming with a flourish, ending with a wicked grin. If I showed any sign that the rhymes put me into a snit, they were intensified. But he knew not to invoke *Ruby Ree* in the presence of others.

He stopped using the nickname when Mom married Jack, and I moved to Halifax with them. Flurries of *Ruby Ree* over the years and then silence.

I missed them.

How I completed the examinations, I do not know. Mama, however, has always been a superb teacher, and the moment I succeeded in banishing the hurdy-gurdy of Granmama's prayer from my mind, I was able to apply the necessary attention. My scores are well above those required for university entrance. I favour Dalhousie, for it would give me the opportunity to live with Aunt Jo and Uncle William.

It was a cold day on the mountain today, so bitterly cold that the community skate on Ezra's pond was cancelled. We all spent the morning in the kitchen, warming ourselves by the stove and the fire. I put rags in Sibley's hair again (she loves her curls but they are difficult to summon!) and then I joined her in a game of Chinese checkers. Eventually, Mama and I enjoyed tea together—a souchong, well-steeped, and a good accompaniment to our cranberry scones. The wind off the bay rattled the window panes in the scullery, but the fire in the hearth crackled in cheerful defiance of the elements.

Conversation turned to my plans for the future. Mama would like me to enter teaching, but I've long dreamed of being an author, the likes of Mr. Dickens. I would not, however, rule out Medicine, despite its challenges. During the service last Sunday, I witnessed Uncle Joseph perform a tracheotomy on young Henry Burrows. A piece of apple, hastily swallowed, lodged in the poor boy's windpipe, and no amount of pounding by his pew-mates could dislodge it. To my dying day I will not forget the fear radiating from him, eyes straining in their sockets, the sweet surrender to relief as the blade cleared the passage to his airways. If only one could live day to day with such a transcendent awareness of life!

"What of your future, Mama? Do you plan to return to teaching?"

"Return to teaching?" Mama looked genuinely surprised. "I may no longer have a husband, but as a woman once married I now have a different station in life."

"You needn't subscribe to convention."

Mama stacked our dishes, and then brusquely pushed herself away from the table. "What will become of society if we don't adhere to certain conventions?" she said.

It did not take me long to counter: "And what will become of society if we don't at times learn to break free?"

It's a cold and miserable day on the mountain, and Ben wants company. I run in a slanting rain down the road, dodging puddles and adjusting my umbrella to wind direction. By the time I hit Ben's doorstep, my runners are squelching and I'm soaked to the skin from the knees down.

"Just a quick game," Ben says. The soapstone chess board is already laid out on a small table in the living room, its pieces in their starting positions. He's perched on the edge of a love seat, his foot newly casted and propped on an old ottoman. He's feeling better these days. It turns out that the original cast had been too tight, and Kaye had finally convinced him to go to the hospital for a new fitting.

My socks and runners abandoned on the veranda, I embed my feet in an old pair of Kaye's slippers. "It'll be a speedy one," I agree, pulling up a chair to the table. "I'm not going to give you much of a challenge."

"Take your time," he says. "You can beat me if you take your time."

"I haven't played in ages."

"I'll bring you back up to speed this summer."

I shake my head. "I've never enjoyed it as much as you do. I didn't come back to the mountain for chess."

He has the first move and his fingers are resting atop a knight. "Why *did* you come back to the mountain, Ree?"

"You know why. The bicentennial celebrations. Jack's inn, too."

He releases the knight, glances up at me. "You didn't have to come back right now. The bicentenary is still a year away and the inn's not even started yet."

It's not difficult for me to address his argument. "I'd been away from the mountain too long. It was time to come back."

Ben moves the knight. "How's Haddon?" he says, not looking at me.

It's the question I've been expecting since my arrival on the mountain. He's asking about Paul Haddon, the boyfriend that I left behind in Toronto. My ex-boyfriend.

The first time I brought Paul to the mountain, two years ago on an Easter weekend, I was excited about introducing him to everyone. There was no doubt in my mind that he and Ben would develop a close friendship. They had pastimes in common: basketball, backgammon, board games like Risk and Diplomacy. Similar interests in fiction: books by Huxley, Orwell, Kafka and Walter Miller Jr. Paul displayed a touch of arrogance at times—it served him well in his profession as a criminal litigator—but Ben's someone who is entirely at ease in his skin, and I knew he would hold his own. The entire weekend was programmed to be an enjoyable one for me.

It wasn't. Ben and Paul circled each other with a cool and wary politeness from the beginning. Both of them made numerous, almost ludicrous attempts to isolate me from the other. Ben suggested that a city *boy* would not enjoy a hike to the "ovens"—a series of caves carved out in the bluffs along the shoreline west of the village. Paul maintained that we rarely had time for each other in Toronto and that I alone should take him to my favourite haunts on the shore. "Do we have to spend every waking hour of the holiday with him?" he said.

"He's like family. And I'm here to see family."

I endured three days of skin-prickling discomfort, paralyzed by my inability to confront either Ben or Paul, and I returned to Toronto with an ill-defined, yet profound sense of loss.

"How's Paul doing?" Ben asks again. "Is he coming down this summer?"

"I broke up with him."

Ben's eyes dance. "When?"

"Just before I came down."

"About time, wouldn't you say?"

I glare at him. "You've never liked him, right from the start."

He shrugs. "He wasn't good enough for you, Ree. He wasn't *ever* going to be good enough for you. I'm glad you finally figured that out."

"You don't have to be condescending."

The look on his face is amusing. *What? Me?*

"You can let me know what you think," I continue, "but you don't have to be insufferable about it."

He ponders the accusation. "Point taken," he finally concedes.

I turn my attention to the chess game. There's no way that I'm going to win.

Christmas 1895—it was the first one without Papa and his boundless enthusiasm for the day's rituals. No tree of pink silk roses and feathered birds graced the parlour. No boughs of greens adorned the mantelpiece. Papa's gift from Granmama, sitting next to the ormolu clock, remained unopened; Mama couldn't bring herself to unwrap it.

We were meant to go to Halifax, to spend the holidays with Aunt Jo and Uncle William, but an ice storm two days before Christmas brought all life on the mountain to a standstill. Glittering ice coated the roads and the rooftops, every tree branch and stalk of vegetation. It gave new and astounding dimensions of power to sunlight, but created an unbearable burden for its hosts. Sinister beauty!

There was no church service today, no rousing renditions of Christmas hymns for which Sibley and I had practised days on end. Sibley and I played cribbage and I read a great deal in Papa's chair by the fire. Mama's joint of beef was a bit over-salted but tasty, and we enjoyed our Christmas pudding.

At the end of the day, I freed a large, ripe orange from my stocking. I peeled it, gritted my teeth as its acidic juices invaded a tiny cut on one of my fingertips. The flesh of the fruit was perfect—tart and teasing to the palate. I closed my eyes and stayed mindful of the explosions of flavour, one after the other, and of the juice slipping down my throat.

Papa can no longer experience these worldly pleasures. I will do that for him, tenfold, if need be.

Paul Haddon reminded me of a child at times, a child that required constant attention. At his worst, he would interrupt me when I read for enjoyment. He respected my need for quiet when I read books or texts for the workplace, but as soon as I curled up with a work of fiction—a highly anticipated pleasure for me—he would initiate a conversation or start firing trivial questions at me.

On the day that I'd told him I was considering spending some time in Nova Scotia—coward that I was, I couldn't yet bring myself to make a clean break—he joined me in the living room late in the afternoon. He'd gone to the office to put in some work for a few hours. Even though it was a Saturday and he wasn't seeing any clients, he had dressed for work, and he'd still not changed into anything comfortable since coming in the door.

He soon eased himself into the armchair, draping one leg over the low arm. I met his gaze briefly, sent a pleading message for peace into those unyielding discs of amber. Strange, flat eyes—a foreign currency. Had I truly once been attracted to them?

"What is it between you and Ben?" he said.

It was not the opening line I'd expected. I reluctantly closed my book and looked up at him again. At least he'd taken off his suit jacket and loosened the tie. "What are you talking about?"

"There's something going on between the two of you. I can't put my finger on it, but it's there."

"There's nothing going on. Ben's a good friend."

"A *good* friend."

"Yes. We're close, because we've known each other since we were kids and—"

"And?"

"That's it. We're friends."

"You're not thinking of going back to Nova Scotia because of him?"

"No, Paul." I felt weary, liquid to the bone. "I haven't seen him in almost a year, and I've barely spoken to him."

"But you write to each other."

"No, we don't. Stop it. I'm *not* on a witness stand and you're *not* cross-examining me."

He smiled then. It was a brittle effort, but it was a smile nonetheless. "Good enough," he said.

I returned to my book. "That's the last I want to hear of it."

He unknotted his tie and rose from the chair. "You've got yourself one summer down there," he said. "Max."

I wring out my socks and stuff them into the pocket of my windbreaker. Shivering, I guide my bare feet back into the running shoes. Just one game of chess with Ben has driven away the rain; I telescope my umbrella back to its portable form. Through the living room window I see Ben hobble off the couch, use the furniture to support his way to me. "What can I do to make you stay?" he says.

"There's nothing." I put my shoulder to the screen door.

"I'll let you win next time."

I give the door a nudge.

"Wait. I'll make you a grilled cheese sandwich. Real shaved cheddar, with tomato slices, of course."

"No more talking about Haddon."

"Hell, no. That would be unappetizing."

I remove the first runner, then the other. Ben grins. He puts an arm around my shoulders. "Take me to the kitchen," he says.

Chapter 8

Affliction sore long time she bore
Physicians came in vain
The Lord was pleased to call her home
And take away her pain

My feet, staked to ruts carved long ago by farm machinery, absorb the vibrations of the machine advancing up the road toward me. I frame the Whitfield house and its shrubbery in the viewfinder of my Pentax. Frail as any centenarian, the house appears to be sleeping. Perhaps it is stoic.

One viewpoint is never enough, of course. I catch a burst of sunlight from a metal brace on the railing of the widow's walk. Sweep to the ancient lilac bush. Capture the stone-ledged window in the tower on the northwestern corner. It is open to the elements and a narrow sheet of plastic, snagged on a nail on its sill, flutters in the breeze like a pennant. Or a signal of distress.

I see disconsolation. Pride, too, not forgotten. And my heart constricts. Yes, the Whitfield house is old, but it does not deserve its fate. It's an historical artifact. It should disintegrate over time, on a schedule imposed only by the winds of the bay.

The excavator comes to a stop in front of the house, ends its ominous song. A brand new "Cat" from the John Deere dealership in Danton, its painted metal is obscured by a veneer of road dust. It is soon joined by a two-man tanker truck from the Fire Hall in Danton. On my walk to the house I had seen the firefighters pumping water from the pond that lies midway between my grandparents' home and the Whitfield house.

The machine operator jumps down from the cab. Smoke drifts towards his eyes from a cigarette that is anchored in the socket of a missing tooth. He nods toward the camera. "You takin' pictures for *The Sentinel*?"

"No. They're for me." I collapse the tripod, return my camera to its case. "Don't take down the lilac bush."

Bemused, the man shakes his head. The cigarette, close to its end, twitches between his lips. "No promises," he says, "but I'll see what I can do."

The vantage point that I choose to view the demolition is a large boulder in the field in front of the house. It's a volcanic throw-away, one that has resisted the efforts of a long line of farmers to extract it from the compacted soil of the North Mountain. Like the roof of the house that it faces, it bears multiple badges of lichen. I settle myself on its highest point, watch as the firemen direct a sweeping arc of water over the house for dust abatement. I commit the house to a final memory.

The operator climbs back into the machine, drives the excavator to the eastern side of the house, and then lines it up as if he is facing an opponent in a duel. Light pulses as he takes one last drag on his cigarette and drops it to the floor of the cab.

He drives forward, nudges the wall with the giant bucket. Above the din of the machine the house groans. He backs up the machine then drives it with full force against the wall. There is the sound of splintering, of fibres disconnecting and disintegrating. A shudder echoes through my body.

The machine retreats. Eternal seconds go by, captured in shimmering water from the hose of the fire truck. And then the bucket of the excavator rears up like the neck and head of a primeval beast. It plunges down through the roof, taking a chimney in its wake, and eviscerates the floor of the attic below it. Shingles, splintered wood, and plaster cascade to temporary shelter one level below. The bucket soars again, this time through pulsing water, swings to the right, and clangs against the iron brace of the widow's walk. Echoes reverberate across the field.

Every muscle in my body tenses, prepares itself for the next impact, as the excavator retreats.

The machine operator breaks into a grin; he performs a "thumbs up" for me before he lines up the excavator again. He executes one push, the bucket grazing the roof of the veranda. Large shards of glass skitter down from the dormer window on the second storey. The columns of the veranda buckle first, and sections of its roof follow suit, sighing as they slide into the empty spaces below.

I can't watch anymore. Hunched over on the rock, I sit there, my body coiling into tension as I listen to blow after blow on the house. Absorb the incessant whine of the machinery. I'm unable to watch, yet incapable of abandoning the house. And I cannot stop thinking of Alyda. She spent time there, hid her journal on those premises. I've travelled the corridors that she once roamed.

The silence that descends almost two hours later is oppressive. I look up; the initial work has been done. The house has been reduced to a giant's game of pick-up sticks. My neck and shoulders are throbbing; my bottom is numb. The machine operator crouches outside of his machine, tying the laces of one boot. One of the firemen tilts his throat to down the contents of a Thermos.

A blizzard of seagulls wheels in from the bay and circles above the house. Strangely, the birds are silent. One of them lands on a rock close to me, its wings retracting into tidy storage by the side of its body. It fixes a passive, chilly-eyed gaze on me. "Vulture," I say to myself. "You won't find any pickings in these ruins."

As I descend the boulder, a movement in the thickets of the tree line at the back of the Whitfield property catches my eye. A young woman, clad in a white blouse and a dark, toe-length skirt, steps out from the bushes and looks to the remains of the house. I squint, shade my eyes with one hand, but I can't discern her features.

No, the sun must be playing tricks on me. It's not a woman. It is a man, and as he starts to walk the property line, his gait is immediately familiar to me. One leg constantly strives to catch up to the other.

I wonder which vantage point Owen Sweeney had chosen as he watched the destruction of the old home.

Deep snow and ice and a hush to the world, and life still urges me on. I am sixteen today and the grateful recipient of a three-tone sketch of Papa that Aunt Helen drew for me. I marvel at the warmth in his brown eyes (deep brown like the rain-soaked earth of summer in Aunt Helen's garden), the stubborn cowlick, and the lower right eye tooth that doesn't regiment itself to the others.

Next to this sketch sits a mountain of die-cuts for my book. I professed appreciation to the gift-givers, but in truth I have already grown tired of these angels! Insipid creatures they are, all of them, with their wide-eyed innocence, rosy cheeks and Cupid's bow lips. They beg dismissal. Give me male angels, ones that possess defined muscles and jaw lines that articulate purpose.

I recall such an entity in Granmama's compendia of sculptural works, depicting a Fallen Angel statue in a rose garden in Madrid's Retiro Park. I gazed at it for a long time, awed by its splendour and power. Lucifer contorts, back arched, as serpents coil themselves around his body. Locks of his hair sweep upward to the heavens, as does one of his wings, and his mouth gapes in anguish. Now, there is an angel for these pages! I must ask Aunt Helen to duplicate this drawing or perhaps devise another one—the archangel Michael in triumph, foot grinding into the neck of Lucifer before he hurls him into Hell? I hope she will oblige me!

Mr. Sweeney leans back in his chair and massages his neck with his fingertips. He's dressed for work: a crisp white shirt, a tie with diagonal black and grey stripes, and grey pants with sharp creases as if they've just been taken off the rack at the store. It always amazes me when a heavy smoker is fastidious about his personal appearance.

He mentions not one word about the demolition of the house.

"I want to know more about the Whitfield house," I say. "You said that it belonged to one of Alyda's uncles?"

He tells me that Alyda's Uncle Joseph was the identical twin brother of her father, Elias. Older brother William, the owner of a rope manufacturing company in Halifax, preceded the twins by almost ten years. All the brothers were successful and well-to-do. Alyda's father had married into money in England; his wife Verity was the only child of the prominent Tew family, owners of dockyards in the port of Southampton. He had also built a successful shipping business on his own and owned three ships: a schooner, *Grace Adelia,* and two barques, the *Athena Majora* and the *Laliah B.* After moving back to Port Carlyle from England, he concentrated on transporting consignments of cordwood to ports along the northeastern coast of the United States.

Joseph, the elder of the twins by several minutes, graduated from Dalhousie Medical School and served as a physician to a large number of communities on the mountain and in the valley. He married Helen Fales, the daughter of a dry goods store merchant in Danton, in 1871, and the house was commissioned by Joseph Teasdale Senior as a wedding gift for his son and his bride.

"And Helen and Joseph lived in the house for many years and passed it on to one of their children?"

Mr. Sweeney shakes his head. "They didn't have any children. Helen was a very frail woman. She'd had polio as a child, and Alyda, who was close to both her aunt and her uncle, spent time at the house as Helen's companion on the days that the housekeeper had off. And in 1897, soon after Alyda died, the Teasdales moved to Toronto so that Helen could receive the most current treatments for her condition."

Dr. Teasdale did not second-guess his decision to leave Port Carlyle; he sold the house to the richest man in the village, Angus Whitfield, owner of the village fish cannery. He was married to a local girl, Fannie, who died suddenly in 1923, thrown from a horse that was spooked by a pheasant. After the accident Angus purchased a smaller home in the village and turned the house on the bluff into a boarding house for workers at his cannery. And when Angus died in 1937, the house was passed on to a nephew, a stockbroker in Toronto. This is the man from whom Jack purchased the property.

I may be finished my studies for the time being, but books of another sort continue to be my salvation. To escape my woes I have only to curl my body into Papa's leather arm chair in the parlour and enter into another world. I will do my chores on time and I will forego a day of reading on Sunday, but everyone now knows not to disturb me when I am in the chair.

*Late last week, I came home from a round of errands to find a rattan reception chair, a hideous thing, grotesque as a giant praying mantis, smugly occupying the space that Papa's chair had once held. Papa's chair—*my *chair— was no longer in the room at all. Frantic, I raced about in search of it and finally found it wedged by the woodpile at the bottom of the garden, a cobweb already spun from one end of the head roll to an armrest!*

"I'm redoing the parlour," Mama told me, "and your father's old chair reeks of tobacco."

"Let it," I said. "It smells of heaven to me."

When Mama left the house to run her errands, I employed the Tattington twins (the lads are of the same build as Papa's chair) to help me restore the chair to its original position. It cost me a bruised foot and a raid on my piggy bank (bribes for the boys), but those were small prices to pay. As for insect chair, I wasn't so cruel as to evict it to the elements, but I did banish it to a dark corner of the drawing room.

"You are rabid, Allie," Mama said, her eyes signing distaste at the sight of the chair. I thought she would force her will again, but she allowed me my victory.

Indeed, I am rabid. Someone must still champion the rights of Papa!

After years of indulging my imagination, I finally have a history of the Whitfield House. The skeleton now has some flesh, so to speak.

"The Whitfields never had any children?" I ask.

Mr. Sweeney shakes his head.

"Did the nephew keep the boarding house going?"

"For two or three years, yes. He planned to move into the house on his retirement, but when his wife dug in her heels and refused to leave the grandchildren in Toronto he started neglecting it. A house of that size requires a lot of upkeep. He may have had money problems of his own, or he might have decided that the house was no longer worth the investment. In any case, you know the ending to this story. It didn't take long for your father to negotiate a good price for the property."

"There were never any young children in that house."

"Not unless they were visitors."

I think of all the incursions that Ben and I made over the years, the fun that we had exploring the house. "I always imagined children running around in it," I say. "I guess because the house is so huge, designed for a large family. Kids would have loved it."

He nods. "It's interesting from a statistical point of view, this business of no children. Think about the odds, especially at a time in history when the birth rate was high."

No children. I feel a pang of disappointment. I think of the scenarios that I have established over the years, the people of my mind that have populated the house. But before I can make any adjustments to my fantasies, Mr. Sweeney says, "There *may* have been one. Not technically a child of the house, but one for the statistics."

His lips break into a half smile. "Alyda Teasdale may have given birth to her baby there."

Chapter 9

A husband dear, a father kind
Virtuous on Earth, to death resigned
Here rests his body in the tomb
To lay till Jesus breaks his gloom

Nan and I participate in a breakfast meeting of the Women's Institute of Port Carlyle in the bowels of St. Luke's. There are only eight ladies in attendance, all of them sixty-plus, comprising a group that has seen considerable erosion over the past decade. I've met these women in the past at museum functions, and I like them. Fueled by a platter of scrambled eggs and baby sausages, I propose a resurrection of *A History of Our Village.*

The first edition of *A History of Our Village* appeared in 1876. The softcover books were updated and republished every five years and finally discontinued at the outbreak of World War II. I have a tattered copy of the first issue, as well as the other three that belong to the late Victorian era, courtesy of my great-grandmother, Sadie Walker Montgomery. Gramps retrieved them for me from a trunk in the attic.

Expecting the ladies to embrace the project as if it were a beloved and long-lost relative, I'm surprised when our postmistress, Willa Adams, says, "I don't see the point of bringing these books out again. Our heydays as a shipbuilding centre are long gone, and we stopped printing them because there just wasn't any interest any more. I'll bet most of them ended up as kindling for the fire."

"But this will be a special edition," I argue. "The bicentenary celebrations will attract more tourists to the area. And so will the Tavener Inn."

"Is that what we want?" Willa says. Her eyes, dark and intelligent, dart above a thin, hooked nose. "Do we want to be another Peggy's Cove?"

"Of course not," Nan says, waving a hand in dismissal of that notion. "Anyway, we're too far off the beaten track for that."

Willa's face is clouded. It occurs to me that Jack may need to make an exclusive pitch to some of the locals. I had assumed that the inn would be welcomed for its job opportunities and hadn't taken into account that there might be a resistance to change.

After the ladies have replenished their cups of tea, I say, "The inn will be a venue for special events like wedding receptions and business retreats, but my father is also hoping to attract tourists who love the beauty of this shoreline and the history of its villages. For those guests we'll have a copy of your book in each room. Some of these copies will disappear, but into travel bags and suitcases, not into the flames of a fire."

"That depends, of course, on the quality of the book," Nan says, avoiding Willa's eyes.

Willa bristles, rises to the challenge. "How dare you suggest—"

I smile, sit back with my fourth cup of dark and pungent Orange Pekoe tea.

Today our postmaster sent me a conspiratorial grin that told me it was here. He did not produce it from behind the counter, however; he knows from previous experience my desire for privacy. I've not yet grown accustomed to small town mores, the incessant need of the village biddies to feed one another's curiosity. I nodded politely to Mrs. Hudson and Mrs. Aylesworth, noted members of the Women's Institute; the latter fashioned her mouth into an O of surprise when I left without uttering a word. Under any other circumstance I would have engaged her in conversation. She bears a striking resemblance to Granmama, and for that reason alone I will spend time in her presence. Not today, however.

I did not go far. I waited round one corner of the building until the two dowagers departed, and then I slipped back inside to greet Mr. Ellsworth. He could not conceal his pleasure as he handed me a large brown envelope.

"You'll not find me doubting the outcome," he said. "Number two ranking in the county, wasn't it?"

It's true; I performed well in the entrance examinations, but I presumed that I was only one of many throughout the province who did so.

I held the envelope to my chest for a moment, trusting its flimsy shield to support my thumping heart, and then my fingers somehow found the way to prise the flap and release its single sheet of paper. We are pleased to inform you . . .

"I'm accepted!" I exclaimed, and Mr. Ellsworth was immediately beside me, pumping my arm and shouting his congratulations. I beamed at him and held the letter to his eyes so that he could see for himself. He looked ready to sweep me up in a jig.

I'm accepted! I'm admitted to the undergraduate Arts programme of Dalhousie University for the school year of 1896/97.

The meeting with the Institute ladies behind me, I pay a visit to Gramps in his spacious work shed. He's tinkering with the colourful guts of an old record player. A mélange of smells greets me—damp wood chips, gasoline for the chainsaw, the scent of whisky-flavoured tobacco embedded in Gramps's shirt. It's his lumberjack shirt, the red, threadbare one with the Rorschach oil stain on the back that looks like an outline of Australia.

"Old Owen just gave us a shout," he says. "He's got something to show you, but there's no need to rush over right away."

I smile at Gramps's use of the epithet "Old Owen." He's only a year younger than Mr. Sweeney, but at the age of seventy-four he's in remarkable shape—almost six feet of hard-packed sinew.

"Tougher than a boiled owl"—that's how one of his war buddies once described him. His eyes are ice-blue, eyes that make a stranger think twice about crossing their owner. He came home from the First World War with his body peppered with shrapnel and had to give up his job of salvage diving. He became an auctioneer instead, renowned from the Annapolis Valley all the way to Halifax.

We settle into two Adirondack chairs just outside of the garage. Gramps pulls out his briar pipe and a pouch of tobacco from the pocket of his shirt, a signal that he's ready to take a good break. That's one of the things I like about him. No matter what he's doing, he makes you feel that you're more important than the task at hand.

"You and Owen Sweeney are about the same age, aren't you?" I ask him.

He nods, crumbles tobacco between his fingers, and drops the threads into the pipe bowl.

"But you're not friends."

"Not friends, but very good acquaintances. We've given each other a neighbourly hand over the years."

"Why not friends?"

"That's hard to say." He packs the tobacco with his thumb, repeats the ritual. "I'd say he's a bit of a loner. He deals with the public in that little museum of his, but he's an outsider at heart. Probably likes it that way."

"What was he like in school?"

"He didn't go to school." A pause. "He only spent one day there."

"Oh?"

"It's not a pretty story, Rianne."

I wait until Gramps is ready; he knows I'm not going to let him off the hook.

He feeds the flame of a match to the tobacco, finally pulls on the pipe. Then he tells me what happened during the lunch hour of Mr. Sweeney's first day of school. A group of grade five bullies cornered him in the schoolyard and dragged him to the boys' outhouse. They upended him, hauled him up over the bench seat, and then repeatedly plunged his head into the hole. They laughed as he gagged and struggled to free himself.

I'm silent for a moment, horrified by the image of the young boy, inhaling and exhaling fear in the stench of the privy.

"Were the bullies punished?"

"Oh, they got their comeuppance, and the principal did his best to convince Alma that he'd be safe in the future. But she pulled him out right then and there and started schoolin' him at home the next day."

"And he never went back to school?"

"Nope. Alma kept him under wraps. I didn't hardly see him again over the years. Both Owen and his mother kept to themselves."

I think of Owen Sweeney, the constant reminder to him of living next to the schoolhouse, all those years. "How could he stand it, Gramps, living just a few steps away from the school?"

"Ah, but it wasn't the same schoolhouse." Gramps explains that the original schoolhouse was right in Port Carlyle. It was a dilapidated clapboard building, and when it was condemned by the school board at the beginning of WWI, Alma offered a building on her property. The huge shed in which her father had once stored antique carriages was meant to be a temporary site, but somehow the school ended up staying there for two decades. When they closed it down in 1945 and started bussing all the kids to Danton, that's when Mr. Sweeney converted it into the museum.

I ask Gramps how he got to know him at all, and he chews the end of his pipe, considers. "I'd say it was when Owen had his accident. That would've been a good thirty years ago. He was out back of his property choppin' down trees for firewood and when he didn't get home by dark, Alma sounded the alarm. Group of us found him soon after, pinned underneath a tree he'd felled. He was hurt somethin' awful."

Mr. Sweeney was fortunate that the trunk had only fallen on the lower part of his body. He sustained a broken pelvis and multiple fractures in both legs, and was in the hospital for almost five months. During that time everybody on the mountain pitched in for Alma. Gramps used to wait outside while she was visiting with her son in the hospital, but after a couple of months, he too started going up to visit Owen. He would only stay for a few minutes, but that's when he started to get a better measure of the man.

"But he never became a close friend," I say.

"Nope. And there's nothin' there you need to understand, Rianne." Gramps taps the bowl of his pipe against the side of the chair and sends a delicate shower of sparks into the air. "That's what Old Owen wanted."

Is it? I can't banish the image of that terrified little boy. And I can't help wondering if he was too damaged by that childhood incident to ever trust another human being again.

I went down to the shore immediately so that Papa could hear the news from me first. Sibley was next; she uttered a war whoop and lifted me cleanly off the floor. Then she told me how much she would miss me and that she was determined to spend many a weekend in Halifax with me.

Mama was at church, Sibley told me, news that was not surprising to me because she had lately taken to going there every morning. To bring composure to her soul, she explained. I didn't find her kneeling in a pew, however. Her voice, low but detectable, drew me to the sacristy, where I found her and our new rector, the Reverend Mr. Zachariah Hamilton, heads bent with but an inch between them, poring over a book of parish records. There was an air of intimacy about them, and I quickly announced my presence.

Mama almost jumped sideways and looked somewhat discomfited, but recovered as I stated the purpose of my visit. Reverend Hamilton was the first to respond. He marched up to me, clasped my hands, and said, "This is indeed uplifting news, my child."

My child! *I pulled my hands from his and was about to object to his form of address, but Mama came to me and embraced me and so I held my tongue.*

"I knew it!" she exclaimed. "Just think of how proud your father would be."

I asked her to leave with me, to return home so that we could celebrate my good news together with Sibley. She hesitated and looked to the Reverend Mr. Hamilton as if she were tacitly petitioning his approval. I turned on my heel.

Finally I heard the tap-tapping of her footfalls.

For years I saved everything I could for my father, determined that one day he would know me and be proud of me. Nan had an old sewing basket in which she stored my report cards, science projects, crafts and drawings from my art classes at school, and certificates from ballet and swimming lessons. Occasionally, I would steal a representative artifact from Nan's stash and add it to a small suitcase that I had found in the attic. The suitcase—locked with a tiny gold key and stored beneath my bed—became the home for cards, letters and sketches that I created specifically for my father. *Here's a picture of me at Ben's tobogganing party. I was frozen to the bone, but that red nose you see is a bloody nose. I went flying headfirst into the trunk of a birch tree!*

About a year after Jack came into my life, I restored Nan's items to the sewing basket. The remaining ones I hurled into a roaring autumn bonfire.

CHAPTER 10

Earth to earth and dust to dust
Calmly now the words we say
Left behind we wait in trust
For the resurrection day

MR. SWEENEY SLIDES a sepia image across his desk to me. "This is the house to which Captain Teasdale brought his family from England in 1895."

The photo shows a grand home, featuring a five-bay front façade, an enclosed three-sided entry porch, and a gable roof. Tall banks of purple and pink lupines in the foreground indicate it was taken in early summer. All the drapes in the windows are drawn, as if the photographer formally posed the house.

It was in the classical Georgian style, Mr. Sweeney tells me. Built by Jacob Teasdale—Elias's grandfather and the town's most prosperous shipbuilder—in 1803.

Nothing about the house prompts recognition. "It doesn't exist anymore, does it?" I say. "What happened to it?"

I learn that it was lost in a fire in 1911. A flue fire erupted in the adjacent house—another sea captain's home—and high winds fuelled the flames. Both houses burned to the ground in the early hours of the morning.

"Alyda's family? Did they escape the fire?"

"There wasn't any loss of life. But Alyda's family was no longer in the house at the time of the fire. They had even moved out of it before her death."

I wait for an explanation, but Mr. Sweeney is not about to offer one. "Be patient," he says. "It's all in the journal entries."

He smiles at me with the smugness of a master puppeteer.

Foul weather has made prisoners of us for days. Today it was no longer raining pitchforks, and so I saddled Sassie to run some errands. She has always enjoyed high stepping through rain puddles.

At my last stop at Bent's, as I was about to pay for Mama's megrim tincture, a stranger hurtled into the store, chased by a rain-studded gust of wind. His black shirt and trousers were soaking wet, driven to the skin. Beads of water hung suspended from his corduroy hook-down cap.

"Chewing tobacco," he said. He removed his cap and shook his head as vigorously as a dog would. "Two pouches of Beech-Nut, if you have it."

I'd not seen him before on the mountain, this young man with hazel eyes, tilting to green. He had a long nose with a faint dip near the bridge, a firm jaw, and lips that were full. Biscuit-coloured hair twisted and flared below the cap. He must have been four or five inches shy of six feet, but for what he lacked in height I suspected there would be compensation in manner.

Dooley Bent did not move to get the tobacco from the shelf behind him. "Ma!" he shouted, and his mother stepped out from a room at the back of the store. She was covered from head to toe in a dusting of flour. It obscured the patterns of her wrapper and apron, but didn't extinguish the flash of silver near her throat: the brooch of The Christian Women's Temperance Society.

"The Bents do not sell tobacco to minors," she said.

The stranger removed his cap and maintained a level gaze. "I'm not a minor, ma'am. Besides, it's not for me. It's for Dugald Roy."

Myra Bent stepped closer, her face sour and unconvinced. She wiped her hands on her apron but only succeeded in transferring more flour to them.

"Mr. Roy's delayed in the back field," he said. "Weather's slowing him down. He wanted me to get here before you closed the store."

"You're the young man he hired to replace Tip Wiley?"

"Yes, ma'am. Leastways, I don't know who Tip Wiley is, but I'm here for the summer to work for Mr. Roy."

Mrs. Bent sent a brisk nod to Dooley, and he moved to fetch the tobacco. I stepped up now to the counter with my purchase. The stranger's eyebrows rose slowly; the eyes beneath them flashed with appreciation. "Caleb Whitelaw," he said.

I introduced myself. He'd come on foot, I soon learned, and although he did not consider the weather a challenge, he accepted my offer to return him to Mr. Roy's farm. He insisted on driving. But first he produced a pocket knife and slit open the pouch of Beech-Nut. He extracted a small amount with his fingers and tucked it to the inside of his left cheek. Then he turned to me and sent me a grin. "Might not be a bad summer, after all," he said.

To the quick of my bones I sense that a story begins.

Sadie Montgomery's editions of *A History of Our Village* have inspired me to learn more about the village during Alyda's time.

The fifth volume of the series contains several photographs of the village's "new" wharf, and today Ben and I find ourselves occupying a bench outside of the village café, looking out to this structure. It was put into place in 1894, the year before Captain Teasdale returned to his birthplace. Ben and I wonder if it may have been a factor in his decision to return to Port Carlyle. How was anyone to know that there would be few glory years left in the village's shipbuilding and shipping industries?

The wharf has a concrete surface now and it's still a working wharf. Buoys, nets and coiled ropes line its length, and three small boats, stranded by the tide, rub shoulders with it. There are a number of fishing boats that did venture out this morning, and they are pinpoints of efficiency, far out on the water. The lobster pound just down the road from us tosses the sweet scent of fresh seafood in our direction.

"The villagers didn't go out onto the pier on the night the *Laliah B.* went down," I say. "The tide must have been out or the wooden planks were simply too icy to negotiate."

"*They soar over the survivors. Over those wretched men glistening with ice frost.* It's hard to imagine that scene on a day like this."

"You've memorized it?"

"A lot of it stayed with me."

The compliment triggers a rush of pleasure. "I like her style of writing," I say. "It has a sense of urgency. And the way she uses dialogue in the entries makes me think she was practising her writing skills. That she was definitely considering writing as a future career."

"You've got something in common with her."

I nod. "And I feel a connection—a connection to someone who's going through the teenage experience and feels a need to write—"

Ben pounces. "You kept a journal too?"

I hesitate. I don't know why; he's already caught me out. "Yes, I did," I finally say.

"Do you ever look back at it?"

I laugh to conceal a *frisson* of embarrassment. "I got rid of it," I say, as I get up from the bench. "I burned it the day that I moved up to Toronto."

Mama summoned me this morning. "Mary Dockley just paid me a visit," she said. "She claims that she saw a young man, a stranger, *driving our buggy yesterday, and that you were sitting beside him, chattering away as if the two of you had known each other since you were babes."*

That old tattler Mary! I was surprised she hadn't scurried here to fill Mama's ear right after the event. And then Mama's lips pursed in distaste when I explained that Caleb Whitelaw was working for Dugald Roy. Was she condemning Caleb Whitelaw by association? Dugald Roy is a tippler, I've been told, and he has a reputation for lewdness when he's in his cups. He has buried one wife and been abandoned by the second. The gossips on the mountain certainly consider him a worthy target. I have only met the man once and the introduction was perfunctory, and so I've reserved all judgement.

Mama said, "This Caleb Whitelaw couldn't find his own way back to the Roy farm?"

"It had started to rain again. And he was soaked to the skin! Would you want me to have a case of pneumonia on my head?"

Mama allowed herself a smile. "Don't make a habit of rescuing young men from the elements," she said. "I don't imagine you'll see him again this summer unless he comes into the village on a quick errand. Mr. Roy might drink to excess, but he runs his farm as if it's a well-oiled machine and he expects a lot of the men that work for him."

I'm sure that Caleb Whitelaw will not suffer unduly; he'll see to that.

Opportunities for another encounter will arise. I'll see to that!

I slow my steps to accommodate Ben as we cross a stretch of shingle towards the remains of the old wharf. He hasn't brought his crutches; they would sink into the grit. It is slow going for him, and he finally collapses onto a driftwood log several feet from the shoreline. He retrieves some flat stones from the area at his feet and skips them out onto the water. "We should have brought Lucy," he says.

The old wharf was the heart of Port Carlyle's shipbuilding industry for most of the nineteenth century. It was left to rot when it was abandoned in 1894, and a winter gale less than a decade later finally dismembered its remaining planks and cribwork. Its surviving stone ballast eventually formed the clasp of a fishing weir. Two men straddle a horizontal pole on the weir today as they repair the netting. They work quietly, and from time to time they share the amber contents of a hip flask that travels from one back pocket to another. The structure sways gently under the slightest shift of weight.

I contemplate Isle of Haute, its escarpment now rising in a deep purple haze before us. Ben tells me about its inhabitants, those settlers of another century whose only means of communication with the mainland was to build a fire. One fire signalled that all was well. Two fires denoted that someone was ill. Three fires signified a need for help, and four fires conveyed that someone had died. He doesn't know who devised this system. I think of how difficult it must have been for the islanders—how anxiety-heightening—to try to summon aid by lighting three fires. Surely it wouldn't always have been possible, especially in the midst of a raging storm, to get three fires going.

"How do you know this?" I ask him.

"I did research before I went there last summer with my students."

Another indictment of neglect. I feel shame for having forgotten his field trip and for not expressing interest at the time. Gramps had told me about it over the phone, as did Kaye in a letter. Among other things, the group had studied a colony of harbour seals just off the island.

Finally, I say to him, "Would you mind going over there again once your cast is off? I'd like to see where the *Laliah B.* went down, but I'm curious about the island too."

"No, I wouldn't mind going back." He smiles. "You know, there are deer mice there—big, dopey mice that have no fear of humans at all. We'll have a picnic and just sit there and watch them come to us."

I settle back against a rock, return the smile. "You're on," I say.

My summer continues with its promise of being a rich one.

CHAPTER 11

Ere sin could blight or sorrow fade
Death timely came with friendly care
The opening bud to Heaven convey'd
And bade it bloom forever there

BEN AND I are the proud new owners of IBM Selectric typewriters, beneficiaries of office equipment upgrades at the tidal power generating station where Ben's father works. Warren, a bear of a man, propped the door open and then carried both machines into the house, each tucked to one side of his body. "You'll love these darlings," he said before he gave us a lengthy in-service on them.

I haven't started using my machine, but Ben is spending hours every day learning how to type via a manual that Kaye picked up for him at the library in Danton. *The quick brown fox jumped over the lazy dog.* Kaye tests him every day, and if he doesn't achieve the words-per-minute goal that he has set for himself, he increases his practice time. He is encouraging me to improve my typing skills.

"You could type up your Alyda passages," he says.

"True."

"You had to type at your job, didn't you? You must be pretty good at it by now."

"I was an editorial assistant. I mainly did preliminary readings for manuscripts." I did have to type at times, but I don't want to admit to Ben that I never achieved a speed of more than thirty words per minute.

Perhaps I should revisit the whole concept. My handwriting is not reader friendly. It sprawls in all directions, as if it's always searching for a definitive style. It's not indecipherable but it requires a lot of attention on the reader's part.

"Let me know when you're ready to take me on," Ben says, grinning.

I should have known. He's wanted to make this into a competition all along.

I type the first passage of Alyda's story, neck extended and shoulders hunched like a vulture. My fingernails drumming the desk as I wait for dozens of applications of Wite-Out to dry. Convinced that there are few authors left on the planet who write their manuscripts by hand, I also type up the first supplementary passage of information gleaned in my research at the library.

My neck is soon throbbing. I stand up, stretch all limbs. It's time to make another visit to Mr. Sweeney. I have something to present to him.

Mama asked Sibley and me to go to the drawing room after supper; she had news for us. Sibley set herself to her embroidery as we waited, guiding a teal blue thread through the corner of a linen tablecloth. She was convinced that Mama would announce an excursion to Montreal. "Don't you recall that she and Papa promised us a trip there once you turned sixteen?"

"Southampton," I said. "I think we'll go back home."

Sibley was so astonished by my speculation that she drove her needle into the fleshy part of her thumb. "For a holiday?" she said.

"No. I mean for always. What's to keep us here now that Papa is gone?"

"His family is here in Nova Scotia. And you're going to school in Halifax in the fall!"

"Perhaps I shall go to school in England instead. If I do stay here, Mama won't be

concerned about leaving me behind. She knows I'll be in good hands with Aunt Jo and Uncle William."

A pear-drop of blood slid into the basin of Sibley's palm. She dabbed it with the lace edging of her handkerchief. "I will not *leave you behind," she said, her voice trembling.*

"No one is to be left behind." Mama sounded brisk as she entered the room, but something in her voice betrayed frailty. She was wearing her black skirt and blouse, but today, for the first time since Papa's passing, she had adorned the blouse with a circular ruby brooch inherited from a great-aunt in London.

She seated herself beside Sibley on the chesterfield, oblivious to the scene of her daughter nursing a wound with a crimson-patched handkerchief. The brooch glittered as she stroked it with her fingers, and the light captured its facets at different angles. For all that she had told us that the news would be exciting, she now seemed reluctant to impart it.

At last she took a deep breath and said, "I'm to be married again."

My stomach lurched, once and then again as if I were aboard a gale-buffeted ship. There was not a word from poor Sibley; she sat immobile as a statue, intently studying her handkerchief.

I was the first to find my voice and I could not contain the outburst: "Not to Mr. Hamilton!"

"The Reverend *Mr. Hamilton," Mother corrected me. The rebuke was soft, but there was intransigence in the undertone.*

Sibley broke the spell that had kept her in thrall. "But Papa's been gone but four months."

"You don't think that your father would wish us happiness?" Mama said.

"Are you sure this is what you want?" I asked her. "Do you truly believe you'll be happy?"

"Of course I will be happy, dearest. How could I think otherwise?"

Indeed, how could she? Papa is gone, and Mama can now cling to a delusion that will see her though this loss.

My presentation to Mr. Sweeney will have to wait. His mother is missing, having slipped out of the house while he was conducting a tour of the museum. He called Gramps to enlist his help, and Gramps has already been in touch with several villagers to organize search parties.

Alma Sweeney is ninety-one and suffers from dementia. I'm not sure how advanced the disease is; exaggeration is always endemic to small towns. I rarely saw her when I was a child. During my teen years

I caught only one glimpse of her as I was leaving the museum office one day—a ghostly mask staring at me from an upper storey window of the house. When I mentioned this rare sighting to Gramps, he told me that he hadn't set eyes on her in about ten years. "She was a beauty when she was younger," he said. "Hair dark and sleek as coal. Cat's eyes. The kind of green that you find on the first shoots of spring."

Mr. Sweeney tells us that Alma is wearing a blue dress and an old pair of moccasins. He is worried, and I can understand why. The Sweeney property comprises almost two hundred acres and poses risks for an elderly woman. Abandoned barbed wire fencing that is woven into wild grasses. And the yawning cellars of two old homestead foundations.

Alma was only sixteen when she and a young man from the village, Leonard Sweeney, eloped to Toronto. A year later word came back to the mountain that they'd had a child. Her frantic parents visited Toronto twice in that first year, intent on locating the young couple. Alma and Leonard always remained one step ahead of them, moving from one boarding house to another.

I drop Gramps off at the Sweeney home, and then I drive to the general store in the village to pick up a pack of Export 'A's for Mr. Sweeney. He had requested them; I suspect he's been chain-smoking since his mother's disappearance. I buy two packs, and as I return to the car in the parking lot by the wharf, my eyes catch a flash of orange further down the shore.

Six years after the elopement, soon after her parents died in a house fire while visiting relatives in Halifax, Alma reappeared in Port Carlyle to claim her inheritance. Young Owen in hand, but no Leonard in the picture. She did not need to make a living, but she practised as a midwife and herbalist for several decades, as had her mother before her. When Owen was young, she always brought him along to the home of the birthing, no matter the time of day or night. The busybodies on the mountain must have had a field day with her disregard for convention. No one openly shunned her, however; her skills were needed and appreciated on the mountain.

I lean my back against the car and observe the shore closely. There it is again. An exuberant flame. Swift extinction. Down by the boulder that's shaped like a massive, stranded whale. I head in its direction, keeping an eye on it, barely mindful of how my sandals navigate the rocks. The elusive orange teases me one more time and it leads me directly to Alma, shielded behind the boulder.

She is perched on a piece of driftwood, eyes trained to the Isle of Haute. Dressed in a loose shift of turquoise blue and a long, orange scarf that rides the wind intermittently.

She doesn't respond when I crouch down by her and place a hand on one arm. Those eyes that Gramps described to me are slightly clouded but still a striking, bright green.

The coloured glass beadwork on her worn-out moccasins glints in the sunlight. The front stitching of the right moccasin is missing, and the exposed big toe has sustained a cut. An iridescent blue fly straddles it as blood seeps into the sand beneath the foot.

"Mrs. Sweeney, I'm leaving to get your son. He's very worried about you."

The eyes turn to me, struggle to comprehend. And this time she responds. "No! Leo's coming. He'll be here soon."

"You can't stay here," I say gently. "You'll roast in this heat."

"Where's Leo?" She grips my forearm with gnarled fingers. "He said he would meet me here at noon. I got here early so he wouldn't have to wait."

"It's already one o'clock. He can find you later at the house, can't he?"

"No! He said he'd be here. He always comes."

The sun reminds me of its strength by burning hot on my shoulders. I ease her hand from my arm, free my ball cap, and place it over the soft cloud of her hair. I notice for the first time a large beige hearing aid, a bulky metal insect wedged into her ear. At least the cap will give her some protection.

"Mrs. Sweeney, don't move," I say. "I'll go and see if I can find Leo for you."

It takes two men to carry Alma from the shore back to the road. She resists with other-worldly strength, kicking and scratching. She bites one of the rescuers, a sturdy fisherman, on the wrist. It is heartbreaking to see her break down into sobs when they reach the road. "Leo will never find me."

A check-up at the hospital in Danton confirms she is dehydrated, and she is given an I.V. infusion of liquids. The cut in the toe doesn't require stitches, but antibiotics are prescribed to stave off possible infection.

Mr. Sweeney phones us that evening to thank us for our efforts in finding Alma. He tells Gramps he has arranged for a high school student from the village to help keep an eye on his mother for the rest of the summer. The student will also perform light housekeeping duties, and that will give him more time in the museum.

Could he not have asked me?

May 1, 1896. It took place today, less than six months after Papa died. A widow should fulfill a year's mourning, but when I brought this to Mama's attention, she slyly replied that there are times when one must ignore convention. I then begged her to at least move the date forward, for June is a propitious month for a marriage. She refused to listen to me. Marry in May and rue the day. *She seems determined to bring unhappiness upon herself.*

It was cold today, cloudy and raw, as we met in the parlour of the manse. The house quivered at times as the wind attempted to pry the boards away from its skeleton. There were only three guests in attendance: Uncle Joseph, Aunt Helen, and Mr. Hamilton's mother (a tiny woman with the wizened face of a monkey, she was bundled into one of the easy chairs.) The officiating clergyman, the priest of the Presbyterian Church in Bridgetown, was Ezra Hamilton, brother of Zachariah Hamilton.

Mama's eyes were clouded with pain. I could tell that she was suffering one of her megrims, but she was stoical and she bore herself regally in her rose-coloured gown. Her hair had been fashioned to a smooth bun at the nape of her neck, and she had a small sprig of narcissi pinned to her bodice.

Mr. Hamilton was garbed for the occasion in a black frock coat, a beige waist coat, a rich brown necktie, grey-striped trousers, and patent leather boots. He seemed more the dandy than a simple country preacher.

Sibley and I wore frocks of navy blue that differed only slightly. We had woven ivory and burgundy-coloured ribbons into each other's hair.

And Noah Hamilton, son and only child of Mr. Hamilton, a stout ox of a young man bearing an expression of ennui, *was almost a replica of his father in sartorial matters.*

A huge gust of wind shook the manse by its scruff, and the five candles in the parlour fought for their lives. The Reverend Mr. Ezra Hamilton waited until their flames stood tall again and then he looked me in the eye, as if he knew that he must have my attention before the ceremony could proceed. He cleared his throat in an ostentatious manner. "Dearly beloved," he began. "We are about to witness the union of this man and this woman in the presence of our God."

That is all that I recall of the ceremony.

I know that this statement might invite incredulity, but it is utterly true. A mind will choose disavowal if it must save the soul.

Mom and Jack were united in wedlock on January 29, 1958 during a torch-lit ceremony on a beach in the Bahamas. It took place on the same day that Paul Newman and Joanne Woodward were married in Las Vegas. Gramps and Ben and his parents were there, as were two university friends of Mom, Jack's father, and his two sisters. Nan didn't fly down. "Someone has to hold down the fort," she said.

There's a Kodachrome photo of us all, taken after the ceremony. Mom, Jack, Ben and I are sitting on the long trunk of one of those palm trees that grow parallel to the sand; the rest of the group is standing behind us. Mom is clad in a knee-length, mint green, scoop-necked dress with wide pleats in the skirt and a sash belt. A froth of crinoline is visible beneath the skirt; a scarlet hibiscus flower threatens to topple from her hair. Jack is wearing a gaudy Hawaiian shirt and white pants; I've got an emerald green sundress with a smocked bodice. Everyone is smiling for the camera except Ben and me. Ben's looking at me, and I'm looking down and fingering a necklace made of tiny, iridescent shells. It was a gift from Jack.

I can't remember the ceremony itself. Mom and Jack exchanged personally-written vows before a Justice of the Peace, who wore a magenta-coloured caftan and could have been Liberace's twin.

"They were beautiful," one of Jack's sisters whispered to me soon after they were pronounced "man and wife." Did she mean the vows or the bridal couple?

I remember nothing of the vows. All I could think of during the ceremony was gunner Greg.

Chapter 12

Mother thou art gone to rest
Thy sins art all forgiven
And saints in light have welcomed thee
To share the joys of heaven

That first year of living with Mom and Jack in Halifax was tumultuous. I missed my life on the mountain. Above all, I nurtured the anger I held against my mother, stoked it like a hot coal in my belly. She had no right to tear down my father, destroy the dreams that I had cultivated over so many years. But the story loomed, insisted that I complete its sequence of events. I turned to Gramps.

He was visiting us in the city at the time, on the last leg of one of his auctioneering tours. Poor man—he looked panic-stricken by my request. He first asked me to accompany him to a corner store, where he purchased a small packet of beef jerky. He was trying to quit smoking at the time, and I think he needed something to calm his nerves and keep his hands busy. After he'd made his purchase, we continued walking through our residential neighbourhood. That was his idea. "I don't want this jerky reekin' up the house," he said. I'm sure he didn't want to sit down in a room with me. Be forced to look me in the eye.

I had asked him to be completely honest with me. We walked for about a block in silence before I said, "When did Mom tell you she was pregnant?"

He must have been steeling himself for the first question; he seemed surprised and relieved by it. "She didn't," he said. "Your Nan's a sharp one. I'm guessin' she noticed some things, and she finally went to your mom and met her head on. You know, when I look back on it all, your mother was awful quiet when she got home from Boston. And then I found her throwin' up outside of the house a couple times in the fall. She said it was on account of her nerves, with school and all. She was tops in her class, you know—always had been—and she was supposed to be the valedictorian at grad. She must have been feelin' some scared at the time."

"She must have known she couldn't hide it forever."

"She was scared, Rianne. You don't think right when you're scared, do you?"

"And then? What happened then?"

He made me wait as he gnawed a strip of jerky to its end. Finally, he said, "Your grandmother took matters into hand, same as she always does. She pulled your mother out of school and she sent her down to the south shore."

"Why to the south shore?

"Well, to live in one of those homes for unwed mothers."

"But why wouldn't she let Mom stay on the mountain?"

"That's not the way things were done back then."

I came to a stop on the sidewalk, forcing Gramps to plant his feet and face me. "What difference would it have made? I ended up on the mountain anyway!"

He didn't look me in the eye. "That maternity home near Lunenburg—it was one of those places where unwed mothers from all over the province used to go to have their babies. And your mother—" He paused long enough to dispatch another strip of beef. "Your mother was meant to go there because that's where babies were put up for adoption."

Another blow, and Gramps must have known it; he still hadn't looked at me as he uttered the last sentence. He crumpled the beef jerky wrapping and stuffed it into his pants pocket. This time it wasn't I who brought the story to a halt.

May 21, 1896. Today was Uncle Joseph's birthday and the anniversary of Papa's birthday. Aunt Helen and Uncle Joseph invited us all, including Mr. Hamilton and Noah, to a dinner celebration. Mama declined, citing that she was under the weather. To my great relief Mr. Hamilton and Noah added their regrets to those of Mama.

Mama has seen very little of Aunt Helen and Uncle Joseph since her marriage to Mr. Hamilton. "I'm busy learning to be a minister's wife," she told me not long ago. At times I wonder if Mama would see recrimination in a face that mirrors that of her late husband.

Sibley was delighted about the prospect of spending a day at Tyne Bluff. She was anxious to play Twenty Questions and Charades and she wondered whether Uncle Joseph would bring out the kites. I had no idea what Aunt Helen and Uncle Joseph had in mind, but I thought of Papa and how he would approve of a day of merriment.

Aunt Helen greeted us both with warm hugs. Uncle Joseph was in the kitchen, driving Martine to consternation as she cooked dinner at the stove. As we stood and watched from the doorway, his nose twitched and flared and then joined forces with a spoon for a final, fact-finding dive. "More onions, wouldn't you say, Martine?" He emerged from a pot of filling for pork pies with beads of moisture clinging to his moustache. Martine, disguising a smile with a scowl, soon chased him from the room with a wooden spoon.

Martine had prepared a feast worthy of royalty. We started with a small bowl of eel soup each and progressed to savoury pork pies, glazed carrots, and roasted potatoes. At the end of the meal we were all as stuffed as a Christmas goose.

There were to be no games after dinner. Sibley fought to hide her disappointment, but then Uncle Joseph announced that he would take us to the island. "I'm not an able sailor as your father was," he said, "but I've arranged for a boat and a skipper to take us there."

Martine had already packed us a picnic basket. It was filled with small pots of gypsy pudding and trifle, white linen napkins, and silver spoons. Before we stepped into the carriage that would take us to the wharf, she handed each of us armfuls of tulips bound in rough twine.

"For the captain," she said.

I have an 11 x 14 enlargement of a photograph of the Whitfield house that I took two years ago. In the late afternoon of a summer's day, cirrus clouds swirl above the roof—tentative brush strokes on the sky's pale blue easel. *Mares' tails* Gramps always calls them.

The photo doesn't hold back on the ailments of the house; they are well documented. But despite the slants and angles, and the skin slaking off bone, the house appears to be holding its own. It retains a sense of self, a projected memory of its significance in the past.

I've mounted the photograph on a piece of dark blue Bristol board, and in the bottom right hand corner I've attached a piece of the lace that Ben retrieved for me just before his accident.

Mr. Sweeney seems pleased with the gift. And in a spirit of reciprocation, he tells me that he has something to show me. He unlocks one of the drawers of his desk, extracts two small leather cases, and snaps them open. "These are ambrotypes of Joseph and Helen Teasdale," he says.

Helen Teasdale obliges the photographer with her body slightly to one side. She has a sweet face—heart-shaped, ingenuous. Her eyes are wide and light-coloured, the brows above them matchstick thin and arched in elegant lines. She has the hint of a smile, the full lower lip not quite meeting a thinner upper one, and she sports a large hat, wide-brimmed with a bow on top. The bow is so enormous that it takes on a life of its own. A fur stole sits comfortably on her shoulders, and a square buckle—part of a collar, perhaps—is visible to one side of her throat.

Joseph faces the camera straight on, no trace of a smile on his generous lips. His dark eyes look startled. He's handsome, with high, angular cheekbones, a long nose terminating in a moustache flourish, and neat ears closely pinned to the skull. He has a side part to his sleek hair and a boyish cowlick that sticks out stiffly like the inverted cap of an Ionic column.

"He looks severe, doesn't he?" I say. "A bit of a wet blanket. But you wouldn't think that from the way Alyda described him at the birthday dinner."

"I've always been someone who won't smile for the camera. And don't forget that people back then had to fix their expressions for a slow shutter speed."

I stare at the photographs resting in my palms. "Where did you get these?"

"Years ago, at an estate sale in Danton. I found them wedged in the back of an old chest of drawers that belonged to Helen's parents."

"And Alyda? Do you have any photographs of Alyda?"

Mr. Sweeney's answer is a disappointing and unequivocal *no.*

"Do you know what she looked like?" Suddenly, it is important to me to know this, as important as the quirks of character and personality traits that he has been giving me.

"No, I don't."

And then he astonishes me by adding the word *yet.*

Uncle Joseph had arranged passage for us on the supply boat to the lighthouse. The ocean was calm, and beneath a vigorous sun it pulsed like a lea of diamonds. Gulls followed us, circling above us in investigative sweeps; they must have mistaken us for a fishing vessel.

While Uncle Joseph helped the boatman and the lighthouse keeper carry the crates from the boat to the lighthouse, Sibley and I searched for a suitable picnic location near the landing spit. The expanse of shore was bleak: driftwood scattered over tumbled black rocks. We skirted bleached branches that curved inward like the ribcages of whales, once frantic, once alive. Eventually we found a few patches of grass by a small pond and there we spread our thick blanket. When Uncle Joseph and the boat captain joined us, we did justice to Martine's picnic dessert.

On departing the island, the boatman brought the boat close to the ledge where the Laliah B. *went down. We all scanned the waters silently; I almost expected to see remnants of the ship still, even though the villagers had salvaged everything they could. Uncle Joseph produced a flask from the inside of his vest and commemorated Papa with a toast. Sibley and I murmured a prayer in turn. Sibley was the first one to release her bouquet of flowers. She flung it as far as she could, and the binding twine unravelled immediately, as if it had been pulled loose by a malevolent force in the water. The tulips scattered in all directions.*

On our return trip to Port Carlyle, the boatman tried to dispel the sombre mood by telling us stories of the island. "It's not as remote as it seems," he claimed, and he recounted the story of the lighthouse keeper's daughter whose marriage took place there in September of 1881, a year after I was born. Two boats brought the officiating reverend and friends and family of the groom over to the island. There was a grand celebration; tables groaned under the weight of pies and other sweets, and a fiddler presided over a dance floor. And at the end of it all there was a shivaree, so thunderous that the mainlanders could hear the serenade of pots and kettles.

Sibley's eyes grew huge with the romanticism of it, but a shadow suddenly flitted across her face. "It might have been a splendid idea once," she said.

I didn't say a word, but reflected what a solace it would be to wed a beloved beau with my father so near. And then a face came to my mind, a forthright face with laughing green eyes, framed by a thatch of wheaten hair. Silly goose, I thought. You know nothing about this man.

But I will. I'll contrive another encounter. Watch me!

After showing me the ambrotypes of Helen and Joseph Teasdale, Mr. Sweeney has another surprise for me: an assignment to "map" Ocean's Edge. The task involves plotting each gravesite, taking a photograph of its marker, and transcribing the marker's inscription in a legible manner. This will be a paid assignment, thanks to the generosity of a benefactor on the cemetery's board. I'll ask Ben to do this with me and give him an equal share of my earnings.

I'm excited about this project. The name *Teasdale* echoes in my mind from those long-ago jaunts in the graveyard with Nan and Gramps. I had already planned to search soon for the gravestones of Alyda's relatives and the villagers she featured in her journal; now this can be done in a methodical fashion.

CHAPTER 13

Brother thou art gone to rest
Thine is an early tomb
But Jesus summoned thee away
Thy Saviour called thee home

WE LIVE IN the manse now, on the outskirts of the village. It's a shabby box of a building with little character to commend it, and its only saving grace is its proximity to the graveyard. Mama claims that the most urgent repairs will be initiated soon, but I'll not hold my breath awaiting the day. In the meantime, an obscure cousin of Mama and his family of five from Southampton are to move into our *home. My only consolation is that the house will revert to my possession when I'm of age.*

The manse offers no unobstructed view to the bay. If I position myself to the left side of the window in Mama's bedroom, I can catch a glimpse of the water between the two houses that line the other side of our road. It is not enough, of course, and I spend as much time as possible down by the shore.

Today, Mama remarked upon my frequent absences, and so I told her how much comfort it gives me to visit the graveyard and to sit by the shore. "I feel closer to Papa there," I said.

Her face grew tight as a sail under wind. She said that I was too morbid, that as a young person I should not live so much in the past. I countered that this was entirely reasonable, that my past life is preferable to the one I live at present. I know she is offended, but I cannot help myself. She is responsible for bringing Noah and Zachariah Hamilton into our lives.

Sibley seems to have welcomed Noah into the family. "Alyda, just think," she exclaimed after the marriage ceremony, "we now have a brother!" I have never wanted a brother, and I have never thought that our family was incomplete without one. Noah Hamilton will never gain my affection, nor will Mr. Hamilton. I am sure the Lord is not *impressed with this particular representative of His upon this earth.*

I still don't know why Mama felt compelled to marry this man. Papa left us well provided for, and if he hadn't, Uncle Joseph and Uncle William would have seen to our needs. Sibley and I are both capable of looking after her and after each other. Could she not see that?

What induced her to marry a preacher with a dour disposition and the facial features of a plough horse? I am in awe of how he transforms his long, sallow face when he preaches—his cheeks actually billow and his nostrils flare. I expect him to start snorting, and shaking his head at any moment. You do not believe me? I confess only to slight exaggeration. I seriously doubt, however, that Zachariah Hamilton ever set any hearts aflutter, and Noah is a true chip off the old block. There is one difference, however. At the age of fourteen he has already exceeded his father's height by a good three inches and his girth by several more. Noah is a brute.

And I do not like the way he looks at me.

Ben finally wants to visit the site of the Whitfield house. Earlier this morning we watched as a procession of dumpsters made its way down our road toward the Port Carlyle road, solemn as a funeral convoy. The contents of the containers were strapped under tarpaulins, but the tip of an occasional beam or board could be seen. Huge clouds of dust followed the procession like a pack of hounds on the trail of a scent.

Ben has jettisoned his crutches. He's used them rarely in the past week and has now dispensed with them for good. He has a hopping gait that is similar to Owen Sweeney's but he can manoeuvre quickly on even terrain.

The Whitfield property doesn't fall into that category. We're forced to take our time negotiating its ruts and rough grasses. A sticky blanket of dust coats the fields and attaches itself to our runners. Here and there, shards of glass and board remnants, refugees from the round-up, poke through the thin layer. A post-apocalyptic landscape, if it weren't for the blinding sun.

The leaves and the blossoms on the lilac bush are also smothered by the film of dust. Ben shakes his head as I start using the pad of my thumb to scrape the leaves clean. I abandon my task when I catch him leaning at a precarious angle over the foundation of the house.

Half of the cellar is filled with water: murky water, blood-tinted from the soil and rust. Blackened and splintered apple crates stand stacked in one corner; a twisted bicycle frame—tires and pedals missing—leans against them. Shattered mason jars send us a faint odour of pickling brine.

The shorn ductwork of the furnace reaches blindly for the sky. The metal giant evokes the memory of an incident that occurred almost twenty years ago, on our first visit to the house. Ben had slipped away from me in the basement as I was examining, in curious horror, the stiff bodies of three kittens. Panic had gripped me when I realized that I was alone. *Ben? Ben? Where are you?* He had launched himself from the shadows behind the furnace with a sustained, guttural roar that hurled my heart to my ribcage.

Ben pivots on the "walking extension" of his cast. "Let's get out of here," he says.

I'm ready, too. The day may be warm and sunny, but the remains of the house cast a pall.

Papa has answered my prayers. I have an escape from the manse, from its stained ceilings, narrow corridors, and constant fog of camphor. Its holier-than-thou Mr. Hamilton! Its skulking Noah!

I'm at Tyne Bluff for two weeks while Martine visits her family in Port Royal, and I'll be here every Friday and Saturday throughout the summer, helping Aunt Helen. I presented a good case to stay there all Sunday as well, but Mr. Hamilton was adamant that I not miss any Sunday services.

It is a joy to take Griff on his runs every day, and he insists on going directly to the field that abuts Dugald Roy's property. It is choked with wild pansies, and I always return with handfuls to feed to Aunt Helen's flower press. On our third day of exploring the field's perimeter, a man finally stepped out of the Roy woodlot. A low growl immediately escaped Griff, but I made him stay to the spot and he obeyed with ill-disguised reluctance.

The man scrutinized an enormous sheet of paper as he slowly walked in our direction. He was clad in the same brown work shirt and black trousers he had worn on the day that I met him at the store. Below the rim of his cap, the right cheek pulsed where his tongue worked the tobacco in its hollow.

"Caleb Whitelaw!" I called out. "You'll dive head first into a cow patty if you don't watch where you're going."

His head snapped up. He smiled. "Alyda Teasdale." He turned away from me and ejected the tobacco into the grass. When he reached me, he removed his cap. Grit peppered his hairline, and a smudge of dirt rested on one cheek. "You've come a long way from the village," he said. "Where's Sassie?"

"Enjoying her oats, no doubt. I'm at the home of my uncle now, on Tyne Bluff. I'll be here quite often until the end of the summer."

"You'll not even be a mile away."

I smile at the thought of it. "You're working hard?"

He returned the smile, lines as fine as cat's whiskers creasing the corners of his eyes. "Sun up to sun down," he said, "with the ungodly total of three hours every day to see to myself."

I nodded toward the paper that he held in one hand. "What kind of work are you doing for Mr. Roy?"

"Sit down with me. I'll show you." He placed a light hand to my elbow and led me to a boulder a few feet away.

He laid out the map on his knees. The paper shook slightly as one knee beneath it moved with nervous energy. "This is a sketch of my cousin's property," he said. "Do you see these squares, here on the southeast end? This is where we're sitting now. I'll be building fencing on these squares, making new paddocks for the cattle."

"Is Mr. Roy buying more cattle?"

"He is. He'll be the first man on the mountain to have Scottish highland cattle. But even if he wasn't to have new stock, Miss Teasdale, you have to rotate what you do have. You can't have it feeding from the same pastures time and again."

"Please don't call me 'Miss Teasdale.' It sounds stuffy. It makes me out to be a spinster."

He laughed. "Isn't that what you are?"

"You cannot condemn me to spinsterhood yet."

"Still, I like Miss Teasdale. *It suits the accent, Miss Come-From-Afar."*

"Allie. Call me Allie."

I placed my hand on the paper to quiet the jiggling knee beneath. He drew in his breath and then rewarded me with a smile of assent.

I join Ben as he heads to the bluff, to an area where a wooden staircase once descended from its edge. Staggered in five levels like an urban fire escape, it connected to a pathway to the house. Nobody seems to know when the staircase was first built, but it rotted away over time, treads and railings dropping like decayed teeth to the shore below. A few boards of the old staircase's landing have survived, but they are black and rotten. Rusted nails and copper-coloured fungi hold loosely to the wood.

"Jack will have to get rid of the landing," he says. "It'll be a liability issue, just like the old house was."

"Maybe he'll build a whole new staircase."

"Great for the inn, but we wouldn't have our private section of the shore anymore."

I can't find the keys when we get back to the car. I could swear that I'd left them in the ignition, but they are nowhere to be found. Ben stays in the car as I re-trace the route we took to the edge of the bluff, keeping an eye out for the glint of metal in the sunlight. Finally, I find the set of keys, splayed in a small depression of earth near the edge. I stoop to pick them up, stand tall again. And my heart suddenly seizes.

A young woman is standing on the edge of the bluff, just beyond the landing of the staircase. Petite and attractive, she is dressed in a dove grey gown with a white sun bonnet tied to its belt. Thick waves of rich brown hair, verging to black, fall to her waist and frame the face of a gamine. My heart still turning on itself, I return her gaze. She has restive grey eyes. Or are they blue? Does the sky have a say in this matter? The sea?

The breeze carries to me the scents of salt and lavender. It plays with my hair, and it collects a few strands of the young woman's hair and fingers it across her face. She pulls back the hair and tucks it behind her ears. Her cheeks are flushed, and I notice now that her chest is rising and falling, as if she's just completed the long climb from the shore. An impossible climb since the staircase doesn't exist anymore.

I stand spellbound as she reaches into a pocket of her skirt and removes a hairpin. She loops a thick train of hair to the top of her head and starts fashioning a bun. When she is finished her work, she releases the bonnet from the belt, places it on her head, and ties its ribbons into a perfect bow beneath her right ear. The look is jaunty.

She takes one step forward, and another, and before I can react and step aside, she has walked right *through* me. A sensation of heat, almost of burning, floods my body. I steel myself to pain, but suddenly it is gone. Breath trapped in my throat, I spin around, but she is no longer there. I make a slow revolution on the spot where I'm standing and make note of all my surroundings. A stand of Shasta daisies glides into view, petals lifted by the breeze. A swallowtail alights on one of the boards on the landing. A pageant of cumulus clouds crosses the bay. The feeling of warmth dissipates; nerve endings send pain signals from my right hand. I look down and open the hand to find that I've driven the keys hard into my palm.

The keys jingle as my shaking hands start the car. Ben doesn't notice; he's busy inserting a cassette into the eight-track player. I brace my arms against the steering wheel and stare at the spot where I last saw the girl. As if by concentrating, I can bring her to life again.

Ben reduces the volume. "Are you okay?" he says.

I turn to him. "Did you watch me as I was walking toward the bluff?"

"I always keep an eye on you."

"Did you see anything?"

"I saw you taking your time as you walked back to the edge. A couple of times you bent down, like you were checking the grass. And then when you got close to the edge, you stopped and you stood there for a while."

"Did you see anything strange?"

Ben's scarred eyebrow attempts elevation. "Help me out here, Ree. What was I supposed to see?"

I look into his puzzled eyes. "It's nothing," I say. "Everything's okay."

I can't tell him, and yet I want to tell him. More than anything I want him to know that just a few minutes ago I stood face to face with Alyda.

Chapter 14

Sleep on sweet babe
And take thy rest
God called thee home
He thought it best

Ben and I are in the kitchen of his home, set to enjoy lunch before starting the graveyard mapping assignment. Baby carrots, green beans, and new potatoes—hand-picked this morning from Kaye's garden—simmer gently in a cream base in a pot on the stove. Small islands of butter glisten among the vegetables of this hodgepodge; they'll soon be soaked up by the sourdough bread that Kaye baked before she left for the hospital this morning. She'd taped a note for us on the fridge: *Eat all you can, kids.*

Ben has already devised a grid system for dividing the cemetery into sections; those grids will be plotted on over-sized graph paper that Warren has given us. Since Ben has become a proficient typist in a short period of time, he's also going to transcribe the notes that we obtain from every headstone.

Mr. Sweeney has given both of us metal toolboxes stocked with chalk for highlighting, soft-bristled brushes, Photo-Flo solution (a non-abrasive cleaning compound), and dowels that are cut at an angle on each end, like cuticle pushers. We'll remove lichen only when it interferes with our reading of the inscriptions. Mr. Sweeney has mixed feelings about removing it from gravestones. Lichen gives off an acid that works with the stone's own chemistry to erode it, and it gradually reduces its host to soil. It may take centuries to achieve this result, however, and in the meantime the lichen protects the stone from other destructive elements.

Ben and I help ourselves to generous portions of hodgepodge and eat silently for a while in appreciation of one of our favourite meals. I use a spoon, but he tears off chunks of the sourdough loaf for ladling. As he comes to the end of his serving, he brings up the subject of Owen Sweeney's source again.

I corral equal amounts of each vegetable onto my spoon. "I don't care where he finds the information as long as he keeps passing it on to me."

"I'll bet it's his mother."

"Alma? No. She's got dementia. She's not all there."

"Think about where she is. If she has dementia, she's living in the past at times. Didn't you say she kept mentioning Leonard Sweeney the other day?"

My spoon makes a thoughtful exit from my lips. "You think she might have known Alyda?"

"Do the math. They've got to be close in age."

"But how would they have met? Alma didn't live right in the village, and Alyda was home schooled. Would they have even moved in the same social circles?"

"You'll have to find out the answers to those questions. I'd say it's worth pursuing them, don't you?"

I use the back of my spoon to chase the pools of butter into the depths of the broth. Ben's right; Alma and Alyda would have been contemporaries. Perhaps Mr. Sweeney has been sitting patiently with his mother for hours at a time, encouraging her to relate the stories as he accompanies her on journeys into the past.

"You've got a cream 'stache," Ben says. Before I can lift a hand, he leans over and gently erases it with the pad of his thumb.

It's not an intimate gesture—surely it can't be—but it sets off a shock. I seize Ben's empty bowl, push away from the table. Walk with unsteady legs to the sink and deposit the bowl with a clatter among the dishes already there.

I cannot even turn to face him as I say, "I'll think about it. I'll think about Alma."

"Good," Ben says. And then, "Could you bring me another helping of hodgepodge?"

His voice is calm, down-to-earth. It allows me to compose myself and return to the table.

It's a daily ritual, climbing up from the shore, through the apple orchard and into the graveyard. As I walk the avenues between the rows of trees, I can spot the obelisks stationed like a phalanx of soldiers on the hill.

At times I wish I had an over-flowing food hamper in one hand and family members by my side. How I miss those days in the cemetery by The Common, Granmama officiating over a picnic in the shadows of the yews. Perhaps I should try to import our custom to this lonely seaside village.

Today, smells of tobacco and sweat and freshly-turned earth drifted toward me, and I could hear the occasional clash of metal on stone. The gravediggers were hard at work, preparing final resting places for little Janie and Myles Handley. The poor man survived the wreck of the Laliah B. *only to lose his footing while tasked to repairs in the rigging of a fully-berthed schooner.*

As for Janie, the excavation would not have taken long, she was that tiny. I see her still at the church picnic Sunday past, as iridescent as a barn swallow in her blue pinafore. She had the most endearing smile and pink spots of hectic on her cheeks when she won a potato sack race. So young and so innocent she was, and yet they will still carry her out of her home feet first so that her spirit will not look back and beckon others to follow.

Beyond the apple trees, as always, I turned and looked to Ile de Haute, its bleak and uncompromising silhouette. I thought of Papa, lying in the frigid waters that surround the isle, his limbs still, his hair and beard streaming in the current. In my mind, his body is never degraded; the creatures of the sea maintain a respectful distance. Despite the activity behind me, I stayed calm and gave good measure to my heartbeats. I was able to close his eyelids.

There should be a marker for Papa in that graveyard, a plot in readiness for the day that the waters let him go. Mama says she will arrange for a memorial in good time, but I know she has gone to loggerheads over this with Uncle Joseph and Uncle William. They wish to provide the funds for a marker that is larger and of a different design to the one that Mama would choose.

And in the midst of this feud a sea captain, a man who performed the duties of his office with clear sight and courage in the throes of a winter gale, does not receive the honour due him.

It's a perfect day to begin plotting the graveyard. Sunshine slants through the gaps of the spruce branches. A light breeze ruffles the leaves of the apple trees. Ben and I aren't the only living occupants here—an army of insects trills in the Queen Anne's lace that borders the orchard. I immediately glance at Alyda's gravesite as we enter through the lichgate. Do I really expect to see her again? The rose bushes close ranks; she's not there, of course. I force myself to focus on our assignment.

We fill buckets of water at the pump by the storage shed; these will dilute the Photo-Flo solution for cleaning the headstones. Nan has given us a clean potato sack filled with soft rags, and I have divided those evenly between our two backpacks. From what I can see of the sack's contents, Gramps will discover that an army of his old flannel shirts is missing.

Ben hands me the sheet for what he has deemed the first section. Its perimeters are determined by the twelve gravesites that extend from the corner and anchoring Celtic cross of my grandmother Addie. This section comprises a smaller area than the one he has chosen for himself. Once I'm finished mapping it, I'll go over to his section and take pictures there.

Adelaide Harris tripped into my grandfather's life outside of Fenway Park in Boston in 1922. A Red Sox fan, Gramps was attending a ball game with a group of buddies from Port Carlyle. He bent over to retrieve a fallen coin outside of the stadium; she was opening her English-style umbrella and accidentally thrust the pointed end into the upper lobe of his right ear. It was his "cauliflower ear"—the one that was permanently disfigured in a bar-room brawl in London at the end of the war. Horrified Addie didn't know this, of course; all she saw was a bloody, swollen mess, and she and her brother insisted on taking him to a physician. Gramps, immediately taken by Addie's vivacity and dark beauty, milked the situation for all its worth. The ensuing two or three hours gave him plenty of time to start stealing her heart.

The light grey stone of Addie's cross displays relief work created by a local artisan—bold trumpet flowers and intricate, interlaced strap work. The size of the stone garnered a lot of speculation at the time it was raised. Gramps is not a pretentious man, and by all accounts he was mortified by the attention. He eventually conceded that in his grief he'd written down "the wrong damn measurements" for the monument maker.

After a high society wedding on Nantucket Island, Addie and Gramps settled into life on the mountain. She stayed home to raise her two children, rode horses in provincial equestrian events, founded an amateur theatre group in the village, and organized church fund-raisers in which her shoo-fly pies were always a huge hit. She swiftly lost her outsider status on the mountain.

The inscription at the base of the cross has long fixed itself in my consciousness, but I transcribe it carefully into my notes: *Adelaide Harris Montgomery / July 22, 1899–August 12, 1935 / Beloved wife and mother.* The rest of the epitaph is a saying of Cicero from 43 BC: *The life of the dead is placed in the memory of the living.*

The family unit was shattered with Addie's death at the age of thirty-six. She spent the last morning of her life cooking a hot luncheon for men re-shingling the roof of the house then slipped from the rung of an old ladder as she was delivering a fallen hammer to one of them. She died instantly of a broken neck. My mother was six years old at the time, her younger brother only two.

Within a month of the accident, Addie's closest friend on the mountain, Rachel Manning, had moved into Gramps's home to provide child care and run the household while he was away on his auctioneering runs. The tongues on the mountain soon took to wagging, leaping to the presumption of an illicit love. Nan and Gramps took their time silencing them; six years would go by before they "tied the knot" in a quiet civil ceremony in Halifax.

I am doomed. Although I scarcely know the man, Caleb Whitelaw persists in occupying every thought of mine. He fixes a gaze on me in mock severity or his eyes crinkle at the corners in rays of sunlight as he grins at me. Today he displaced almost every word of the homily that flew at me from the pulpit.

"All wicked men shall perish in the pit of devouring flames!" Mr. Hamilton's voice swooped across the pews like a raptor in pursuit of its prey and finally sank its claws into my brain and annihilated all thoughts of Caleb. Overcome by his imagery, Mr. Hamilton paused for a moment to wipe his brow with a handkerchief that was already sodden with sweat. He glared in accusation at his congregants, and a few of them obliged him by squirming like maggots on their stone-hard seats. I would have sworn upon the prayer book in my hand that my stepfather was uplifted by his words; he would be a gleeful observer of the damned.

"I'm leaving," I whispered to Mama, before sliding to the edge of the pew. "It's far too hot in here, and I cannot breathe." Noah, seated directly behind me, could not stop me. His hand lunged for my wrist, but I was too swift for him. I bolted down the aisle and through the open doors.

I paused for a moment at the edge of the woods and considered returning to the church. I could have sat outside on its well-worn steps, and claimed that I felt the onset of a fainting spell. After all, the air within that building was fetid; all the dried lavender in the world could not erase the stench of sweat and the day-old gammon on Noah's breath.

No, the evergreens beckoned me, and I stepped willingly into their shadows. A thrush sang—liquid notes of beauty—until it broke its song to gauge my progress, and the distant chorus of Lift Up Your Heads, Ye Mighty Gates *soon slipped into the void. I travelled quickly then, moving westward away from the church and the village, allowing my feet to carry me to the edge of Dugald Roy's property. Mr. Roy and his workers never attend church; perhaps I would be afforded a glimpse of Caleb.*

My heart quickened when I saw him, but I soon realized that he was not alone—another man was working alongside him. The two men appeared to be wearing coats and bulky gloves even though it was a warm day. I soon saw the reason for this: they were replacing the old rail fencing with barbed wire. Caleb was performing the most difficult part of the task, unfurling the wire, while the other man was nailing it to the old posts.

I was about to turn away when Caleb saw me and raised his hand in greeting. He leaned to his partner, stripped the gloves from his hands, and bounded across the field toward me. He was scarcely out of breath when he reached me. "No dog?" he said.

"I've come directly from church."

"You'll not think poorly of me for working on the Lord's Day?" He jerked his head in the direction of his fellow worker. "My cousin respects no lord but himself."

"I've disturbed you. Will he treat you ill for this?"

He smiled, ignored my question. "Do you know the ovens?" he asked me.

"Yes, of course."

"Then meet me there tomorrow," he said. "Seven o'clock in the evening. The most westerly one."

"Wait . . ."

"Seven o'clock." He was already striding back to the fence; he didn't once turn back to spare me a glance.

Dare I meet him?

It is a painstaking task photographing the headstones. Time and again, when the lettering is worn and shallow or if a marker is shaded by a spruce tree, I resort to an old make-up mirror of mine, a large oval that tilts on a base. I balance the mirror on my clipboard and angle it to reflect sunlight onto the stone or to create shadows that will provide contrast.

After more than two hours of camera work and note-taking, I complete my section of the graveyard. Ben is still at work in his section, and I join him in front of an obelisk. He's used a thick stub of chalk to highlight some of the inscription letters. The stone marks the final resting place of Effie Greaves, *departed this earth on the ninth day of April 1862 at the age of twenty-one*:

Cheerie go I to my Maker
Rid at last of ills and woes
Now shall I be a Partaker
Of Heaven's splendour fair as a rose

"What do you think, Ben? 'Heaven's splendour' is 'fair as a rose' or 'Effie' is 'fair as a rose'?"

He considers. "Hard to say," he offers, "but I'd go with 'Effie.'"

I read the passage aloud, attempt to make the extra syllables flow. "It's a clumsy piece of doggerel, isn't it?"

Ben's pen pauses in mid-transcription. He looks up at me. "Dog *what?*"

"Doggerel. Verse that's trivial, with forced rhymes. Like that Ruby Ree stuff you used to spout."

"You call that trivial?" Ben stares at me, as if he's sizing me up. And then, in a low voice, he croons, "*Ruby Ree on a shootin' spree! Taking lots of photographs, one, two, three! She takes 'em to the left; she takes 'em to the right. She takes 'em . . . um . . . she takes 'em in the morning and she takes 'em in the night!"*

I laugh, shake my head. "I rest my case."

Ben takes his turn at reading the epitaph aloud. "Seriously," he says, "it serves its purpose. It's just trying to make sense of something that defies understanding."

"*Cheerie go I.* I can't believe she'd happily go and meet her maker at that young age. Maybe it was written for the benefit of the family. To make them feel better."

"Or she just might have been a staunch Christian. What if she wasn't afraid to die, because she believed in God's will and an afterlife?"

"Then she was lucky."

As those words escape me, I realize I'm envious of Effie Greaves. The admission startles me. I've always been comfortable with my agnosticism. I did go to Sunday school at St. Luke's one year, encouraged to attend by my best friend at the time. I loved everything about it: the pageants, the hymns, and the stickers, glossy, lace-edged like postage stamps, which were awarded for flawless recitation of Bible verses. I can't remember now why I stopped going.

"Ree?" Hand cupped above his eyes to protect them from the sun's glare, Ben is staring at me. He's left-handed, and I notice that the side of his hand is blackened from ink settling into the skin.

The detail puts my thoughts to flight. I direct my attention to the settings on my camera. "Let's get this done," I say.

The last gravestone of the section is a large tablet marker; its central carving is a dove. Wings tucked for aerodynamic efficiency, the bird plummets headfirst from the sky. The edges of the inscription are eroded, framed by patches of black and orange lichen. Ben removes most of the lichen with a dowel, and once again I use the mirror to highlight the lettering and make it more decipherable.

Eudoria Mae Chesney
February 20, 1839–November 23, 1857
Beloved wife of Stillman A. Chesney
&
Infant daughter
Born and Died November 23, 1857

Sleep little baby sleep
Not in thy cradle bed
Not at thy mother's breast
But with the quiet dead

Born and died. Does that mean that the babe wasn't stillborn—that she drew air, even for a moment? And was the mother still alive when she was born and able to hold her, even for one precious second?

An infant daughter without a name. Perhaps that was Stillman Chesney's way of challenging the pain. He had a child once, but she died on the threshold of life. She didn't live long enough to earn a name.

Is that the way the family of Alyda felt? The baby—simply *a babe*—didn't live long enough to merit a name?

To curl hand into fist in a corner of one's mind?

To clutch at memory?

Sleep little baby sleep. The verse is not doggerel. It's not trivial at all.

CHAPTER 15

Reader pause, behold your fate
Death will arrest you soon or late
Your dearest interest is to have
Your bliss secured beyond the grave

MR. HAMILTON, SEATED behind the desk in his study, motioned me to stand before him. "Your mother," he said, and he stopped to clear his throat ostentatiously. "Your mother and I have decided—" Once again he paused, no doubt to inject suspense and drama into the proceedings. Lord in Heaven, the man is pompous!

It came to light that I was to be punished for leaving the church during his sermon (arguably not *an act of delinquency). I am to meet with Noah every morning, from Monday to Thursday, to tutor him in science and mathematics for two hours. It's evident to me that Mr. Hamilton sought and found a pretext to assert his authority over me. Tyrant! Petty despot! It was later, through Sibley, that I learned that he first wished to rob me of the latest addition to my book collection,* Middlemarch. *I'd only just received it a few days ago as a gift from Granmama.*

After Mr. Hamilton dismissed me, he and Mama had a furious quarrel in his study. I had left the house by then (gone to the shore to ease my spirits), but Sibley stood the entire time with her ear glued to the door. Mr. Hamilton insisted the book be taken away from me, not only as chastisement, but also because he feels it is unsuitable for a young woman of refinement! I must remember to hide The Picture of Dorian Gray *before he appoints himself as my censor.*

Sibley told me that Mama stayed steadfast and argued on my behalf. She supported my claim of feeling unwell and disagreed with the confiscation of a gift from Granmama. I'm glad to hear that she spoke up, for she surrenders far too often to her new husband.

Mr. Hamilton finally agreed that I would provide lessons to Noah, commencing at the beginning of the week to come, and that would be sufficient. I'm ecstatic that Middlemarch *is still safely in my hands, but I dread the sessions with Noah. Already my belly feels tighter than a Gordian knot.*

I return to the edge of Tyne Bluff and the remains of the staircase, hoping to—hoping to what? Alyda didn't present herself in the graveyard the other day. Surely I can't recreate my experience of seeing her in this location.

I sit there in the grass for over an hour, arms clasped around my knees, bare toes nudging the rotten boards of the landing. I turn often to peer over my shoulder, as if I suspect Alyda will move stealthily toward me and make a playful effort to startle me. She doesn't oblige.

My thoughts turn to Ben, to his thumb gently banishing the hodgepodge cream from my upper lip. And I think of another incident on an island more than a decade ago, of my response to it and the inevitable shift in our relationship. I groan, thrust a foot against the rough slats of the landing, causing them to splinter and collapse to the ground. The old boards call to mind a safer memory, of a time when the staircase was still operative and served as an escape route for Ben and me.

It was a warm summer day, with an overcast sky. A dull band of pewter on the horizon. It made it easier to scan the waters, and after an hour of serious beach-combing, we sat down on a massive boulder close to the water's edge to watch some harbour seals. There were six or seven of them, their heads sleek and stolid in the water. "Don't say a word," Ben whispered, and for the next hour we became simple outcroppings of the boulders. I remember how peaceful it was, how impatience and boredom for once didn't gnaw at me.

I would choose a seal, observe it until it dived beneath the water, and try to guess its point of reappearance. One seal, on the periphery of the group, stayed below the water for an exceptionally long time. Ben once told me that seals would expel all the air from their lungs for long dives and then use stores of oxygen from their bloodstream and muscles. When the seal returned to the surface, it would "top up" on its oxygen supply.

Eventually, the seals, curious about the change in their territorial landscape, began watching *us.* They came closer, receded, advanced again, as if they were daring each other to approach the strange hulks on the rock. And by the time they got tired of trying to make sense of our presence, the rock was surrounded by water. Flotsam swirling around our knees, Ben and I squelched our way in heavy jeans and runners to the staircase.

The stairs were rickety, and the distance to the top looked intimidating. "Maybe we should climb up on a boulder and wait for a helicopter," I half-joked.

"Waste of resources." He smiled and made an "after you, ma'am" gesture.

"You don't want to go first? Test the slats for me like a gentleman?"

"Ah, but what if one breaks and I hurtle into you? Nope, you go first."

It was easier than I'd thought, once I got started. Ben, to his credit, didn't try to make me go faster. He did, however, give me a running commentary of the splendid vistas he was enjoying.

I didn't look back. Every time that I stopped to get my bearings, I focused on the plants that had somehow secured footholds on the sheer face of the rock. Marvelled at their survival skills. That excursion up the old spruce had prepared me, after all.

When I got to the top, I felt dizzy. I immediately lay down in the rough grasses near the edge and closed my eyes. Clouds scudded across my eyelids, made way at times for the indistinct orb of the sun. The grass kneaded and tickled the nape of my neck, my elbows.

Ben rustled into a spot beside me. I turned to smile at him. His hands were clasped behind his head; his teeth clamped a long filament of rye grass. It bobbed up and down like a fishing line.

"Feeling okay?" he said.

"Why wouldn't I?" I closed my eyes again, but the clouds were pulling back on their dizzying run. They were horses on a carousel now, slowing to an inevitable stop.

"You did it," Ben said.

"What do you mean?"

"You made it up those stairs."

I opened my eyes. "It was no big deal."

"I could tell you were scared."

"No, I wasn't."

Ben was silent. The stalk of grass jerked one last time, dropped from his lips. He rolled over onto his side, facing me. "Give yourself some credit," he said.

He looked me in the eye, dared me to lie one more time.

He was not at the oven when I arrived. Had I heard him correctly? Had I been so intent on seeing him that I hadn't taken proper note of time or place?

No, I had not erred in the location. He'd been there before. It wasn't just the tell-tale scent of his tobacco that flourished in the dampness. His presence was there; he had made that oven his own.

I paced its entrance, constantly checking in both directions, even though I assumed he would descend the bluff where it tapers to the shore. The path there is steep, but in good weather it is passable. And while my eye was upon that path, a hand slid along my waist, and I jumped. I laughed to banish the fear that had darted through my body. "You're late," I accused him. "Where did you come from?"

"The stairway," he said. "I was in the village first, fetching a wheel bearing for Dugald." He held a plank of wood and a rolled blanket to his side. He looked particularly handsome today, his face scrubbed and his hair combed free of tangles. A moss green, ribbed jersey with a deep roll collar brought liveliness to his green eyes.

"Did anyone see you?" I asked him.

"Why? Am I not allowed to use the stairway?"

"Yes, of course. It's there for all to use."

He regarded me for a moment, his head slightly cocked. "Are you ashamed to be seen with me, Alyda Teasdale?"

"No. I asked only to see if someone was following you. My stepbrother, Noah, is a stick-tight these days."

"No spying stepbrothers that I could see." He balanced the plank on two large rocks

and spread the blanket upon it. "And this is far and away from the curious crowd in the village." He motioned me to join him on his bench.

We talked at length, that is to say, he did, because I peppered him with questions about his life. He was reluctant at first to answer them, maintaining that he hadn't led an interesting one. He was born and raised in Sydney, his father had been a coal miner, and his mother had her hands full with eleven children. Eleven children and amongst them, two sets of twins! He was the oldest of the lot, he told me.

I could not imagine a household of that size. "It must be very lively," I said.

"Chaotic. It doesn't help that my poor mum's not well—she gets bad bouts of the rheumatism. She's a brave woman, though; soldiers through everything."

When I asked him next about his father, he averted his gaze. He was dead, he told me, and he spoke with such an absence of feeling that I feared for him. I laced my fingers through his, but his hand resisted mine. It happened four months ago, and no, he would not talk to me about it, nor would he talk to me about him.

Should I have persisted? Surely he would have felt better if he had spoken to me about this. I too have lost my father. His face, however, was a storm and it daunted me.

To break the impasse, I asked him to tell me about his brothers and sisters. He appeared surprised by my interest. Every one of them, I assured him, and that is when the storm dissipated. We would start with his wee brother Ian he told me, and so he did.

I cannot remember each name now, but I will ask him again and create a list of the members of his family. I wish to know everything about him!

As I leave the bluff, I pay another visit to the site of the Whitfield house. The second post-demolition clean-up crew has been thorough. Except for the grey rocks that once formed its foundation, every sign of the house has been obliterated. The cellar has been filled with soil, level to the tops of the right-angled lines of stone. The soil is dark, dotted with small, smooth stones and the gnarled skeletal fingers of root systems.

I sit down on the southeast corner of the foundation, close to the lilac bush. Large clusters of pale purple flowers rise to the sky like goblets offered for a toast. The scent is mind-numbing. I remove my socks and runners and plant my feet in the soil.

I look across the fields to the line of thickets at the back of the property and Owen Sweeney comes to mind, travelling along the line after the demolition of the house. And I remember, too, that I had mistakenly seen a young woman—perhaps it wasn't a mistake, I think with a start. Perhaps that was my first sighting of Alyda. The young woman watching the destruction of a beloved home.

Where do ghosts go when their property is destroyed? Are they finally forced to enter another realm?

Light pressure on my shoulder. I jump, let my breath escape as I realize who it is.

Jack joins me on the stone foundation. "I have an idea," he says. He reaches down, scoops up a handful of earth then lets it fall in a fine shower from his hand. "This whole area would be perfect for a garden."

I consider the squares and rectangles, all in varying sizes, and envision the growth they would support. "It's even nicely sectioned off," I agree. "We could put vegetables in the front parlour and in the drawing room. That's what we'd want most of, wouldn't it be?"

Jack nods. "Herbs in the kitchen . . ."

"Perennials in the library." I picture tall strutting flowers that strive to outdo each other in height and vibrancy. "We need at least a few of those. I want poppies and lilies and delphiniums. And hollyhocks, of course."

Jack smiles. "We can even extend the gardens, if we want to, and plant things like perennial shrubs to keep our lilac company."

"Raspberry bushes. Can they be moved? If they can, I'm sure Nan would let us transplant some of hers. And currants."

"All good. I want to hire a chef for the inn who's used to working with fresh, local produce. That can be one of the selling features of the restaurant."

"And we can place the flowers on the dining room tables. It might even be nice to have a bouquet waiting in each guest room during the summer."

Down the road a short distance, where beams are being fitted for the framing of the inn, the high-pitched clamour of a saw begins. A minute later a breeze brings a fine mist of sawdust to our future garden. It settles on the soil and shimmers golden in the sunlight.

I feel a surge of affection for my father. Jack and his dreams. My feet dig into the soil until they are no longer visible. They're taking root, assuming ownership of the project that will take place there.

CHAPTER 16

In the silent tomb we leave thee
Til the morn when Christ appears
Then with joy we hope to greet thee
Far beyond this vale of tears

GRAMPS HAD MADE his contribution to my birth story, and I resolved not to cause him any further discomfort. He'd invoked Nan's involvement in the story, but it wasn't until the week before I left for university in Toronto that I finally approached Nan. This time she relented and gave me her insights into the story. To my surprise, I learned that Kaye also played an important part in it.

March 16, 1946. It's a raw and bitterly cold day on the mountain. The wind is icy and dirty snow lines the ditches; winter still has the mountain by its throat. Ben is two years old, and Kaye entrusts him to Warren as she and Nan drive cross country to the south shore to visit my mother. The two women are also on a fact-finding mission. They've heard rumours that the provincial government is threatening to close down the Ideal Maternity Home, the small institution in East Chester in which Gwyneth Montgomery has been living since the beginning of January.

An elderly woman, her face lined with exhaustion, greets Nan and Kaye. She's a midwife who lives on-site and she dismisses the reports about the home. Nan, however, is beginning to develop an uneasy feeling about the place. The home has always been austere, but now, to the background chorus of an inconsolable baby, it has a seedy quality to it, a marked sense of deterioration.

Gwyn is sitting on her bed when Nan hesitates at the entrance to the room; in a smooth few seconds she picks up a snow globe from her bedside table and hurls it across the room at her stepmother. Nan instinctively ducks, and Kaye, who is directly behind Nan, receives the full force of the object on her right cheek. The snow globe shatters as it strikes the floor, ejecting its miniature replicas of reindeer and evergreens.

"Sorry," Gwyn says. "That wasn't meant for you." She turns to Nan, who is staring at her, appalled. "That's for leaving me to rot in this hell-hole," she says, her voice remarkably calm.

Practical Kaye sets out to find ice to apply to her injury. She procures an ice bag from the kitchen and is disturbed to discover mouse droppings on one of the counters. She decides to conduct a tour of the rest of the home. As a nurse who has probably been exposed to worse, she is shocked by what she sees. Sailor mops stand abandoned in pails of dirty water. There is only one small bathroom, located on the second floor, and it is filthy. Chamber pots have not been emptied in some of the ground level rooms, and the stench of urine is overpowering. Two screaming babies are unattended, their mothers pale and listless on dingy bedding.

Nan is waiting at the front door when Kaye completes her inspection, and Kaye tells her that Gwyn cannot remain in this house of horrors. It's too late to drive safely back to the mountain; they'll stay overnight at a hotel in nearby Lunenburg and pick up Gwyn in the morning.

It was at this point that Nan brought her telling of the story to an end. A friend from the village had come to visit her, but I wouldn't have pushed her to continue the story once she was free again. I simply assumed that my mother was granted her wish to return home to the mountain. To have her baby there.

*Mr. Hamilton continues with his unfailing knack of approaching me when I am soul-tethered to a good book. I have always dreaded these moments and the ensuing conversations that lurch along like a carriage on a rutted country road. Today, upon seeing my book's title (*No Name*) he allowed that he had read it, as well as Wilkie Collins' better-known pieces,* The Woman in White *and* The Moonstone. *Purely for investigative purposes, he explained: he had to apprise himself of his parishioners' literary tastes and warn them of inappropriate reading matter.*

He nodded toward the book in my lap. "Collins is wearisome," he said, "in his preaching about society's ill-treatment of unmarried mothers and their illegitimate offspring."

"It's a subject that is worthy of everyone's attention," I protested. "Neither party deserves censure."

Mr. Hamilton gave a dismissive wave of his hand. "Collins only spoke from a bully pulpit because he felt guilt," he said. "The man fathered three children and didn't have the grace to marry their mother."

"She became a pariah for that, no doubt. Do you consider that just?"

"May I remind you of chapter twenty-three in Deuteronomy? The second verse clearly states that a bastard shall not enter into the congregation of the Lord; even to his tenth generation—"

I half rose from Papa's chair. "You're not listening to me! I was specifically espousing the rights of the mothers."

"Like their illicit children, they possess none; nor should they."

I clapped shut my book and rose from the chair.

"You will not leave this room without my permission," Mr. Hamilton said, his voice struggling to maintain a controlled pitch. "We have not finished this discussion."

"I have," I said.

I sailed by him and out of the room.

I stand on the doorstep of the side entrance to the Sweeney home, ready to test Ben's theory about Alma's knowledge of Alyda. In my hands is a Corning Ware container filled with a casserole of chicken and dumplings. I inhale its deep bouquet of rosemary before I knock on the screen door. "Mr. Sweeney?" I see him at the kitchen table, leaning back in a wooden chair, his head wreathed in a nimbus of cigarette smoke. "My grandmother's made something for you and your mother."

Mr. Sweeney stubs out the cigarette in an ashtray and hoists himself out of his chair. He opens the door for me, stretches out his arms to accept the pot. I move it out of his range and slide past him into the kitchen. It's the first time I've ever been inside the Sweeney home. "How's your mother?" I ask him. "Has she recovered from that day down by the bay?"

"She's doing fine."

I conduct a quick survey of the kitchen. Every inch of counter space is taken by cake-mix boxes, canned fruits and vegetables, tinned ham and tuna, and a large bowl of licorice All-Sorts tinged with dust. An old ironing board stands in front of the window, its rusty surface home to pots of ivies and spider plants. Stacks of dishes, nesting cups, and soup tureens conceal the oilskin cloth on a large table. Judging by the overhang, the table cloth sports a motif of roosters, hens, and eggs in wire baskets. It looks as though Alma's about to conduct an inside yard sale.

Mr. Sweeney spreads his arms in an all-compassing gesture. "I'm not allowed to put anything away," he says. "I've tried."

I lift the lid from the casserole dish and release a cloud of fragrant steam. "Let me give this to her," I say. "Do you have a bowl and a spoon?"

"I'll take it in to her." He tries to wrest the casserole dish from me, but I pull it out of reach, dance away from him.

"Mother's resting in bed and she's probably not hungry right now," he says. I resist, insisting that I personally deliver Nan's supper to her. Alma's bedroom adjoins the kitchen, and I've already caught a glimpse of her through the door.

"You won't be able to talk to her," he adds. "She's misplaced her hearing aid."

Alma is at sea in a massive four-poster bed with a teal blue velvet canopy. There are matching velvet drapes, cracked slightly to admit a nominal amount of light. I've heard that this was once the birthing room because of its proximity to the stove and the water pump. Alma would usually attend to her maternity patients in their own homes, but sometimes the women would come to this house.

The room is a busy one. There are paintings of pastoral themes—grazing sheep abound—on the scarlet, flocked wallpaper. A coat rack exhibits a collection of hats. Porcelain dolls, teddy bears, and stuffed animals of all sizes spill from shelves and over the edges of two antique sofas.

Alma is sitting upright in the bed, her hands resting primly on the quilt bedspread. Mr. Sweeney seats himself on the side of the bed and slides a teak tray under his mother's folded hands. The tray holds a folded cloth napkin and a spoon. He gently tucks a roaming wisp of hair behind his mother's ear. "Rachel Montgomery made you some dinner," he says, deepening the pitch of his voice.

Alma cocks her head toward me. There is no recognition in those arresting green eyes. "That's mighty fine of you, Rachel."

"I'm not Rachel, Mrs. Sweeney." Owen catches my eye, tugs on his ear. I raise my voice. "Rachel's my grandmother."

"Who is my grandmother?" She seems not the least bit surprised by the absurdity of the question.

"Rachel Montgomery is *my* grandmother." I tighten my grip on the bowl of chicken and dumplings, struggle to repress nervous laughter.

Alma leans forward and taps the tray with the palm of her hand. "Are you going to stand there all day, Rachel, or are you going to give me my supper?"

"Of course," I say. "I mean, here it is." I slink to her bedside, like a child chastised, and place the steaming bowl on the tray. Alma tucks the napkin into the collar of her flannel nightgown. She adjusts it, smoothes it with her hands. She places one hand on the spoon, but doesn't lift it. "Where's my water?" she says.

Mr. Sweeney stands up immediately. "I'll get it for you, Mother."

"And Owen?" He pauses at the doorway, without turning around. "Take that next cigarette outside, do you hear me?"

He'll be gone for at least a minute or two. Will that give me enough time to make reference to Alyda?

I was late today, frantic that he would no longer be there. We'd not missed one tryst in our cave yet, despite his demanding work schedule and our dependency upon the tides.

But he was there and my heart stilled. I caught a glimpse of his hair, gold-spun like the sun, in the shadows. Not one to be at rest while he was waiting for me, he had fashioned a low wall of rocks at the entrance to the cave. The rocks were heavy; he had chosen ones that could withstand the power of the tidewaters.

He broke into a grin as I approached. "I was setting to leave," he said. "I thought you'd forgotten." He was covered in a fine mist; his skin appeared moist and cool. I wanted to lay my hand on his cheek, but I dared not.

"Mama wouldn't let me go," I said. "She had one task after another for me to do."

"She suspects something."

"No." I said it with confidence, as if that would impart truth to it.

Today he could not sit. He paced the confines of the cave as he told me of his dream to one day own a cattle farm, as his cousin does. "Dugald told me that he'll give me a section of his land some day, when I've paid my dues and learned all that I need to know about animal husbandry."

"Do you trust him?"

"Yes, of course I do." He took my hands into his. "I'll be here, Allie. Someday I'll be here on the mountain year round."

I felt duplicitous; I've not told him that some of my plans for the future are well-laid, that I may never come back to live on the mountain. It was not the right time to do so; it would have been cruel to impinge upon his fervour.

And so I allowed his happiness to uplift me. He commanded centre stage, and I applauded his performance. And when we left the oven—he scrambling up the pathway and I rounding the bend of the bluff to take the stairway—I at least felt contentment.

It was not to last. About a hundred feet before me, at the edge of another oven, the sun made bold strokes of a shadow that had become familiar to me. I stiffened.

Noah squatted close to the entry, looking not the least bit sheepish for his sin of following me. He is but a boy, and if he weren't such a massive beast I would have seized him by the scruff of his collar and attempted to shake some sense into him.

"You are despicable, Noah," I said.

He stood up to full height, and he glared at me, a frown etched between jousting eyebrows. "He's not one of us. And you, Allie, meeting him on the sly—you give yourself airs, but you're no better than a trollop."

"Watch your tongue! I'll conduct my friendships as I see fit." I wheeled about and walked with studied care to the stairway.

Has a game of daring been declared between us? I cannot allow Noah to gain the upper hand.

Mr. Sweeney's quick re-entry with the glass of water supports my decision to wait. But he leaves the room again, and tension rises in me, urges me to execute my plan.

I cannot bring myself to interrupt Alma while she is eating her meal. Soon after she has finished it, however, the kitchen door squeaks open then closes with a prolonged yawn. Mr. Sweeney escaping to have another cigarette?

Now is the time. I push the food tray to the bottom of the bed. Then I lean down, close to Alma's ear. "Mrs. Sweeney, do you remember Alyda?"

Her body suddenly tenses; the shoulders wing forward.

"Alyda," I repeat. "Alyda Tea—"

"A *ladder*!"

I jump back, startled by the intensity of her response. Alma's face is contorted. I don't know if she's in pain or struggling to focus on something. "Poor Addie," she continues, her hands now plucking at the quilt. "There she was, sprawled like a rag-doll. Face in the dirt."

"Please. I wasn't asking about my—"

"Joshua just awailing and the others stunned into silence. Sweet Mother of God, I'll never forget the sound that man was making."

"Can we talk about something else, Mrs. Sweeney?" I try to sound brisk, matter-of-fact. I feel ill. For the first time in my life someone has fed me images of my grandmother's death.

Alma levels her cat's eyes at me. "He shouldn't have let her go up that ladder."

I glance at the doorway and pray that Mr. Sweeney will stay outside. "Mrs. Sweeney, I'm sorry." I feel terrible for causing her such distress. I sit down on the bed; my hand hovers two or three inches above hers. I'm not sure if she will respond positively to contact. She's shaking now. Fear starts to insinuate itself through every nerve in my body. What if she has a stroke or a heart attack?

Alma opens her mouth. She runs her tongue along the delicate trenches of her lower teeth. Then, in a voice that belies any frailty she barks, "Owen!"

The screen door slams open. Mr. Sweeney launches himself into the room, his face taut with fear. He sends an accusing glance in my direction. "What's going on?"

Before I can cobble together an explanation, Alma corrals her thoughts. She looks up at her son then bears down with her eyebrows. "Don't just stand there! Pull the ladder off Addie!"

Mr. Sweeney reaches the bed in a few quick strides. "She's all right, Mother. Addie's all right. Josh is seeing to her right now."

The fear begins to recede from Alma's eyes. "You're sure of that, Owen?"

Mr. Sweeney meets my eyes, jerks his head in the direction of the door to signal that I should go. His face betrays anger now; it's clear that he considers me the source of his mother's distress.

As I leave the room, I hear his voice, low and soothing, "I'm sure, Mother. I'm absolutely sure."

CHAPTER 17

Sweet pleasure only blooms
And then it dies
Leaves friends to mourn
For friends beyond the skies

"FLAT EARTH OR round?" I asked Noah. He slouched into his father's office, taking the chair that was closest to the door. "To which school of thought do you belong?"

He stared at me, a stunned bunny with hooded eyes and a slack mouth. He recovered in time to say, "You cannot be serious."

I feigned a notation on a sheet of paper on the desk. "I just need to determine how much you do know and what I must teach you."

"I won't stand for any ridicule."

"I'm not mocking you. I need to review with you a number of basic concepts. I shall assume that you consider the earth to be round. Now, dinosaurs and human beings—did they live in different epochs or together on this earth?"

"Together, of course." He fixed his eyes to his lap for a moment, in concentration. "Genesis 1:25 tells us that God made the beasts of the earth after his kind—"

I interrupt him before he continues the recitation. "Genesis gives us a tidy allegory.

Your ancestors did not tread earth with those lumbering beasts. We are talking of millions of years of separation."

"Father won't stand for this."

I shrugged. "He appointed me your tutor. Tell him, by all means. I'll be happy to be relieved of my duties."

Noah stood abruptly and moved his chair back with an ear-thrashing scrape, then just as suddenly he reclaimed the chair and sat down upon it again. He looked grieved. "Continue," he said.

I didn't question his behaviour. The two hours flew by quickly; I confess it was entertaining to disabuse him of a number of erroneous notions. As I gathered together my papers, I asked him, "Are you comfortable now with Mr. Darwin's theories?"

"I know enough about them to write what's needed on the examinations. That's all that matters to me."

I shot high my eyebrows. "Your practical nature triumphed over your convictions. Is that why you decided not to report me to your father?"

"No, that's not the reason why." He licked his lips, swept away the moisture with the back of his hand. "I had a vision of you and the farm drudge together. Every hour that I'm with you is an hour away from him."

Daft boy. It seems he has no idea how hard Caleb works on the Roy farm, and how hard he and I must fight for the time we spend together.

Ben and I escape to the graveyard almost every day. He takes this project seriously. All his notes are meticulous, and he types both his and mine on the same day.

Yes, the epitaphs are often bleak and melancholy, but Ben—scientist Ben—finds beauty in the formality of the language and the religious overtones. He tried hard one day to think of a word that best describes the verse and finally settled upon *earnest,* a word that is delightfully apt.

Sometimes he reminds me of an archaeologist who has stumbled upon a major discovery. "Ree! Over here!" His hand had been brisk in motioning me to join him. "Look at this—six kids in one family who died within two weeks of each other. The youngest was only seven months old." He had slid the palm of his hand over the raised inscription dedicated to baby Clementine Drury, gently as if he were closing the eyelids of a just-deceased. "Makes you wonder if they all died of the same disease," he had said. "Can you even begin to imagine what those parents went through?"

Today, as I come out of a stretch to ease the kinks in my muscles, my eye catches movement in the distance. Ben's hand is particularly urgent this time. The obelisk he is mapping is of a deep red marble, capped by a draped-urn finial that seems almost top-heavy. A memory of a long-ago graveyard jaunt flares before I even see the name *Teasdale* engraved in block letters just above the base. My eyes immediately rise again to the inscription:

In loving remembrance
of
Susannah Elizabeth Teasdale
Beloved wife of Joseph A. Teasdale
who departed this realm May 16, 1863
aged 42 years

Her sun has gone down
while it was still day
Be ye also ready
for in such an hour
as ye think not
the Son of Man cometh

Judging by the dates, this must be the mother of William, Joseph and Elias Teasdale. How old would the twins have been when she died?

A tug of the arm; Ben steers me to the next side:

William Annandale Teasdale
February 22, 1819 – September 19, 1886
Beloved husband of Susannah
Noted citizen
of our village

A candle flickered brief and wan
It soon let go its light
And from my deathbed, ill and frail
I entered into night

And now Ben propels me to the third side, ready to present the *pièce de résistance*:

To perpetuate the memory
of
Captain Elias M. Teasdale
Son of William and Susannah Teasdale
Who died in honour at sea
in the just execution of his office
during the loss of the Laliah B
and remains forever lost in the deeps
November 28, 1895

"Alyda's father got a marker, after all," Ben says. "*Died in honour.* That makes it a fitting memorial, don't you think?"

I'm not sure if I agree with his assessment. "It's okay," I say. "There's not enough personal information for my liking—no date of birth and nothing to indicate that he was married and had a family."

"And no verse."

"That, too."

An ant has found its way onto Ben's arm. Bewildered, it moves cautiously through the maze of fine hairs. "The information about the captain's loss at sea," he says, "is similar to what you'd find on a cenotaph."

"It looks like that was more important to his family—to his brothers, in any event."

The ant gets blown to the grass. Gently. "Maybe it was their way of showing disapproval of Verity's remarriage," he says. "Still, it's a decent memorial."

I'm not convinced. "There weren't any money problems in the family. The very least the Teasdale family could have done is erect something solely in his honour."

"We weren't there, Ree. There may be a reason why they chose this route."

My list of inquiries inevitably grows.

I suggested that we adjourn to the outdoors for Noah's lesson today. I had in mind to place him under one of the apple trees by the graveyard, arrange for an apple to plunge onto his head, and pray that it would drive inspiration into him. It worked well for Isaac Newton.

Noah looked horrified. "I won't go near the graveyard," he said.

"Why not? Are you afraid of ghosts?"

A flush stole across his face. "They exist," he muttered.

"Of course they do. But I don't believe they mean us any harm."

"Father says there are children buried there who weren't baptized and buried before sunrise. They haven't been admitted to heaven."

"How does your father know that the children weren't baptized?"

Silence.

"If they aren't in heaven, where are they?"

"I don't know," he admitted. "They float. Somewhere. They have no home."

"Did your mother believe this?"

"Yes, she would have. She was always of the same mind as Father. He made sure that she and the baby were buried in proper fashion."

"Your mother died in childbirth?" I surprised myself by adding, "What was it, the baby? A boy or a girl?"

"A girl. I had a sister once."

I briskly gathered my books and papers into my arms. I would not give in to his attempt to cultivate my sympathy. "We're going to the graveyard, Noah," I said. "Do you really think our God would punish innocent babes?"

Mr. Sweeney looks dapper today. A new pair of wire-framed reading glasses clings to the bridge of his nose as he peruses figures in an accounting ledger. Even though the temperature is in the mid-seventies, he's wearing a crisp white shirt and a navy blue blazer with a crest on the single pocket. A stiff white handkerchief in the pocket adds a flourish.

I'm concerned about the reception he'll give me; this will be our first meeting since the incident with his mother. The scenario of my grandmother's death continues to haunt me, as does Alma's response to it. I constantly replay the incident in my mind, reshape its nuances. Mr. Sweeney doesn't raise it, however, and I soon begin to relax, reassured that we'll continue our collaboration.

After a lengthy discussion about the last two completed journal entries, I ask him, "Why didn't you tell me about Joseph and Susannah's obelisk? It's good to know that Alyda, in some fashion, got her wish for a memorial for her father."

"I knew you would eventually find it on your own." He removes his glasses and tucks them in the pocket of his blazer. "Go to the museum in Danton if you want to find out more about the Teasdales. They have records for Ocean's Edge that date to 1903."

"Why are the records there? Shouldn't they be in your hands?"

"They should be. But since the turn of the century the funds for the cemetery have come from benefactors in Danton, business people who also sit on the board of their museum." A wistful half-smile. "I can't compete with that."

"Will those records tell me when Captain Teasdale's inscription was engraved and who commissioned it?"

"They'll tell you that the inscription was carved in 1902 by Rigby St. James, the same man who did the engraving for Alyda's tombstone. As to the name of the person who commissioned it, the records don't provide that kind of information."

1902. The inscription for Alyda's father was etched into the Teasdale family obelisk five years after her death. Not only did she endure the loss of her father, she did not live to see the desired memorial to him.

It is all so patently unjust.

"Go to it, Noah. Open it for me."

He was trembling as he unlatched the lichgate and swung it to one side. A layered fog was beginning to roll in from the bay. It would soon create the perfect ambience for our school room.

I knew exactly where to take him for the first stage of my lesson. The tall tablet marker, near the east end of the orchard of apple trees, belonged to Captain Enoch Sabean, who had died twelve years before. Beneath the crude etching of an anchor, it stated: A gale that stormed throughout his life / Washed over him and eased his strife.

"Do you know anything of this man, Noah?"

"No." And then, with added petulance, "Should I?"

"Was he lost at sea?"

"No. I don't know. It doesn't tell us if he died at sea."

"Then what did he die of?"

Noah read the inscription one more time. "I don't know," he said, his voice flat yet emphatic.

"Speculate." I did my best to quell the frustration in my voice. "Please."

"I don't know," he repeated. "This has nothing to do with my schooling!"

"Yes, it does. I find that your biggest impediment to learning is your inability to look at things in different ways. Your mind is as rigid as one of these tombstones."

He looked pathetic and frightened; it was evident he hadn't understood one word of mine. I took pity upon him and directed him to another tombstone to start afresh. The epitaph for Eliza Gates rivalled Enoch Sabean's in its short length and obscurity. In slanted, florid script, on another double-height tablet marker, it told us: In fortitude was not a queen / But in our hearts she's as one seen.

"What does the word 'fortitude' mean?" I asked him.

"Courage."

"Do you think that the person who chose Eliza's epitaph had a synonym for courage in mind?"

He shrugged his shoulders. "How can we know?"

"We can't. All I want you to do is conjecture, Noah. What do you think?"

At last he humoured me; he studied the entire inscription again. "She was only nine years old," he said. "Surely they didn't expect her to be courageous in the face of pain or hardship?"

I felt a tingle of excitement. "Continue."

He frowned. "Perhaps 'fortitude' in this case means 'stamina' or 'endurance.' Could it be about her young age?"

"Bravo!" I almost clapped him on the back. At first he looked mistrustful of my approbation; he must have assumed once again that I was mocking him. He studied my face carefully and finally nodded.

"Let's go home now," he said. "It'll be a choking fog soon. We shouldn't be here."

"You could strike me blind and I'd still be able to lead you to any tombstone upon request. Just one more epitaph and then we'll consider it a day."

Mist swirling about us, I led him to the tombstone of Nathaniel Banks. It was a simple slate tablet with the ever-popular weeping willow motif and the stark announcement: Died in collision with a steam engine. *Nathaniel was only nineteen years old on the day of his death in 1879. The way in which he died was indisputable, but the circumstances behind it were not. I asked Noah, "Was poor Nathaniel distracted? Tired or careless? Booted or shoved into eternity? What are your thoughts?"*

He looked solemn now. "Again, we cannot be certain," he said, "but perhaps he set out to take his own life."

I smiled. "Consider the lesson for the day done."

Nothing is etched in stone.

The museum in Danton is one of the few buildings in town constructed of brick. It comprises two storeys and its façade is concealed by dense layers of ivy. A wide flight of steps leads to the cracked Doric columns that flank its entrance, a wooden door that rivals those found in medieval castles for its aura of impenetrability.

An employee of the archives department is ready to assist Ben and me. Mary-Anne Bell doesn't look a day over fourteen. She is short and vibrant with energy, and her eyes have assumed an exotic slant, thanks to the over-efficient elastic band that encircles the base of her pony tail. She leads us into a side room with a long table, heavy wooden chairs, and several rows of back-to-back filing cabinets. A pervasive smell of lemon-oil furniture polish clouds the air.

Ben and I seat ourselves at the table, and Mary-Anne brings us a rectangular book, similar in size to Alyda's scrapbook. "I thought you'd be interested in seeing this first," she says.

The book is cloth-bound and olive-coloured, with a dark brown cross weave. A large water stain, orbited by several smaller satellite stains, holds centre ground. I catch a whiff of mould. "It's a record book for Ocean's Edge," she continues, "covering the years from 1853 to 1903."

The information in the book was compiled by one of the graveyard's caretakers, a woman by the name of Martha Munro. Her brother, Daniel Munro, was the sexton of St. Luke's and the head of the cemetery association. Martha did the paperwork associated with the cemetery and also filled the journal with notes of a personal nature on each resident of the graveyard.

I open the book randomly to a section in the middle and my eye immediately catches the name of Jane Elizabeth Hiltz. This must be the little Janie from one of the earlier journal entries, the one who died a year before Alyda.

Janie of the bright blue pinafore. Her headstone is one of several recumbent lambs in Ocean's Edge, one of a "flock" of gravestones that marks the deaths of several children in one year. Scarlet fever, I surmised. Or diphtheria.

The page is yellowed and brittle. Martha Munro's handwriting is small and precise, spidery thin. An ink blot rides the *z* of *Hiltz*, but doesn't obscure it.

Jane Elizabeth Hiltz is written in a left-hand column, along with the notation *b. 30 January 1891 / d. 26 June 1896.* Below that is the epitaph:

I have not years enough in me
To be by life beguiled
Tis cruel that I must part this life
When I am but a child

In the right hand column, immediately opposite the name, is a list of entries:

316 (B. Holtby and Son)
3rd daughter of Adam Hiltz and Anna Sampson Hiltz
Sister to Adriana, Molly and Hector
Model for Lily's Taffy Sweets and Dr. Malleby's Soothing Cough Syrup
Summer milk ailment

Touched by these random and personal details of a young life, I ask Mary-Anne, "Why did she note down this kind of information?"

"I'm not sure. I've never come across other records like this. Perhaps she thought people in the next century might be interested in trivia like this from an historical point of view."

"What was summer milk ailment?"

"It was a bacterial infection from drinking milk that wasn't pasteurized. Diseases like scarlet fever, cholera or tuberculosis usually come to mind when we think of the 1800s, but the summer milk ailment wasn't an uncommon cause of death back then."

"And the 316? B. Holtby? What do they stand for?"

"That's the plot number and the name of the stone engraver."

Beside me, Ben shifts his weight. "Alyda," he says, with uncharacteristic impatience. "Find Alyda."

I turn the next three pages and Alyda's name leaps out at us from the top of the following page:

Alyda Faith Teasdale b. 16 January 1880 / d. 3 June 1897

As in other entries, the full inscription of the tombstone is noted. The personal data are as follows:

339 (Rigby St. James)
Elder daughter of the late Captain Elias Teasdale and Mrs. Verity Hamilton; stepdaughter of the Reverend Mr. Zachariah Hamilton
Sister to Sibley; niece of Dr. Joseph Teasdale and Mrs. Helen Teasdale
Pianist; erstwhile student at Dalhousie University
Drowned

I stare at Mary-Anne Bell, my voice throat-snagged. It is Ben who finds his first. "Alyda *drowned*?" he says.

"We'd assumed she'd died in childbirth," I explain to Mary-Anne. As I read the notation that belongs to the baby, I run my fingers along it.

339 (Rigby St. James)
Unnamed infant boy b. 31 May 1897 / d. 6 June 1897
Son of Alyda Faith Teasdale
Causes unknown

Mary-Anne looks confused; she must assume that Mr. Sweeney has already given me an overview of Alyda's life. I describe the nature of my sessions with the old man.

"If Mr. Sweeney isn't giving you all the information you need," she says, "then I'll see what I can do for you on my end. We have newspaper archives here for the *Danton Chronicle* and the *Port Carlyle Sentinel* dating back to the mid-1800s, and I can look up articles on Alyda Teasdale's death for you. Just give me a few days, though. A short while ago we packed all those files in boxes because they'll be going to another floor."

Ben and I express our gratitude to Mary-Anne and exit from the dark stillness of the museum onto its sun-washed front steps.

"Owen Sweeney's playing a game," Ben says, as we descend to the street. "I'm not sure why he is, but by suggesting that we come here he's changed one of the rules. He's decided to relinquish some control."

Ben may be right.

And I'm particularly pleased with the "discovery" of Mary-Anne Bell. I've acquired another source for my book.

CHAPTER 18

One by one our friends pass o'er
To the bright and peaceful shore
And they join in glad surprise
The glorious anthem of the skies

"YOUR MOTHER ALMOST died."

Kaye told me this as she sat on my bed, calmly rolling pairs of socks together to tuck them into my suitcase. I would be leaving the next morning to attend school in Toronto, and she'd come into the city to say good-bye to me.

She looked up at me when I didn't reply, regarded my face carefully. I'd disciplined it to be impassive, but Kaye was never one to be fooled. "Come here," she said, patting an empty spot on my quilt. "Rachel tells me you haven't heard the whole story. Sit down with me."

I did as I was told.

Gwyn was experiencing vaginal bleeding, but had not told anyone in the home about this. When Nan and Kaye arrived from Lunenburg that morning, Kaye immediately knew that something was amiss. She detected the metallic odour of blood and saw that Gwyn was horribly pale. While Nan was in the office arranging for Gwyn's discharge, Kaye pulled the covers from Gwyn and found the sheets soaked in blood. She ordered a nurse's assistant, hesitating in the doorway, to call an ambulance. The young woman, eyes pooled in fear, didn't move an inch. "I can't do that," she said. "We don't have permission to—"

Kaye had already stripped an empty neighbouring bed of its clean sheets and was starting to pack them around Gwyn. She sent rolled-up, bloody sheets flying across the room to the doorway. The young woman stepped back, aghast. "Then find someone who can make that call," Kaye said. *Now.*"

Gwyn was taken immediately to the women's hospital in Halifax. She had placenta praevia and had lost considerable blood by the time of her arrival. An emergency Caesarian section saved her life and that of the baby.

Rianne Adelaide Montgomery weighed in at an impressive three pounds, eleven ounces, with the customary respiratory problems of a preemie. Adoption wouldn't be an option for a while.

Nan and Kaye visited the new mother in the hospital the next day, Nan bearing a lavish bouquet of pink roses. Gwyn refused to bury her nose in the flowers (pink roses were her favourites) or acknowledge them as a gift of joy.

"I got a good look at the baby," said Kaye, who had been smuggled into the neonatal intensive care unit by a friend from nursing school days. "She's beautiful." Tension bristled in the room. Kaye kept trying to steer the conversation into neutral territory. Eventually she had to acknowledge defeat.

"I'm going back to school in the fall to finish my grade twelve," Gwyn said. "And then I'm going to university."

And Nan, her voice equally blunt and rising, replied, "Do whatever you want. But that wee little girl isn't leaving our family."

The home that I escaped, the Ideal Maternity Home, plied an illegal trade in infants between Canada and the United States for almost two decades. It's believed that babies which were considered unmarketable—those who were sickly, physically or mentally disabled, or of mixed race—were starved to death on a diet of molasses and water. Some of the bodies were thrown into the ocean or burned in the home's furnace. Others were buried in butter boxes—wooden crates from a local dairy.

At the time of my mother's stay, the home had already been shut down once but had started operating again as it appealed a conviction of violating new adoption licensing laws.

An ultimately healthy child and the achievement of her dreams—my mother was granted both. But the fates conspired against Alyda.

"Consider yourself lucky," Nan has said to me on a number of occasions. Knowing Nan, it wasn't just in reference to a butter box fate.

We've met many times now in the oven and on the boundaries of Dugald Roy's property. Oft times, Caleb signals that he's free to meet me by sounding the call of a nighthawk. It's an eerie whistle, akin to the rushing sound of the male bird as he first circles high then plunges in a dive during courtship display.

For our rendezvous today I brought along Griff and a picnic basket filled with soda bread, cheese, and a handful of late strawberries. Caleb is always hungry and grateful for the food that I bring him.

He was waiting for me, pacing the edge of the bluff. His hair dazzled in the sunlight. Over a few short weeks it has turned from harvest wheat to almost white.

It was peaceful on the bluff, the waning sun still warm on the skin. We sat on the grass and listened to the song of the cicadas. He took all the strawberries but one from my basket, and soon dispatched them with a few gulps. Then he leaned to me, and his tongue, hot and scented with the ripe fruit, tickled my ear.

"Stop," I said, my voice trembling. "No more!"

He heeded me and he pulled back; his face gauged mine carefully. "You mean it," he said.

I exhaled a ragged breath. "I do." I blush even now to recall my fierce response.

Caleb shrugged away his disappointment and threw a generous piece of cheese to Griff. Then he jumped to his feet and walked swiftly to the edge of the bluff, to an area where a giant spruce lists to the bay. He looked back and grinned at me then leapt with spring-loaded grace, just like a wildcat, into the air beyond the bluff edge!

He was gone! He was truly gone. There was not a sound from him or the sound of an impact, but perhaps that was because I could not hear anything for the roaring in my head and Griff's endless barking.

And then a movement stayed me. The spruce was quivering, and as I looked to it, a patch of blond hair suddenly skimmed the top of the cliff. I stood up, and my wobbly legs took me to the edge, and there was Caleb, hanging from an extended root of the spruce like a trapeze artist. His chest was heaving and his arms trembled with exertion.

"Griff," he managed between his teeth, and then, "Stand back."

I hooked my arm around Griff's neck and we retreated several feet. Seconds later, Caleb hoisted himself up and twisted his body to the side like a pole vaulter, to the exact degree required to land him on the edge of the bluff. Behind him a portion of its edge crumbled and hurtled to the shore below.

He rolled himself a few more feet away from the edge. I pounced upon him immediately and pounded him mercilessly with my fists. Griff circled us, barking and adding a chorus to my fury. "You blithering idiot!" I shouted. "How could you do something so utterly senseless!"

He curled into a ball to protect himself from my blows. His body shook with laughter. "Enough!" he finally gasped.

I called a truce, for my hands were throbbing. Caleb remained in position for a minute; perhaps he was deciding whether I still posed a threat to him. Then he rolled over and sat up. "I didn't mean to do it," he said.

"You're a liar." I recalled the pacing steps, the arc of his body as it launched to the sky and then plummeted like a wild duck riddled with buckshot.

"All right," he admitted. "I've been here before and I tested the root."

"You did this before? You knew that the tree would support you?"

"I did. You're not impressed?"

"No. Should I be impressed by someone who behaves much as a five year old?"

He laughed. "You want a lily-livered beau?"

"Beau? You presume too much, Caleb Whitelaw."

He came to me, fell to his knees, and put his arms around me. "What would impress you, Allie mine?"

"A sense of responsibility."

"Tell me you don't mean that. You're only saying that now because I frightened the daylights out of you."

I remained silent, rigid beneath his arms.

"I told you, I made sure that I'd be safe."

"You couldn't know that the root would stay strong a second time," I said. "All the trees on the edge have an uncertain hold."

"Then I would have plunged to the rocks below and deserved my fate."

His tone of voice was light to the heart, but it sent a chill through my body. He meant what he said, I was sure of it, and I could not abide his way of thinking.

We all have a precarious hold on life. We must cling to it with all the forces we can muster.

On the agenda today is a trip to the shore. I load a small cooler packed with food and drinks into the back of Gramps's Jeep. A bag filled with firewood and kindling joins it, along with several sticks for roasting hot dogs.

Ben's already seated on the front steps of his house, Lucy at his side, when I swing by. The sun glints off his mirrored aviator sunglasses. He's growing a beard. The skin beneath his cast is itching mercilessly, and he's decided that nurturing a beard will distract him and stop him from going insane. Five days' worth of stubble now, he tells me with a grin. The beard looks good on him—it gives him an air of *gravitas.*

We drive slowly along the sand-and-gravel shore road west of the village. The window is down for Lucy, and fine dust settles on us like a fog rolling in from the bay. About two miles in we arrive at a meadow, a small clearing between two dense woodlots. Nailed to a tree at its entrance is a crudely etched *No trespassing* sign. It doesn't deter all of the locals, many of whom know that the meadow isn't private property, but it reduces overall traffic to that part of the shore. Ben and I have often had it to ourselves.

The Jeep noses its way first through a rutted path in the meadow, then negotiates a narrow rock-and-dirt road that slopes down to the ocean. It's my favourite spot on the bay, a showcase of boulders and ghost-fingered driftwood. There are four ovens set into the bluff on this stretch of the shore—Alyda and Caleb's cave is the last one. It is on the other side of a promontory, at a considerable distance from us. Close to the first oven a long, narrow waterfall streams down the rocks and glitters in the sunshine.

Ben won't be able to negotiate the rocks close to the water. He makes himself comfortable on a driftwood log on the upper reaches of the shore. The sand in this area is coarse, studded with small stones. The log itself is almost obscured by an invasion of morning glory vines. A fire pit beside it shows signs of recent use; it's filled with charred roasting sticks and dimpled orange peels.

Lucy, attention hog that she is, immediately demands a game of fetch. I find a good piece of deadwood for Ben and he starts tossing it to her, throwing it far and high. She streaks across the sand, her tail a plumed arc above her back. Once she's stationed below the stick, she takes a flying leap into the air, twisting body and head to capture it. She gets sidetracked from this game of aerial catch twice, first to pay homage to a dead crab, and then to devour the remains of a sand-coated roast beef sandwich. We have to wait until she's finished doing justice to that one.

I leave Ben and Lucy to their game and go down to the shore to explore the shallow tidal pools among the rocks. Almost immediately I find a creature trapped in one of them. It looks like a starfish, but the arms aren't as thick as those of one. I call up to Ben and describe it to him—the bluish centre, the long and thin arms with bands of green and brown. The arms are in constant languid motion.

"Sounds like a Daisy brittle star."

"That's really what it's called?"

"Would I lie to you? Show it to me."

Stalling for time, I inspect the brittle star in its tidal pool. I've never come across one on this expanse of the shore before. "Two of its arms are shorter," I say.

"How many does it have?"

"Seven."

Ben whistles. "They start off with five. It probably lost a couple at one point and had to regenerate, but then its body just kept producing."

I look down on the Daisy brittle star, equipped by nature with this special survival mechanism and then left stranded, at the mercy of predators, in a tidal pool.

"Hold it up for me," Ben says.

I bend down and grasp the end of one arm with tentative fingers; the brittle star slackens. It feels cool and moist, rubbery. I slide it up and out of the water, almost even to my waist, but then I lose my grip and it plunges back into the tidal pool.

"Ouch," Ben says.

I crouch down, observe it anxiously. It lies motionless for a long time, but finally its arms begin to stir again. "She's okay," I reassure him. "Did you get a good look? Was it a Daisy brittle star?"

"Yup. Now that you've decided it's a *she*, pick her up again and take her down to the water."

"Do I have to? She's in lots of water until the tide comes back in."

"What if a gang of seagulls comes along before then?"

"You're joking, right?"

"We might have some badass seagulls in these parts. You never know."

He's putting me on, I'm sure of it, but I take a deep breath and bend down. This time I grasp Daisy firmly by one arm, closer to the centre disc, and then fling her like a Frisbee into the ocean. Caught by the crest of a wave, she bobs briefly then sinks out of sight. I wipe my hands down on my shorts, sniff my fingers.

Ben laughs. "She's not going to give you some rare disease."

"You never know and I'm about to serve lunch."

"I've been dying to know what's in that cooler."

My picnic consists of a pack of hot dogs, buns and condiments, potato salad, carrot sticks, grapes, and a bag of Oreo cookies.

"No marshmallows?" Ben feigns disappointment.

"Don't be greedy."

Ben cooks his hot dogs, all three of them, to blackened, blistered crisps. My two hotdogs barely taste the fire. They emerge, sleek and shiny, with two tawny stripes. Lucy is in full mooching mode, swivelling her head between the two of us.

I finish the picnic with the grapes and then lean comfortably into the warm, solid incline of a rock. Lucy completes a self-administered massage among the rocks and stretches out among them. Ben trawls his skewer through the low-key flames of the fire as he cooks yet another hot dog. Ash flakes drift lazily upward then stop suddenly, suspended in the air, as if they are deciding where to go next.

"What's on your mind?" Ben says.

I glance over at him, wishing that the sun glasses didn't obscure his eyes. "That Daisy brittle star," I say. "I can't stop thinking about it. It got a reprieve today, but it's still going to end up in the gullet of some predator. It's no more equipped to avoid its fate than any animal that's low on the food chain. Take snowshoe hares, for example. They get to change their coat colour from summer to winter for camouflage and they run in a zigzag pattern to complicate things a bit for a predator, but—"

"What are you getting at?"

"I'm not sure. But the odds are stacked against them. Against *us*. I'm sure this idea isn't an original one, but don't you wonder sometimes if someone or something up there is just playing games with us?"

Ben reaches for the ketchup. He grins at me. "Not on a magnificent day like this. On a day like this I just let it all go."

He always makes everything sound so easy. And I don't think it's a guise he puts on for my benefit—for the most part, things *are* easy for him. Ben accepts that the universe is an imperfect place. I beat my head against walls.

I have to find a way to adopt his perspective.

Caleb is away from the mountain for several days, gone to Yarmouth in the company of a fellow worker from the Roy farm. They are entrusted to fetch certain materials for the farm, but when I inquired as to the nature of these materials, Caleb declined to say more. I am now doubly annoyed with him as his leaping from the bluff still rankles. He has five more years to my sixteen; am I unreasonable to expect less childish behaviour from him? Perhaps it's for the best that we enjoy a break from one another.

I asked Aunt Helen today if she would render a fallen angel for my journal, but she immediately rejected the proposal. I persisted, believing that modesty might be the grounds for this. It is deplorable how insensitive I am at times. Truly, anyone else would have heeded the look of profound dismay upon her face, but I chattered on, oblivious to her discomfort until she finally raised her voice (Aunt Helen always speaks with the softest of tones) to inform me that she simply wasn't at ease with the subject. I apologized, and she was immediately her old self again. "I'm content with my flower cards, Allie," she said.

I resolved to make amends, and so I later brought her generous crowns of fireweed and meadowsweet and fed them to her old press. She sat with me as I performed this task and suddenly she placed a hand on mine. "Your hands are as brown as a nut, Allie," she said. She looked at me intently and continued, "And your face is ruddy, too. Are you not protecting it from the sun?"

I pressed my fingertips to my cheeks and felt a deep warmth course to them. "I lost my bonnet the other day," I said. "The wind carried it away as I was trying to adjust the ribbons."It was an ill-prepared lie, but if Aunt Helen was mistrustful of my explanation, she did not show it.

"What does your mother say to this?"

I thought of Mama and her complexion of a consumptive, achieved by diligently avoiding the outdoors. "You can be sure she hasn't paid notice," I said. "There are other things she now considers more important."

Aunt Helen, true to her diplomatic nature, declined to comment on my observation and its tone of bitterness. She smiled and simply granted that my skin had a healthy glow.

A quiet day often dictates a peaceable night. It is not so for me tonight. Halfway through the night I'm assailed by a nightmare. Perhaps those existentialist musings at the end of my picnic with Ben have something to do with it.

It is late evening, and storm clouds obliterate the horizon. I'm standing at the northern boundary of the graveyard, looking out to the ocean, where a tombstone slab floats upon its choppy waters. Suddenly, the slab lists towards the shore, and a pair of hands rises from the water and grips one side. And then the owner of those hands bursts out of the water and struggles to achieve a greater hold on the slippery stone. Alyda is panicking, salt water burning her throat as it chokes her. I can feel every muscle in her body straining, vibrating.

A body brushes by me, almost knocks me to the ground. A man hesitates briefly at the edge of the water then tears off his corduroy cap and tosses it to the ground. As in all of my dreams that demand fight or flight, I am paralysed. But I can still find my voice. *Caleb!* I shout. *Do something!* He doesn't need this directive, of course; he's already hopping for balance as he struggles to remove his shoes. He plunges into the water, starts swimming with frantic strokes toward the slab and the girl who has slipped beneath the waters again.

I awake, hands clenched. My heart threatening to leap out of my chest.

Light penetrates the crack beneath my bedroom door. I sit up and gulp air for my frenzied heart. As my heartbeats steady, the fridge door squeaks open, closes. A spoon strikes a mug and liquid splashes into a pot. I hear the *skritch* of a match and then a soft *whoosh* as an element of the gas stove is ignited.

It's not long before Nan arrives in my room, bearing a huge mug of cinnamon-scented hot chocolate. Nan's cure for everything.

Chapter 19

I slept on the shore of time
But was not permitted to stay
God proferred me joys more sublime
His angels conveyed me away

The postman arrives on our doorstep today, bearing two items for me. One is a registered letter from Toronto with the return address of Paul Haddon's law firm; the other is a postcard of a dog-sled team silhouetted against a spectacular sunset.

Avoidance is always a good short-term solution for anxiety, and so I set Paul's envelope aside. I turn my attention to the postcard that my mother has sent me from Yellowknife.

In small, cramped script Mom tells me that she's fine and that the work is gratifying. She thanks both Paul and me for the time spent overnight at our apartment before she flew to Yellowknife the following day. "I can tell Paul's going to be around for a long time," she writes.

I sit down at my desk, pull a pad of stationery from the drawer, and begin a letter to her. At first it hints at a trial separation from Paul, but then I crumple that sheet of paper and start anew. This time I make it clear the break is permanent and that the decision was mine.

How can I begin to explain it? I do so by describing an incident that occurred early on in our relationship. It was the fall of 1969, and I participated in a massive protest at Toronto City Hall against the war in Viet Nam. In the company of fellow students and faculty members from the university, I'd carried a sign that read: *Kill for peace?* Paul was enraged when he learned of my involvement. "You made a bloody fool of yourself," he spat out, and then he didn't speak to me for a week.

There's no need to revisit this, even for my mother's sake. I destroy that sheet of paper as well and simply tell Mom that Paul was stifling me, that I'd felt I was losing a part of myself. I imagine her rejection of my argument: "Really, Rianne! What's that supposed to mean?"

The explanation of the breakup expedited, I find a strange need to continue writing. I tear another sheet from the pad and before long I find myself describing the Alyda project and how it has affected me. *She was only sixteen when she got pregnant, the same age as you. When I'm working on the journal entries, I manage to feel okay—I'm keeping her alive, even if it's only to take her through some rough times again. Sometimes, though, I can't stand it, knowing that she had to die at such a young age and that the baby died too.*

Soon I find myself typing copies of my birth story passages to enclose. *I had to finish the story, Mom. Gramps, Nan and Kaye all gave me something to work with, but you'll see I've taken a fair degree of literary licence. Now I'd like to hear everything from you.*

I want her to separate the fiction from the facts for me.

I simply want her to respond.

Much as I confess to pique over Caleb's conduct, I find that I miss him. At times I catch myself smiling in remembrance of his prank. Jumping off a cliff for me! Perhaps it did have greater meaning than that of a school-boy stunt?

This afternoon I visited our oven. A slippery new growth of algae required the plank's turning and there, snagged in a sliver of wood, was a long piece of moss green yarn. Without doubt it had come from Caleb's jersey, the one he had worn during our first meeting there. I fashioned the yarn into a ring on one finger, enjoyed its snugness, and envisioned myself wearing a band of eternal devotion one day. Then I closed my eyes for a long time, listened to the waves lapping the shore, and breathed in Caleb's comforting tobacco scent.

Upon my return, Mr. Hamilton sought me out, rapping like a demented woodpecker on my closed bedroom door. He had a message for me: Uncle William and Aunt Jo had invited me to spend a few days in Halifax with them, to explore the university campus and to purchase school supplies in advance. Without consulting Mama (she was next door, visiting our neighbours), Mr. Hamilton had sent away the bearer of this invitation, a good friend of Uncle William who had come to do business in our village.

I tried to close the door on his smug face, but he had moved one foot forward, no doubt to prevent my doing so. "You are committed to your obligations to Noah," he said, "and so I respectfully declined the invitation on your behalf."

Respectfully declined! *Unctuous, lying, interfering killjoy . . . if only I'd had the courage to use language that spoke to my fury!*

I denied myself such revenge, but did manage to administer a different kind. Schooling my face to indifference, I replied, "Quite right, Mr. Hamilton. I'm well prepared to wait for September." And as his nostrils flared at my use of the title 'Mr. Hamilton', I added, "I shall enjoy the sweetness of anticipation."

He withdrew his foot then, and I immediately closed the door. He waited a moment—was he trying to dredge up a response to my comment?—but then he stomped down the hallway and descended the stairs. Stomped! Truly, like a two-year-old in the throes of a tantrum.

How dare he deny me a visit with my *family! How dare he!*

Paul's envelope no longer daunts me. I'd been concerned at first that it would contain a legal document, but it's a personal letter, written on a grey sheet of company stationery.

"Come back now, Rianne" is his opening gambit. There is no conventional salutation. He's found a job for me through a friend who is launching an independent publishing company. I'll be an editor, he says, not an editor's assistant, and he has underlined the word "editor" not once, but twice. He can't absolutely guarantee me the job, of course, but if I come back to Toronto immediately he knows there will be a positive outcome.

Come back, Rianne. You must be bored to tears by now. I need you.

He's never at home anymore. When he's not at the office, he's running his heart out in the back ravine or catching a bite to eat on the Danforth.

Usually he ends up at Strombo's, dining on moussaka and chewing the fat with Big Nick. Sitting in the corner, at the table with the candle wedged into an empty bottle of Retsina—*our* corner.

I can't continue. The man who is a foe of sentimentality is verging on maudlin. I shake my head in disbelief. Then I methodically deconstruct the letter to a small pile of confetti. A broad sweep of my palm feeds it to the wastepaper basket beside my bedroom desk.

He doesn't truly miss me. I know why he wants me to come back to him.

Absence makes the heart grow fonder, it truly does. It also whets our senses, brings memories into sharp and desired relief.

He wished to kiss me!

I leaned back in the grass on the bluff and lifted my face to the evening sun. A breeze stirred the hairs at the back of my neck. The chorus of the cicadas took possession of my body, made my blood hum.

He made a soft sound of pleasure as his teeth bore into the strawberries, and the air around us quivered with their heady scent. He leaned to me then, gently brushed my hair away from my ear, and my blood began singing to a higher pitch. The tip of his tongue touched the tip of my lobe—or did it? It soon removed all doubt, sweeping smoothly in an arc below the ridge of my ear.

A shudder—heart-jolting—stormed through my body. How could a move so elegant, so designed . . . ? Ecstasy—I wished to die from it!

He knows only, senses only, the fear that made me sit bolt upright and warn him to desist.

Did I wish to kiss him? I did. God in Heaven, I did.

I was twelve years old the summer that Kaye and Warren took Ben and me to Prince Edward Island for a week. We stayed at cottages near Brackley Beach and spent most of each day exploring the island—golfing, visiting lighthouse museums, gorging on lobsters and strawberry shortcake at church suppers. Despite Ben's protests, we took in all of the *Anne of Green Gables* attractions and L.M. Montgomery's gravesite in Cavendish.

At the end of our last day, Ben and I picked up some snacks at a nearby canteen and went down to the ocean one last time. The sun was still warm on our skin; laughter floated to us from a game of volleyball further down the beach. Ribbons of pink and crimson spanned the western sky. We climbed to the top of one of the sand dunes by the ocean. A red fox exploded from a fan-shaped thicket of marram grass, the coarse fur of its tail swiping my leg as it made a panic-stricken escape between our two bodies.

In the space between two thick patches of the grass we scooped out bowl-shaped depressions to create chairs in the sand. The sand was still warm to the touch at first, and then cooled and turned moist as we dug deeper and deeper. Silt wedged itself under our fingernails and clung to the webbing between our fingers. When we'd finished shaping our chairs, we ran down to the ocean to wash the sand from our hands. We carefully evaded the jellyfish that had called a convention so close to the shore. I took a head start to race Ben back to the top of the dune, but as usual he won by several lengths. By the age of fourteen he already had the legs of a sprinter.

Laughing, out of breath, we settled ourselves into the sandy depressions and faced the reflected, dancing light of the ocean. Two monarchs sitting on their thrones.

Ben cracked open a bag of potato chips. I slipped a Kit Kat chocolate bar out of its wrapper and snapped off one of the fingers. The chocolate was soft, on the cusp of melting.

"Have you ever had chocolate-covered pretzels?" Ben said.

"No. They don't sound all that great. Do you like them?"

"Yeah, they taste pretty good." He leaned toward me. "Here, look at me." He took the Kit Kat stick from my hand and started painting my lips with it, as if it were a wand of lipstick.

"Don't move," he said and, "No, don't lick it off," as the tip of my tongue emerged instinctively. "Not yet." He selected a large chip from his bag and rubbed it against his lips. Then he leaned over and planted a firm, but lingering and decidedly salty kiss on my lips.

I didn't see it coming. Didn't anticipate the sudden, piercing sweetness deep in my belly.

"What did you think?" Ben's eyes displayed such longing that I felt another jolt.

What did I think? I couldn't think at all at that moment. Was he asking about the combination of sweet and salty? Was he asking what I thought of my first kiss?

I had to look away. I wiped away the studs of salt and the chocolate with the back of my hand. Then I continued to play it safe. Digging my palms and my heels into the sand, I hoisted myself out of the depression. "Give me plain old chocolate any time," I said. I started to scramble down the dune at a diagonal.

"Hey, where are you going?"

It didn't take long for Ben to catch up to me. He grabbed me by the waist, staggered the few remaining steps to the bottom of the dune, and spun me around until I was dizzy. Then he let go, and to steady me and to steady himself he placed his hands on my shoulders. He was panting, laughing at the same time. Sweat spiralled down from the neckline of his T-shirt.

I still couldn't look at him. As soon as he caught his breath, he ruffled my hair. Tousled the top of my head as if I were his favourite five-year-old.

"You didn't have to run away," he said. "I was just kidding around."

It's the only time I've ever caught Ben in a lie.

I brought Paul Haddon to the mountain five times. He's aware of how much my family and the Allenby family mean to me. He doesn't know, of course, the story of the time that Ben kissed me. It's an anecdote that a girl keeps to herself or reserves for her closest girlfriend. It happened once; I made sure it never happened again.

And the passage in which Alyda recalls Caleb's strawberry-scented kiss—I neglected to show that one to Ben.

Chapter 20

Dearest sister thou hast left us
And thy loss we deeply feel
But tis God that hath bereft us
He can all our sorrows heal

I HAVEN'T ONE close friend in this village, even though I've met girls of my age at church and they all seem bright and good-natured and eager to befriend me. Friendship is not something to be taken lightly, however, and I'm not sure I would be able to confide in these girls.

Should I make an effort? No, I'm content to leave things the way they are. I could not ask for a better friend than Sibley. My sister is a wise soul, and a kindred spirit to me. She cajoles me into high spirits, consoles me when darkness sets in and floods my heart, takes me down a peg or two when that kind of reckoning is needed (more times than I would care to mention here). Best of all, she gives me her peppermint sticks!

This afternoon, Sibley and I took advantage of an empty house to pierce each other's ears. We had talked at great length of doing this for one another, but took time to muster the courage to do the deed.

Sibley insisted on doing mine first. Fortunately, the coals at the front of the stove were still hot. Seated in the king's chair, a towel draped over my left shoulder, I watched as Sibley dipped the end of a hat pin in the coals, waited for the searing heat to subside, and then brought the pin tip to the spot of ink on my lower left earlobe. "Now?" she whispered. She clamped her tongue between her lips in concentration.

I steadied my feet and gritted my teeth and gripped the ends of the armrests; nodded. And bore the pain valiantly with the softest of screams as the pin bore through flesh.

Sibley looked overcome, and so I did my best to minimize the ghastliness of the experience. "Quickly, do the other one!" I said. She found the courage and steadiness of hand to pierce the other ear; still, I bit my tongue the moment the pin drove through the flesh.

That is when Uncle Joseph marched into the room!

Sibley jumped like a scalded cat and we both screamed. Uncle Joseph swiftly took command, blotting the blood, poking Sibley's embroidery thread through the fresh holes to keep them open, and then applying alcohol to the wounds (something Sibley and I had not even considered).

Sternly, but with a gleam of indulgence in his eye, he told Sibley she would have to wait for her torture. He needed me to accompany him on one of his calls.

That salty kiss on Prince Edward Island laid a claim on me. It was a sword of Damocles, and a guilty pleasure. It wasn't always Ben who triggered a jolt: it could be a Kit Kat bar, the grainy texture of sand on skin, the glimpse of a fox streaking into the ditch beside the Port Carlyle Road. Ben was never aware of this—I made sure of that.

These were feelings that I managed on my own. I had a friend in the village dating from early childhood, but I'd found out over time that she couldn't keep secrets. And my school friends in Danton had evolved into bullies as they approached their teen years. *We know you're keeping something from us, Rianne.* Their eyes always accusing me of insubordination. During my last year on the mountain I spent as little time as possible with them.

It was soon after I moved to Halifax with Mom and Jack that I found a way to suppress my feelings for Ben: I acquired a boyfriend.

Grant MacKay was stocky, with deep brown eyes and dark, wavy hair that fell almost to the shoulders. He was a member of the "in" crowd, and my new girlfriends in the city considered him a catch. He played lacrosse as well as hockey, and liked science fiction and comic books. His kisses were dry and timid—as if he were afraid they would bruise my mouth. That didn't pose a problem for me. In all other respects he conformed to my concept of a boyfriend.

I thought of telling Ben about him, but the words never coalesced. Over time, I convinced myself that he didn't need to know and he wouldn't want to know.

Grant and I had been together for about a year when we left my house early one Friday evening to visit friends in the neighbourhood. We were laughing about something idiotic—I think I'd put my foot in the wrong shoe, twice, as we were getting ready to go out. We were holding hands.

And suddenly there was Ben on the front path, walking briskly toward us. Glowering.

I immediately slipped my hand from Grant's. I was so startled to see Ben that I didn't ask him what he was doing in the city. My voice ragged at the edges, I started introducing Grant to him.

Ben didn't wait for the end to the introduction. His arm shot out and his fist caught Grant squarely on the mouth. Grant collapsed, reeling back against the pillar of the front porch. He slid to its base, taking strands of ivy with him. Blood trickled from one side of his mouth. Shock registered on his face. As it must have on mine.

I crouched down beside him and wiped away the blood with a tissue that I'd found in my pocket. My hand was shaking. I looked up at Ben in disbelief. "Are you out of your mind?"

Ben had stepped back. There was a strange look of incomprehension on his face too. The fist was still in position for another go. "Jesus," he said. "I'm sorry."

Grant groaned. A bubble of blood appeared at the corner of his mouth, burst, and snaked to his chin. I fished for another Kleenex, applied it. I didn't look at Ben this time, but I asked him, "What on earth got into you?"

"Mom's got cancer," he said.

No. Please no, I thought. I teetered for a moment on the balls of my feet.

And from the corner of my eye I could see Ben's hand, clenching and unclenching. Knuckles and tendons briefly surging then sinking below the surface of the skin again.

I stood up. I couldn't hug Ben, but I ran my hand down his left arm and when it reached his hand, he seized it and squeezed the life out of it.

Uncle Joseph had come to fetch me, to assist him as he attended to a ghastly bite wound. I was horrified to learn that the victim was Robbie Gibson—dear Robbie, who has the eternal age of a six-year-old; who has been locked into the mental age he possessed on the day that he slipped beneath the wheel of a cart; who walks with a rolling, staggering gait that inspires misunderstanding in those who do not know him. He's in his late thirties now, and beneath untidy locks, threaded with silver, he usually displays a rapt, child-like expression, as if the world still has everything to offer him.

Robbie was lying on a cot in the kitchen when we arrived, his mother kneeling beside him, whispering, "Soon, soon, sweet boy, he'll put everything to rights." The man's lips were compressed in pain and his thin chest rose and fell in paroxysms.

He'd been attacked without provocation by a massive cur-dog ("why didn't the dog like me, Ma?") as he'd picked potatoes in their garden. It was fear, Uncle Joseph believed, that was compromising his breathing now, and not the gaping eight-inch wound on his right thigh.

The injury was grave, however, and Uncle Joseph suspected hydrophobia. "I can think of no other explanation for the animal's behaviour," he said. My heart pitched as I recalled our gardener's son at Tew House who died an agonizing death of the ailment, many years ago.

This time, however, something could be done. With loving but firm hands, Mrs. Gibson and I held Robbie down as Uncle Joseph first cleansed the wound and then cauterized it with silver nitrate. Robbie was brave, the dear soul, but I shudder still to think of what is to come. He's on his way to Halifax now with Uncle Joseph and Aunt Helen, and in short time he will receive daily injections into his abdomen, of two weeks' duration at the least. But he will live, of that Uncle Joseph assures me.

A thousand wasps buzz beneath my skin tonight, frantically seeking a route to the surface. I feel as I did on the day that Uncle Joseph cleared young Henry's airway in church. I will not sleep, nor do I wish to. I relive horror and I relive elation. I am alive.

Bachelor of Arts or Bachelor of Science leading to Medicine? Once again, it matters not. The world is my oyster!

I didn't have to break up with Grant. Warren immediately arranged to pay for the necessary dental work, with the understanding that Ben would gradually pay him back for it. And Grant was quite willing to forgive me my crazy friend.

I didn't break up with him because I was slow to shed the embarrassment of that encounter with Ben. Ben needed me; that quickly became apparent. Kaye had a stage two breast cancer, and he had a difficult time dealing with the diagnosis. He insisted on accompanying her to Halifax, to all of her appointments with the oncologist, to the surgery and radiation treatments, even though his father was always present and sometimes other family members and friends as well. Ben would call me to give me a schedule of her appointments, and I always made sure that I was available to him at some point during the day, even if it meant skipping school. Often Kaye and Warren would stay overnight at our place, so we saw each other in the evenings as well.

Mostly Ben and I walked. We climbed to the top of the Citadel numerous times. We took walks in Point Pleasant Park, the Public Gardens, the old burying ground of St. Paul's, and along the waterfront. Any place that was in reasonable walking distance of the hospital or my house. Sometimes we didn't say anything for long periods of time. At the end of our time together Ben would always say, "Thank you, Ree." In an oddly formal manner, as if I had performed a special service for him.

Aside from one inquiry about the state of Grant's mouth, about a week after the incident, Ben never brought up his name again. Nor did I.

There were other boyfriends like Grant over the next several years—short-lived relationships that served no purpose other than my need to repudiate Ben's kiss. I finally increased the stakes with Paul Haddon in Toronto, staying with him for three long years. Enduring steady erosion to my happiness and sense of self-worth.

Watching the "pansies" on my wrists blossom.

Chapter 21

The seas shall waste, the skies in smoke decay
Rocks fall to dust and mountains melt away
But fix'd His Word, His saving Power remains
Thy realm forever lasts, Thy own Messiah reigns

"Does it need to be an angel, my contribution to your scrapbook?"

"No, it needn't be an angel." I was more than happy to abandon that theme, delighted that Aunt Helen would bring a fresh tone to my book. She sat down beside me on the stone bench in the lily garden, a spiral book in one hand and her Japan-lacquered box of paints, brushes, and pencils in the other.

We tossed about ideas. I vetoed my portrait; she declined to provide one of herself. I suggested watercolours of wildflowers, but she promised to provide me with pressings instead. We finally settled upon a sketch of the house.

How quickly she rendered it with her charcoal stick: windows and door blossoming in an oblong box; three columns each side, anchoring to the front porch; the hint of the side veranda; the widow's walk with its elaborate railing; the three chimneys jutting from the roof; the finials on the gables and the gingerbread trimmings; and then, there I was upon the widow's walk, eyes shaded to a magnificent sunset upon the water (or so I imagined).

Exquisiteness! She has a formidable talent, my dear aunt. "Would you oblige me by making another one?" I asked. "I would like to hang one in my room in Halifax."

My throat ached. Aunt Helen knew better than to say anything; she put her arms around me and laid her cheek to my hair, and we sat there in the floral-scented warmth of the garden, just like that, for a long time.

Two o'clock in the morning on a cool night in August. The cicadas are still. Most of the mountain dwellers are in bed, heartbeats slowed to a faint but steady tempo. Sleeping bags slung over our shoulders and Thermoses in hand of hot chocolate laced with amaretto, Ben and I make our way to the top of a small hill behind his parents' home. Lucy makes a quick note of our final destination then abandons us to explore the thickets down by the creek.

We've already been outside for half an hour, pacing the property to let our eyes adjust to the darkness. It is a night of the Perseids, and the sky is already alive with meteors playing their high-spirited games of tag.

Ben and I wriggle into our sleeping bags in a depression at the top of the hill, rest our backs against the small incline. A motorcycle speeds by on the Port Carlyle Road, gunning it down the slope to the bay. Silence rushes in again. The barn owl that resides in a nearby tool shed glides over us, eyes impassive in its heart-shaped facial disc. The night air feeds our nostrils with the smell of moist, freshly-cut grass.

Ben takes a swig from his Thermos. He pulls out a piece of paper and a stubby pencil from his jeans pocket. He's going to keep track of the number of shooting stars that he sees between two and three a.m. The last time he made note of the number, six years ago, he saw a total of 147. He's hoping to beat that record this year.

He orients himself to the Little Dipper and once he's identified each star in the constellation, he tells me that he's ready. I wind up my Minnie Mouse alarm clock, place it on the ground several feet away from us, and bundle an old sweater over it to muffle its torturous *tick tock tick tock tick tock.* "Go!" I say. Ben notches the first meteor on his scrap of paper.

I have an hour to kill, an hour in which I'll be silent and confine my movements so that I won't interrupt him. My toes are already itching, my back chafing against the compact earth beneath it, despite the barrier of the sleeping bag. I try to concentrate on the shower of meteors above me, but their endless play soon becomes commonplace. Each one evokes less awe and soon melts into the vast nothingness beyond it. And in a netherworld between consciousness and sleep, a white light sears my mind and the reel of my recent nightmare begins to play again.

Sputtering, thrashing, Alyda fights to climb to safety on the slab. Caleb hurtles by me and soon plunges into the water. I stifle a sob in my throat and scrape the earth by my side with my fingers, forcing awareness of its stubborn, grass-matted resistance. It does not blunt the horror.

"Let's give it a new ending." Nan has often told me this after I've experienced a nightmare. Can I make Caleb reach Alyda and assist her onto the slab? To what end? It didn't happen in the manner presented in my dream, but Alyda drowned.

The alarm clock rumbles beneath the sweater. I startle, lean across the grass to squelch the ringer. Ben turns to me and I train a flashlight on the paper. He counts twice to make sure of the numbers, and at the end of his second tally I hear a fervent "Damn!" He's toted up a disappointing 138.

"There's always next year," I console him.

"What were you thinking about?" he says. "An hour is a long time for you to be still."

"Alyda." But I can't bring myself to tell him about the nightmare. Instead I mention the most recent entry in the journal and Aunt Helen's drawing of the house. "The sketch is essentially gone," I say. "The outlines of the house are barely distinguishable."

It's harrowing, the diminishment of everything associated with Alyda: the absence of a portrait; the delicate condition of her scrapbook; the destruction of the houses in which she once lived. Even her resting place is concealed.

"Everything about her has faded away," I say.

Ben's voice bridges the darkness: "You're doing everything you can to bring her back to life, Ree."

That's all I need. It's finally time to tell him. "I've seen her," I say. "I've seen Alyda."

"*What?*"

Relief sends its sweet juices through me; I've finally said it. "I saw

Alyda. That day we went over to the edge of the bluff, where the steps used to be."

I have his full attention now. He slides up out of his sleeping bag, clasps his knees with his arms.

"What do you mean by *saw*? You saw a woman in the field who looked like Alyda might have back in her day?"

"The woman I saw was Alyda. I *know* it was Alyda."

I can sense that he's looking intently at me. I can't read the expression on his face but I'm sure it must be seasoned with scepticism. "How did you know it was her?" he says. "What was she doing? Did she say anything to you? Did you touch her?"

I laugh. "Not so fast." I recount everything that happened to me in the field that day. And when I tell him how I felt when she walked right through me, I again experience the burning sensation that extends to all my extremities. "Do you think I'm crazy?"

He hesitates just long enough for me to reach over and punch him playfully on the arm.

"No, of course not," he says. "I'm just trying to figure out a reasonable explanation for this."

"Just for once I want you to stop being the scientist."

"So, you want a non-reasonable explanation."

My breath suddenly catches as Lucy glides out of the shadows towards us. A body lies limply in her jaws. "No!" I hiss. "Go away!" Lucy turns abruptly and the rag-doll of a rabbit—I can see its long ears now—jerks in harmony. The two of them disappear down the hill into the underbrush near the creek.

"Did you see that?" I shudder.

"She can't help it."

"I know. But I wish she'd keep her hunting prowess to herself."

"Reincarnation . . ."

"Ben, please. Don't joke about it."

The spell has already been broken by Lucy's disruption, the warmth that flooded my body chased by a chill that sends me back down into my sleeping bag. "There's only one explanation for it," I say. "I'm so caught up in this whole Alyda thing that I've imagined her into existence. It's probably a writer's trick."

I say this, but I haven't convinced myself. Everything was so vivid, so *real.*

Ben leans towards me. He trails a blade of grass across my cheek. I inhale the sweet scent of the clipping, then an intimation of chocolate and alcohol as he leans even closer. I hold my breath.

And then he's gone.

He's on his back again, face to the heavens. He slides down into his sleeping bag and clasps his hands behind his head.

"Run with it," he says. "If Alyda's real to you, just run with it."

I have no choice. She's inside my head now.

A quiet re-latching of the front door, and Griff and I were outside. The night air was as soothing as a mother's hand on a feverish brow. Mars, a flaming crimson orb, gazed down upon us. In close proximity to it was the hero of the evening, Perseus, who tonight would hurl cosmic javelins across the night sky. It was deathly quiet as I navigated the fields, a lantern in one hand and an old quilt slung around my shoulders.

Caleb was waiting for me. A sudden outburst of light in the heavens illuminated him, standing by the boulder, and the trail of the fireball continued to define him.

"Did you see that? Did you see that?" I could scarcely speak for excitement. "We've come at the right time."

Caleb drew me into his arms. "You missed me," he said, brushing my hair with his lips.

"You were gone but a few days." I could not deny the truth, however; I had missed him, and it did my heart good to be with him again.

Griff had immediately burrowed into the grasses to resume his sleep. I spread the blanket at the base of the rock, and Caleb and I eased our backs onto its natural incline. A shooting star appeared out of the west and streaked across the firmament above us. It was soon followed by another. Perseus was an archer now, his sinewy arm pulling arrows from a quiver and feeding them to the bow for rapid release.

"It's frightening to think of how vast the universe is," I said. "It always makes me think of what else may be up there. What do you think, Caleb? What is up there besides heaven?"

He made a sound of derision, low in his throat. "There's no heaven."

"No? Then where do we go?"

"Six feet under. A banquet for worms and maggots and other crawling creatures."

And then almost immediately he squeezed my arm. He turned his head to me. "Your father—"

A stone lay wedged between my heart and my ribs. "Do you truly believe that's all there is?"

"When we have no proof—" His voice trailed into silence. He must have been afraid of offending me again.

He continued, however. "I don't like to think of it, Allie," he said. "That's one reason why I never go to that graveyard. I haven't any need to, of course; I don't know anyone who is buried there. And it's a constant reminder of death."

"I see the graveyard as a constant reminder that these people once lived, that we should do everything that we can to keep these people in our minds as the breathing, laughing, crying souls they once were."

"Murdering, conniving, thieving . . ."

I smiled. "That, too. Sometimes that makes them even more interesting."

Caleb was silent for a few moments. Then he said, "You wouldn't think that about my father. You would spit on his grave."

Now he finally told me. The elder Whitelaw—Caleb would not speak his name—was a coal miner and a drunkard. "Those were the two things that meant the most to him. Family wasn't one of them.

"Six months ago I faced up to him outside our house when he came home from a night of drinking. I needed to keep him away from my mother; she was still hurting from one of his attacks the week before."

Caleb paused; his throat fluttered against my hair as he swallowed. "I got in one good right hook, but my father drove his fist into my gut and threw me to the wall outside the house. And then he pulled a brick from a pile that stood there in the alley and he drove it into my collar bone." He expelled a bitter laugh. "That cost him. He finally pitched back and landed on that pile of bricks."

Caleb was silent again. I felt his heart pounding against his ribs. At last I found the courage to ask him, "And that is when he died?"

He laughed again. "No. He had a few hours to live yet, if you want to call it that. I left him there on the pile of bricks, arms and legs flung in all directions. He wouldn't be a threat for at least a few hours. And a neighbour found him there in the morning, stiff with the rigor. Fingers curved and black like the talons of a hawk. He'd choked to death on his own vomit."

"I cannot begin—"

Caleb stirred beside me. "I may not know what the heavens hold," he said, "but

I'm grateful for justice on this earth." He exhaled with a puff that sent a shiver along my scalp.

I turned to him, let slip the top two buttons of his shirt; widened it to the shoulders, and slid my fingers gently over the expanse of chest just below his throat. Not far from the heart, I felt the scar of the wound. It was a deep gouge with a ragged lip to one side. My heart swelled with compassion. I wished for a way to restore his skin to a pristine state, to return him to a history of innocence.

I kissed the scar, gently grazed it with my lips. I lifted my head to his. His lips bent to mine and he kissed me. He kissed *me! And finally I had no qualms. I returned that kiss with an urgency that was equal to his.*

Something nudged me, produced a deep and throaty growl. I sat up with a start; Caleb laughed and sat up, too. He eyed Griff carefully. "You can go back to your dreams," he promised the dog. "We'll behave as you wish now." And he laced his fingers through my hair and drew my head to his shoulder.

Aunt Helen and Uncle Joseph were in Halifax; I only stayed at the house to see to Griff's needs.

Caleb needed me. Should I have offered him refuge for the night?

What does Mr. Sweeney think of these passages? It was difficult reviewing Alyda's musings about the strawberry-scented kiss with him, and I continue to admit to a low level of discomfort. What could he possibly know about the sensibilities of a young woman?

"What made Alyda behave like this?" I ask. "Her actions are inconsistent with the mores of the time."

The old man has been tracking a ladybug on his pencil; it's now negotiating its length as if it were a gymnast on a balance beam. He glances up at me. "Meeting with a man without a chaperone along?"

"That, yes. And leaving the house at night."

"She scolded her mother for conforming to convention."

"That's true. She was a bit of a rebel."

The ladybug briefly flexes its wings for takeoff, but then decides to continue its journey along the pencil. "Could you see her as a suffragette in Halifax?" he says.

"Yes, I imagine she would have become one, had she lived. She definitely shows feminist leanings in her writing. But at the time she was meeting Caleb she was trapped in the hothouse atmosphere of this little fishing village. And she was still an upper-class, Victorian woman. A girl, really—she was only sixteen."

"Have you always been the perfect child, Miss Tavener? You've always told your elders exactly what you're doing and you've never lied to them?"

Heat steals across my face. "No, of course not," I admit. "But Alyda lived in a different era."

"Have you ever lost someone you loved?"

I shake my head.

"Neither have I." He watches the ladybug as it makes a return trip on the pencil beam, then lifts his eyes to me again. "Grief," he says. "Can you not imagine that it might lead to recklessness?"

I think about his observation for a moment. "Yes, grief could lead someone to behave irresponsibly, but I'm not sure you could apply that description to Alyda. Remember her reaction to Caleb's jumping from the edge of the bluff?"

"Still, she was impulsive at times."

"And she was a non-conformist." I consider the implications of both our statements. "If we take into account her age and her personality, her actions might not be that unusual."

Mr. Sweeney smiles at me, a rarity for him. The ladybug exercises her wings one last time and takes flight.

Chapter 22

My friends and children all adieu
I leave you in God's care
And though I never more see you
Go on, I'll meet you there

This morning I engaged in a whirlwind of activities with a number of the Port Carlyle villagers.

First, I checked in on a gathering of the Women's Institute and came away with several draft-copy chapters of *A History of Our Village* to edit. A quick scan revealed a story about a lighthouse ghost, a series of letters from a local hero of World War II, and a crossword puzzle with a "Pirates and Privateers" theme. Perfect. Sales worthiness is now a component of the project.

Next, I met with the village quilting circle and proposed a festival of quilts during the bicentenary summer. Ideas swirled. The ladies already have a good store of quilts, but they also settled on a motif of abstract humpback whales for a giant celebratory quilt.

Finally, I met with a group of local artists and artisans, Port Carlyle's "Angels of Art," in a cottage close to the old wharf. They've already started producing paintings and pottery items for the bicentenary, but I was interested in taking a look at their photo collection, which dates back to 1878. I'll pool items of their collection with those in the care of the Women's Institute and Mr. Sweeney's museum, and create a "Then and Now" exhibition.

Awash in tea, I drive to the Sweeney home to "rescue" Nan's casserole dish.

"I've never seen a house so splendid," Caleb said. It was not the first time he'd seen the house, of course, but it was the first time he had made such an observation.

"Never?" I challenged him. "They must have houses as fine as this in Sydney."

"They do. But there is something different about this house. It's the way that it stands on the bluff. It—" He paused in his struggle to find the right words. Finally, he said, "It struts."

His description was apt. I smiled at him. "You're a poet!"

He rolled his eyes in mock horror. "Now you've done it, Allie. I'll have to keep my opinions to myself."

"Come!" I grasped his hand. Aunt Helen and Uncle Joseph would not return from Halifax until later in the day. I had not asked him to return to the house with me last night (head triumphed over heart), but now I would be bold and invite him into the house. "You must see the view from the widow's walk," I told him.

He was not so easily led. He brought me to a stop at the doorway to the parlour, and I saw that he was awe-struck. His eyes settled first upon the oil painting of the old harbour, its ships riding the golden hues of a sunset; they travelled next in admiration from a phonograph to the leather globe of the earth on its stand, the globe that once belonged to Papa.

"Let me look at the globe," he pleaded.

"Later!" I tugged his hand. "Widow's walk first."

"Must you always have your way, Allie?" He was grinning as he resisted, pulled me to him. "Globe," he whispered into my ear, gently, for the piercings still cause tenderness.

"Widow's walk."

"If you must," he said, and before I could marvel at how swiftly he capitulated, he added, "And then you'll reward me with a kiss."

The door from the cupola opens to a view of the northeast, to the bay and to the upper reaches of our village huddled upon its shore. I braced my hands on the railing and ushered the salt-laced air into my lungs. "Didn't I tell you?" I exclaimed. "The view is glorious!"

The highest features of the village lay like the charms of a bracelet scattered along the dark edges of the spruces, against the backdrop of the bay and Ile de Haute.

"Two tern schooners in the harbour," said Caleb, nodding to the colourful pennants that flew from the tips of their masts.

"Union Jack at my house." It streamed at full body above what was once my house, the house of my father.

Caleb's hand suddenly grasped my wrist. "Look to the end of the road," he said, his voice low. "Someone is coming."

"Noah!" Even if that horse and buggy had been a mile away, I would have recognized its occupant by its outline.

I did not need to urge Caleb to the door of the cupola. We clattered down the staircase, I raising my hem to my knees and praying that I would not fall. At the landing I paused to reclaim my breath. My heart was jumping, and I was trembling like a child in a ghost circle on All Hallows Eve.

Caleb's arms encircled me. "Be calm, Allie," he said. "He didn't see us; I can swear to that. His eyes will have been on the road."

It was his strong and steady heartbeat that I felt now, not mine.

Over the last several days, during my meetings with Mr. Sweeney in his office, I've forgotten to mention Nan's casserole dish. She needs it now. This may give me an opportunity to see Alma again. I'm torn between the desire to see her and the fear of causing her further distress.

As I pull into the museum parking lot, I see that Mr. Sweeney is busy conducting one of his tours. Alma's student helper is on the front steps of the house, watering a large pot of geraniums. She doesn't know where the casserole dish is, but she invites me to go inside and search for it.

I quickly locate the dish, on a chair right by the kitchen door. As I retrieve it and prepare to exit the house, a loud rattling noise claims my attention. I follow its source into the parlour, where Alma is standing by a small table.

The table supports a large glass bowl, filled with dozens of shore stones. Beside it sits a copper kettle, pocked with tiny dents and polished to a warm glow. Alma curves her hand into a scoop, dips it into the bowl, and releases her fingers as she draws it up again. The stones stream through her fingers, rattling against each other and the walls of the bowl.

It's a satisfying sound to me. As I continue to watch, Alma grasps the kettle, lifts it to a good height, and pours water over the stones. The colours in the bowl surge.

I step back to leave the room, and Alma suddenly freezes, kettle in hand. I stand quietly, ready to apologize for startling her, but she turns and looks at me without recognition and without fear in her eyes. "Come here, young lady," she says.

She returns the kettle to the table, fishes a stone out of the bowl. Seating herself on a button-back couch by the table, she motions to me to join her. The gesture is a command.

Alma rolls the stone between the palms of her hands. "Do I know you?" she says.

"I'm Rianne Tavener. I met you down on the shore one day, and then—" I can't continue, cannot refer to the visit that took place beneath this roof.

"Ah, you're a new friend, then. I made a new friend on the shore once and this is a stone that I collected that day." Alma releases her fist to display it for me. The stone is about the size of a ripe plum—rust-coloured, with pockmarks of slate grey and a liberal dusting of quartzite.

"I was down by the old pier collecting periwinkles," she continues, "when I saw a girl sitting on the whale rock. It was starting to spit rain, but that girl, she continued to sit there, all huddled up and looking out to the island. The rain was soon smacking down so hard that it bounced off the rocks, so I went up to her and I yelled at her, telling her that we needed to get into one of the ovens. She didn't pay mind to me, so I took her by one arm, practically pulled her off the rock, and helped her up to the nearest oven.

"That girl was about my age and I knew her to see her. I'd never been introduced to her but I'd seen her at least a couple times in the village, and with that fancy cape of hers I knew she had to be one of the Teasdale girls."

A Teasdale girl. I glance down to the hands in my lap so that Alma won't be aware of my mounting excitement. The pulse in my wrist throbs with anticipation.

"We stayed in that oven for at least two hours," she carries on, "sitting on rocks and talking for a long time, even after it'd stopped raining. She was going to be leaving for Halifax soon, to go to school there, and she was excited about that. Sad, too. She was going to miss her younger sister."

Footsteps sound; the front door opens. "Mother?" Owen Sweeney calls.

"Allie," I say. I keep my voice low. "The girl's name—was it Allie?"

"Yes, it was." Alma regards me in astonishment. "Did you know her too?"

I'm saved by Mr. Sweeney's entrance into the room.

Dark stains marched across Noah's vest; he smelled of wood smoke and sausages. Mama had asked to see me, I was told. There was nothing to worry about, but she wanted me to come and spend the night.

I left water for Griff and a note for my aunt and uncle, and when I was seated beside him on the buggy, he said to me, "Do you still see him?"

A chill feeling of resignation came over me. "We've talked of this before, Noah. You've no business to ask me this."

"I'm your brother. I'm interested in your well-being."

"You're my stepbrother, *and almost two years younger than I am. You can put all your concerns about me to rest and enjoy your childhood."*

He stiffened beside me and flicked the reins gratuitously on Sassie's back. But he was silent now. The air was light this afternoon, with only a faint salt tang. It gave energy to Sassie and she kicked up clouds of dust as she trotted down the roadway.

As we turned into the road to the manse, he said, "Sibley misses you."

The comment stung me. It implied that Sibley had spoken in confidence to him, and I didn't want to know if this was so. "We spent good time together the other day, and if it weren't for your lessons I would have more to spend with her."

"You brought those lessons upon yourself. Sibley works hard. She has a lot to do."

"You can't help her?"

"Woman's work?" He did not conceal the contempt in his voice.

"What do you do the day long, Noah?"

"You know what I do. I work in the carriage house. Today I polished Sassie's saddle."

"But you also meet with Algernon and Teddy for several hours."

"There's no harm in that."

"None whatsoever. But if you're so concerned about Sibley, I suggest that you free a minute or two from your busy schedule to help her."

I climbed down from the buggy, and as I reached to fetch my bag, Noah's hand grazed mine and then rested upon it. "Allie, I'll carry—"

My hand jerked back as if it had been put to a flame. I grasped the bag and pulled it out of his reach.

"Allie!"

I turned around, taking sweet time to do so.

*His face was flushed, and mottled with anger. "If I see you with him one more time," he said, "*you'll *be the one given a lesson."*

He's a coward. It takes no effort on my part to read his bluff.

I can't stop myself. My anxiety has been mounting from the time that Alyda first expressed reservations about Noah. *And I do not like the way he looks at me.* I ask Mr. Sweeney what happens. Does Noah Hamilton catch Alyda with Caleb again? And if so, what happens?

He frowns. "I prefer to keep doing the passages one at a time."

"I need to know."

"You don't want to know yet."

It's my turn to frown.

"Don't be disingenuous, Miss Tavener. You've told me you want to be a writer, but I think you've placed yourself in this girl's shoes for another reason. You want to re-create her life for her, experience it at a gut level.

"How could you possibly *think* the way Aldya does when you know what is going to happen to her?"

CHAPTER 23

On youth's bright morn her spirit fled
And left her body with the dead
She fell beneath Death's chilling hand
To bloom immortal in a fairer land

NAN HAS ASKED me to take her to the graveyard. It would have been Addie's seventy-third birthday today, and she wants to lay a bouquet of flowers on the grave. She'll probably choose several stalks of wine-tinted hollyhocks, Addie's favourites. Gramps already paid his visit to the grave earlier in the day. As he always does, he went alone.

It has been raining intermittently for several days, and as we turn into the gravel road that leads to the graveyard, the Jeep suddenly dips into a pothole. I tighten my grip on the wheel as it bounces back onto the road. "Sorry about that, Nan. I should have been paying more attention."

Nan has braced her hands on the dashboard but she is unruffled. "Nothing like living on the edge," she says.

I slow the Jeep to a crawl. "Did Addie know Alma well?" I ask. "I found out a short while ago that she was there when Addie died."

"Yes, Alma was there. She'd just come up to the house to deliver a couple of cherry pies for the roofers. I wouldn't say that she knew Addie well. Owen and Alma were never ones for socializing much, but they did know about obligations to the community."

"You were there, too?"

"Yes, I was. One of the roofers was my beau. I'd lost my first beau in the war and after years of grieving for him, I'd just started going out with a new young man. Of course I was there to help Addie with the luncheon, too."

"Alma got really upset talking about it."

"Of course she did." There's a vein of anguish now in Nan's voice. "It was horrible. And it was—"

My conscience takes a run at me. "Nan, I'm so sorry. I never stopped to think." I grind the gears and lurch to a stop at the lichgate.

"It was my beau," Nan says. "He was up on the roof and he—he was the one who dropped the hammer. Of course it wasn't his fault. Really, no one was responsible. You could never stop Addie once she'd set her mind to something. It wasn't my beau's fault, but it ended things between us."

I'm at a loss for words. This all happened so long ago, and I know that Nan has been happy—still is happy—with Gramps. But Nan has extracted a Kleenex from her sleeve and she's now dabbing her eyes with it. I need to say something.

Nan sniffles and turns to me. "Open up that gate, Rianne. We haven't got all day."

I climb down from the Jeep and swing the gate to the side.

Sibley was ill; that is why I had been summoned home. She was bedridden with a fever and a cold in the chest. She had complained of feeling indisposed at the time she pierced my ears, but I thought that may have been a ploy to wiggle out of our agreement.

When I entered Sibley's room, I found Mama sitting in the wicker chair by her bedside. Mary Dockley was also in attendance. The old crone was applying a mustard poultice to Sibley's chest; the odour was so strong that my nostrils prickled. Sibley was ghostly white save for crimson petals on the ridges of her cheekbones.

I asked Mama why she hadn't called for Dr. Hall, and she answered in a voice that was far too calm for me, "Mary knows what to do. I didn't want to be troublesome."

I turned to leave the room. "I'm going now to fetch Dr. Hall."

"No, Allie." It was Sibley, her voice scarcely a whisper. "Please stay. I'm much better, I swear. I'm on the mend. I don't want you to go away."

"But what if it's something more serious than the grippe?"

"It's not," Mama said, vacating her chair. She motioned that I should occupy it. "She has never been in danger, and the fever has now broken. I only called you home today because she has been asking for you. It was Noah who offered to fetch you."

I sat down beside Sibley, torn in my desire to stay with her and to have a physician confirm for me that she was truly out of the woods. She was such a woebegone figure, adrift in the middle of her bed. Her hair was damp and thin strands of it clung to the pillow like sea algae to a rock. I clasped her hand.

"You'll stay?" she pleaded at the end of a fierce fit of coughing. Her hand was clammy and as light as a newly-fledged bird.

I smoothed back some strands of hair from her forehead. "I'll stay."

I hope Nan will continue with her reminiscences, but as soon as I turn the vehicle onto the track leading to the western end of the graveyard, she grips my arm. "Look," she says, and I follow her pointing finger to the section of the graveyard where Alyda's grave lies. The rose bushes surrounding the paralysing stone are gone.

I bring the vehicle to a lurching stop and leap out of it. I start to run, weaving through the gravestones as if I'm competing in an obstacle race. A sodden cushion of leaves takes my feet out from under me, causes me to slide awkwardly to the base of a tombstone. *The Lord was pleased to call her home.*

Nan shouts something behind me, but the words evaporate. I quickly bring myself to my feet and continue my run, not even stopping to remove the leaves that must be clinging to my bottom. And when I arrive at Alyda's grave, chest burning from fear and exertion, I find that the slab is intact. Twigs, leaves, and petals dot its landscape, adding more texture to the patchwork quilt of lichen, but it doesn't appear to be damaged in any way. It's only the rose bushes that have been destroyed, hacked to pieces and strewn in all directions. An old-fashioned scythe—bruised petals clinging to its blade—lies about two feet from the head of the stone.

"Don't touch it!" Nan expels the words in a rush as she finally catches up to me.

She places herself between me and the stone, determined to thwart any foolhardy behaviour on my part.

"Don't worry, Nan. I haven't." I put my arm around her shoulders. She's shaking.

"Don't touch it," she repeats, as if she hasn't heard me. "Keep your distance."

I move my arm from her shoulder and look into her eyes. "You don't believe all that nonsense about its paralysing powers, do you?"

Nan's eyes blaze. "I don't want you taking any chances, Rianne."

I look toward the southwestern corner of the graveyard, to the tool shed. Its door is hanging by one hinge. "I wonder who did this? What were they trying to accomplish?"

Nan snorts. "Some idiot who got wind of the legend, I'd say. It wouldn't be anyone from these parts. We know to let sleeping dogs lie." She takes a deep breath then turns to fetch the flowers from the Jeep.

In the instant my grandmother has her back turned to me, I stoop and swipe my hand across a corner of the stone. I feel nothing. As I keep an eye on Nan's retreating back, I crouch down and lay my palm flat on the stone's surface. Again, my hand and arm feel perfectly normal. I feel decidedly silly for testing the stone.

I wonder what the cemetery association will do about the destroyed rose bushes. Perhaps they'll replace them in an effort to keep the legend vibrant for my graveyard tours. I hope they'll decide to clean the stone, remove the lichen that is burrowing into its mass, playing havoc with the lettering of the inscription. Visitors should be able to view it.

Even a legend has its lifespan.

Nan returns with the flowers, and I choose a cornflower stalk to adorn Alyda's slab. As we set out to place the remaining flowers on Addie's grave, I say, "The paralysing stone and its powers—that's all just superstition."

Nan doesn't question the source of my conviction. "Superstition," she says, "is what you call keeping an open mind."

Sibley was much better today; she could even sit up without support. I washed her face and hands with a soft cloth, dabbed lavender water behind her ears, and brushed her hair until it shone and crackled with life again.

"Play the word game with me, Allie," she said. I went and fetched the egg timer from the kitchen and the dictionary from Mr. Hamilton's study. She opened it at random just past the middle, and then held it upright as her eyes scanned the columns of words. Finally, she nodded her permission to begin, and I inverted the egg timer. "Mezuzah," she said. "It's a noun."

I wondered if it was a medical term. She often likes to try those on me. "Mezuzah," I said, letting the word ride my tongue. "It's a boil or a carbuncle. A hideous growth usually found on the end of one's nose."

Sibley smiled and then doubled over, driving her arms into her midriff as a coughing fit claimed her. I gently rubbed her back and waited for the spasms to subside. "No, it's not," she finally said. "You're just trying to make me laugh, Allie."

"Well, it almost worked, didn't it? Let me think. It's a person who is condescending and self-righteous." I lowered my voice. "Our stepfather believes that he is God's gift to humanity. He is a mezuzah."

"Stop it, Allie." Sibley's smile had widened to a grin that would put the Cheshire cat to shame. "He's not that bad, truly."

I glanced at the timer. The sand had almost squeezed through the neck. "A musical instrument from Arabia!" I shouted. "A Muslim holy man! An exotic fruit that is similar to a pomegranate!"

Sibley shook her head. "None of those. But you were getting close when you guessed a Muslim holy man. It's a parchment of religious texts that is attached to the doorpost of a Jewish house."

I smiled. "One for you, Sibley."

And now it was my turn. My random opening of the book fell to a section of "E", and I chose the word effleurage. *I gave it a flourish. The particles of sand started their journey to the bottom of the timer.*

"It must have something to do with flowers," said Sibley, who is a good student of French. "I surmise that it's the art of arranging flowers."

I shook my head.

"Then it has something to do with waste materials." She considered for a moment. "The factory discharged an effleurage of chemicals into the town's river."

I shook my head yet again, and Sibley bit down on her lip. "I can't think!" she exclaimed. "The fever has muddled my brain."

"It's just a game," I said. "It's not important." I placed my fingers on her cheek and traced its outlines with a light, circular motion. "Effleurage is a type of massage that uses a circular, stroking movement. It is often used in childbirth."

"Had you heard of the word before?"

"No," I admit. "We've not had experiences with childbirth in our family, have we?"

"Do you wish for children one day?"

"Yes, I do."

"I want at least four, perhaps five. Wouldn't it be grand if we could have our first ones at the same time?"

Dear Sibley, so eager now, her face glowing. "Five children—you're an ambitious one!" I said. "I think I'd be content with two. In any event, we are both going to find ourselves handsome young men, who are truly God's gifts to humanity, and we are going to present them with healthy, bouncing babes."

Sibley lay back against her pillow, smiled at me, and then proceeded to produce a cavernous yawn.

I flew from my chair to the bed and clapped my hand across her mouth. Her eyes grew wide as I maintained a firm hold and then finally loosened my grip. "Bless you, Allie," she said.

How often have I yawned freely? It must be countless times, but the Devil has not yet taken advantage of this welcoming entry way. Or could it be that he already has?

Cover your mouth when you yawn, lest the Devil enter your body and snatch your spirit away!

Mr. Sweeney blows his nose with the finesse of a foghorn, and drops his handkerchief into an out-of-sight receptacle next to his chair.

"Do you believe in superstitions?" I ask.

"Of course not."

"God?"

"Jury's still out as far as I'm concerned."

"Poor Alyda. She kept working hard to separate faith and science, but she had to be on constant alert for these centuries-old notions."

"She had to deal with uncertainty, Miss Tavener. That's what keeps us really and truly alive, don't you think?"

CHAPTER 24

One precious to our heart is gone
The voice we loved is stilled
The place made vacant in our home
Can never more be filled

I SAW HIM in the distance on the Roy property, bent to the fencing again, head and broad shoulders stooped to the task. It was a tremendous relief to see him, for I wished to explain why Noah had come to the house that day.

He did not, however, raise his head to greet me, and I increased my stride, curious to know what held his attention. When I was but a few steps away from him, I saw that it was not Caleb. Dugald Roy, kneeling to the grass as he secured a pole in the ground, glanced up at me. "Miss Teasdale," he said, weighing upon the word 'miss.' "What can I do for you?"

I stepped back to escape a sour vapour of whiskey. "I expected your cousin here," I said.

He stood up and wiped his hands on the hips of his trousers. "I've put him to work in the old barn for a few days."

I forced my eyes away from a large blemish on his right cheek, a grey lake with dotted islands of blood. "I want only a few moments of his time."

"You're not to go to my barn."

My hackles stiffened. "No?"

"No one is to disturb my workers."

"I'll stay but a moment."

"You will not set foot on my property, Miss *Teasdale."*

We stared each other down, both steadfast in our refusal to compromise. In my heart, however, I knew that my stubbornness wouldn't yield the desired result. It was not long before I ceded ground and turned to the direction of Tyne Bluff.

"Do you have a message for the boy?" he said.

I paid no heed to his question. Quivering with rage, I took a deep breath to compose myself and set myself to the road.

Here's how our dear Martine would put it: "Who does he think he is? Jesus walkin' in the meadow?"

Ben's free. The cast is history.

"How does the foot feel?" I ask him.

"Weird. Like it's not really attached to my body."

Two days after my trip to the graveyard with Nan, it's a sizzling hot day in the valley. The smell of deep fat fryer grease permeates the centre of town, creeps stealthily into the pores of our skin. The pavement on the road buckles and shimmers as waves of heat dance above it.

"Are you going to get rid of the beard?" We're on our way to a café that's only a block away from the hospital.

"Don't know," he says, stroking his chin. "I'm kind of used to it now."

"I like it."

"In that case—"

At Julie's Bakery we park ourselves at an outdoor picnic table that has an umbrella. Ben orders two butter tarts and a Coke; I opt for freshly-squeezed orange juice and a double fudge brownie.

Ben says, "What would they have done for my foot in Alyda's day?"

"I'm not sure. Some kind of splint, I guess. You wouldn't have been motoring around the way you have been over the last few weeks."

"I'd have been hobbling around in my laboratory."

"Hunched over. No, wait—hunch-*backed*."

"Hair long and stringy."

"Chemical burns all over your lab coat."

"Nope. Blood spatters. From animal sacrifices."

I laugh. "You're impossible."

He grins. "Can I at least have blood-shot eyes?"

"How about a maniacal gleam in them?"

"Speaking of maniacal, any word yet on who mowed down Alyda's rose bushes?"

"No." I use my straw to fish out a pip from the orange juice. "I asked Mr. Sweeney this morning, but he claims he has no idea."

Ben has already reduced both of his butter tarts to a few flaky crumbs on their plate. "Now that you know Alma is his source, are you going to try to see her again?"

"I don't know. It worked out well the other day, but I don't want to upset her again. I honestly thought she was going to have a heart attack that first time."

"That's because she thought you were talking about a specific event, something that wasn't a good memory for her."

I create a fork grid on the icing of my brownie then duplicate it in the opposite direction. "What if I make the same mistake?"

"Next time don't ask any questions. And don't mention the name Allie or Alyda, of course. Maybe she'll start talking on her own again."

I shake my head. "I don't know if that's such a good idea."

"Think about it, Ree. Mr. Sweeney has given you detailed explanations about the journal entries. She must be talking about the past all the time to him."

"He's her son. He has the right to those stories."

"And you're working on a book." Ben eyes me over the rim of his Coke bottle. "You're not going to give up that easily, are you?"

I poked my head into Uncle Joseph's bedroom. He was fast asleep, his legs tangled in one thin sheet that draped over the edge of the bed. The heat in the room was stifling. Shoes in hand, I negotiated the stairs, avoiding the third one from the bottom with its unforgiving creak. No fresh experience for me, this was; I felt as calm as a veteran thief.

Aunt Helen, on the day bed in the library, was also oblivious to the world. Her hair bloomed on the pillow; one arm was flung across her forehead. Griff, on the hooked rug by the window, immediately sensed my presence, rose, and came to my side.

The air was cool and invigorating outside, and a full moon rode high in a sky that was clear. Griff and I would visit the Roy farm so that I could see for myself Caleb's lodgings for the summer. Yesterday, upon my asking him what the arrangements were, he told me that he has a room in the old barn. "It's clean and comfortable," he added, when he saw my horrified face. "It suits me."

"As if you were one of the animals," I protested. "He has no right, your cousin, to treat you in that fashion. His house isn't small. He must have room for you there."

He shook his head. "Don't make a case of this, Allie," he said. "I much prefer to be away from the house where I'm answerable to no one." Still, I felt compelled to see the room for myself.

Dugald Roy has two barns: a new building that houses the cattle and an older one that is used to store machinery. The boards on the older building are weathered and shrunken, and it was through this building that I saw lights flickering as I crested the hill. I heard barking, loud and sustained, a cacophony that could not have come from the bloodhound bitch that Mr. Roy owns.

Griff uttered a low growl as I approached the building warily. Something was not right and my skin prickled in disquiet. It was not only barking I heard; it was growling and snarling, and these sounds were accompanied by shouts, sounds that were vulgar at times. I stopped and recoiled in disgust, certain now that Dugald Roy had convened a show of dog fighting.

I prepared to return to Tyne Bluff, but a movement near the barn door captured my attention. A man was standing there, and although he was not fully illuminated by the lantern hanging above him, I recognized him.

I stayed Griff, and he settled discontentedly to the side of the road. Caleb's back was to me when I stepped around the corner of the barn; I had resolved to surprise him. I was but a foot away when he wheeled upon me and drove his fist with iron force into my right shoulder. I reeled back, losing grip on my lantern, which plunged to the ground and shattered.

"Allie! No! Allie!" His voice was a thousand miles away, beneath the sea. He knelt beside me and he pulled me to his chest and I groaned, for even though he could not know it, he was causing me greater pain. "I saw a shadow. Thought it was someone who meant me harm," he said. "Why didn't you call out to me?"

My shoulder throbbed in ugly fashion. Face wedged against the stiff wool of his sweater, I tried to catch my breath after the shock of the attack. Suddenly a high-pitched squeal penetrated the roars on the other side of the wall behind me, and I shuddered convulsively, an echo of the pain and the fear in the animal that had uttered the sound.

"Get me away from here," I hissed. I pulled away from him and tried to stand, but I didn't have full wind yet.

Caleb guided me to the ground again. "I can't," he said. "I must stay by the door."

"You're a lookout."

"Yes, I'm the lookout. And, like you, I don't want to see what goes on inside." Coins jingled in his pocket as he ran his fingers through them. "They pay me good wages for this."

I rubbed my shoulder. "That's far more than any lookout would ever earn, by the sound of it."

"That comes from the odd wager. And I've earned far and above what Dugald's given me these two months," he said with pride.

"You think that is money fairly earned, betting on the lives of dogs!"

"It's for us, Allie. I'm doing this for us so that we can go away together."

"Go away?" What could he possibly be thinking?

He looked so earnest, so assured of himself when he said, "You need to get away from here, away from Reverend Hamilton and Noah. I understand why. They cause you considerable grief, and I want to take you away from them."

I knew then that I must get away, away from that hellish barn and its dying dogs and Caleb's solemn and frightening intensity. I took a deep breath and flinched as the pain seemed to separate the shoulder from the arm. "I'm going away in the fall, Caleb," I said. "I've not told you this before, but I'm going to school in Halifax."

My eyes could not meet his again, for now he looked as someone who had endured a blow—a harsh and unexpected blow to the gut.

I forced myself to stand. I had to get away.

If Mr. Sweeney is surprised to see me in his office for the second time in one day, he doesn't express it. He begrudgingly allows me five minutes with Alma. "She's not well today," he says. "I don't want anyone tiring her out."

"Five minutes," I confirm.

Alma is in a nightgown, but she's out of bed, rearranging her doll collection. "I've left them too long," she says. "Completely forgot about them in July. I hope they haven't got into any arguments."

Two dolls are cradled in her arms. "Let's see, Caroline," she says, addressing the doll to her left. "You haven't been with Lucinda for a while, have you?"

I ease myself into a chair by the doorway to watch her. She hums tunelessly and talks under her breath as she moves the dolls. At one point she puts a doll into place only to exclaim a few seconds later, "No! That won't do!" The doll is rotated yet again.

She treats each doll with respect. Readjusts hats, guides stray locks of hair into place, irons dress wrinkles with the palm of her hand. She even kisses one on the forehead. "Rebecca came from one of my birthing mothers," she explains to me. "A lot of these dolls were gifts from my mothers. I guess word got round the mountain pretty quick that I loved dolls."

She brings the doll to me, and that is when I notice that Alma's hands are covered in scratches. Slender, crimson bridges that cross the venous waterways. They look like the superficial swipes of a cat's claws.

I admire Rebecca, and I wait until Alma is finished posing the dolls before I ask, "What happened to your hands, Mrs. Sweeney?"

Alma seats herself on the edge of the bed, runs her index finger along the back of one hand. She peers closely at the patterns on the translucent skin as if she is seeing them for the first time. "I don't know," she says.

"Those marks look like scratches."

"Scratches? I don't think so. They don't hurt at all."

"Were you in the graveyard this week?"

"Graveyard?"

"Yes. Someone cut down the rose bushes around Allie's grave. Did you do that?"

"In the graveyard?" A low throaty chuckle. "I won't go near that bone yard until I'm good and ready."

Is she being canny? Is the slippery memory a convenience or a defence at times?

Sometimes I wonder if it's all a game and she knows that she's besting me at it.

Later, as I leave the house through the mud room, I stop and give the room a methodical examination. I check the soles of all the shoes on the wire rack. I look inside the wicker laundry hamper and in the belly of the old wringer washer. I even turn the coats on the hooks inside out. Mr. Sweeney has been thorough.

I am even more scrupulous. In the end, I poke a corn broom under the washing machine. One of its bristles spears the fragrant, velvet remains of a rose petal.

It's time to give Mr. Sweeney his third visit for the day.

Candlelight flickered in the drawing room and in Uncle Joseph's bedroom. I ran toward the house, my shoes snagging in the dips of the field and my heart galloping like a quarry that must outrun its foe. A horse was tied to the front porch, a dappled gelding that I knew belonged to the village constable. Aunt Helen wasn't to be seen, but Uncle Joseph stood at the drawing room table, inspecting the contents of his medical bag.

I ran to the side of the house and braced myself against the wall, willing my heart to settle. My shoulder ached fiendishly. What would I tell them? That I couldn't sleep for the heat? That once outdoors, I kept walking a mile and yet another mile and more?

I slipped open the side entrance for Griff and me, and placed the new lantern that Caleb had given me on its shelf. I slid along the wall in the gloom, around the corner into the front hallway, and blinked into the flame of a candle held aloft by Aunt Helen. She stood in her silk dressing gown, its corded belt sweeping the tops of her slippers. "Allie," she said softly. "I'm sorry if we awoke you. We did our best to stay quiet."

Griff and I had not been missed! Before I could ask about the purpose of the police officer's visit, Aunt Helen asked me, "Did you see the flames from your window?"

"Flames?"

"One of Dugald Roy's barns is afire."

My heart clenched; my throat was so dry I could not utter a word.

Uncle Joseph joined us; he placed a calming hand on my arm. "There was a gathering in that barn tonight," he said. "They may need me."

A horse whinnied. Aunt Helen opened the front door, and in the distance, we saw Constable MacCallum leading Uncle Joseph's horse from the stable.

"Let me come with you," I pleaded.

"No, Allie. Not this time." Uncle Joseph snapped shut his bag. "It will be no place for a young woman."

Aunt Helen took my hand in her hand. As the men mounted their horses, I saw the flames from the fire, punching high into the darkness. The first ashes, delicate as snowflakes, melted upon my skin.

Lord and Father, let him be safe. Lord and Father, bring him back to me.

Mr. Sweeny is polishing his old gunmetal file cabinet when I arrive at his office. He finally catches sight of me when he stands back to examine his handiwork. He immediately stows the dusting rag into a drawer at the side of his desk.

"Do you have any more questions about this morning?" he says. He remains standing and makes no motion for me to sit down.

I shake my head. "I just came by to say hello to your mother."

"She's really not well. It's good you didn't keep her long."

Everything about our conversation is banal, and yet there is tension in the room, the vague outlines of a stand-off. Or am I just imagining this? "I've been thinking about what happened to those rose bushes in the graveyard," I say. "Have you talked to the police about it? That's vandalism, isn't it?"

He frowns. "I don't think the police need to be brought in on this. None of the gravestones were damaged."

"I suppose. But who do you think might have done something like that? Only the rosebushes were destroyed, so it must have been someone with a specific interest in that gravestone."

"I've already told you. I have no idea." Each word is clipped.

"No theories at all?"

"None." There's an edge to the word, an intimation of warning.

Good. I've finally gotten under his skin. "What is the cemetery association going to do now? Will they put a fence around the stone or will they have some new bushes planted?"

The questions are reasonable, but Mr. Sweeney's eyes project fury. He takes a step toward me, his body rigid with the effort of controlling itself. I step back and reach out to grip the back of a chair. For a moment I wonder if he'll eject me from his office.

Just as quickly he relaxes again, wipes a chain of sweat beads from his brow and takes a calming breath. "I think we might leave things the way they are," he says. "You want to highlight Alyda Teasdale on the tour; we may as well give people something to look at."

It's exactly the answer that I want, and yet I continue to feel contrary. Perhaps it's a childish resentment of his refusal to confide in me. "Aren't you concerned that the stone may get damaged over time from those people who want to test the theory?"

"We'll keep an eye on things," he says. "And so can you." There's a faint hue of exasperation in his voice, but his annoyance is well checked.

Clearly he has defeated me. I motion to go, but he says, "Wait! I have good news for you." His eyes are alight with excitement now. "I have a good idea now what Alyda looked like. "

I wait silently. I'm tired of his manipulations, his incomprehensible agenda.

"She was quite small and slight, probably not much more than five foot three. Delicate facial features, apparently quite pretty. A young Audrey Hepburn, from what I understand." His eyes invite reciprocal enthusiasm.

I say nothing. I will not give him the satisfaction of feigning interest, of asking him one more time the identity of his mysterious source.

"Her hair was a rich dark brown and her eyes were blue-grey."

I have a simple response for him. I look him directly in the eye and say, "I know."

CHAPTER 25

It is God's will that I must see
So soon life's setting sun
With joy I acquiesce and say
Thy will not mine be done

I FOUGHT ALL day to stay awake, anxiously listening for the wing-call of the nighthawk. It came at last in the early afternoon. Fortunately, Uncle Joseph was still asleep upstairs in his room, and Aunt Helen was resting in the library, deep in the embrace of Morpheus. I made my way quickly to the maple copse, eager to see Caleb, to know that he was well.

He pulled me to him immediately, concerned to know how I had fared after the blow to my shoulder. It was tender, but the pain could be borne, I assured him. The odour of smoke still clung to his hair and his clothing. He had a wound on his cheek, rake marks caused by the claws of a frantic terrier that he had rescued, he told me. I put my hand to his face, but he brushed it away. "Why didn't you tell me that you're bound soon for Halifax?" he said.

"I didn't want to think of leaving you. But I must leave soon for school and you must return to Cape Breton."

"No. I'll follow you to Halifax. I'll find work there."

"Your mother needs you, Caleb."

"She has my brothers and sisters. She has her mother."

I took his hand. "Did you think in all honesty we could find a way to stay together?"

He pulled me to him and slid his fingers along a strand of hair that had escaped its pins. I felt a delectable shiver course through my body. He kissed me, again and yet again, hungry, angry kisses—kisses from a cache of endless reserves.

"No more," I finally said, almost choking for air. Tears welled, threatened to flow.

"I have a duty to my mother," he said. "I have a duty to you as well."

Another shiver darted through my body. He truly loves *me.*

Alma Sweeney is in the hospital with pneumonia. Perhaps she caught a chill when she went to the graveyard. I've often thought about that occasion. Did she slip out of the house again without telling her son? Did he suspect this time where she was going? Did he help her destroy the rose bushes? Above all, I want to know why she felt the need to do away with them.

I check in at the hospital in Danton and find that visitors are permitted to visit her. Competing odours of tomato soup and disinfectants follow me to the end of a long corridor that terminates in a cinder block wall. A large poster, peeling away from the expanse of grey, exhorts me to donate blood.

Inside the semi-private room, sliding curtains in a faded floral design are drawn around Alma's bed. I quickly avert my gaze from the only other occupant of the room, another elderly woman, whose breathing sounds like a wind-driven tin can tripping along a stony road. I peek through the crack between the two curtains that surround Alma's bed. Alma, propped like a doll against a bank of pillows, appears to be sleeping. On the bedside table stand a glass of water and the bowl of stones from her home. Her son is sitting beside the bed in a simple chair, a folded newspaper on his lap. His lips are pursed as he concentrates on a crossword puzzle.

Mr. Sweeney's head jerks up as I slip through the opening in the two curtains; he doesn't look pleased to see me. There's a distinct hangover of tension from our last meeting. "I know," I had said in response to his description of Alyda. He had recovered quickly, however, and didn't ask me to repeat myself. I'm sure he'd convinced himself that he had heard incorrectly.

"There's no point in staying," he now says. "She's been sleeping the whole time I've been here."

"Is she going to be all right?"

He nods. "If we're lucky, she might get out by the end of the week."

I sit down on the end of the bed. Mr. Sweeney ignores me as he continues to solve more of the crossword puzzle. After a few minutes have gone by, he stands up abruptly and tells me that he has to return home. "There's really no point in staying," he repeats. "She'll just sleep through your visit." He kisses Alma on the forehead and then he brushes past me.

Alma has colour—her cheeks are a pleasant pink and the pouches beneath her eyes are a bruised shade of purple. The scratches on her hands are still a vivid red, the skin beneath them a milky white and blue. An IV needle bores into the surface of one hand. Oxygen tubing wings from her nostrils. Her breathing doesn't sound laboured; she's in much better shape than her room-mate.

I settle into the chair that Mr. Sweeney vacated and become so engrossed in my *Ms.* magazine that I'm not aware of the moment when Alma first awakes. A faint, prickly sense of being observed finally makes me look up.

Her eyes, wide open, are staring at me. They really are a beautiful, remarkable green.

"Are you ready to listen to me now?" she says.

I nod, let the magazine slide to the floor.

Alma leans towards me. "Allie told me a secret today."

"Oh?" I'm afraid to breathe.

"I can't tell you." The words are delivered with a gossip's air of superiority. "She swore me to secrecy."

I exhale. "That's okay. I don't want to know."

"She needs me. Allie needs me!"

"It's good that you can help her."

Alma grips my wrist. "She's pregnant, you know. She can't have that baby."

I nod in agreement. "You'll know what to do, won't you?"

"Oh, yes." Alma slants me a sage look. "I'm the only one who does."

Outside the window of Aunt Helen's study, the rain leapt from the roof and sheeted down the pane like a waterfall. For a moment I fancied myself as a traveller of an earlier century, huddled in a cave by a dying fire, waiting out the storm. Aided by the light of a lantern, I sat at the marble table and wrote a letter to Granmama. It was cold in the tower room, but the lantern emitted some heat and an old quilt provided comfort on my shoulders. The room rang hollow; since Aunt Helen's leg has worsened, her flower presses, scrapbooks, and painting materials have all been removed to the library.

I glanced often to the grove of maples. And finally, when the heavy rain had tapered to a drizzle, he was there, a phantom pacing in the gloom of the trees.

"You're a fool," I told him, when I'd beckoned to him and he came running to the house. "You'll catch your death in this weather! Did you think that I would brave the elements to come meet you?"

"You've got an umbrella. What's a drop of rain to an English lass?" He grinned. "And don't deny that you'd be pining for me if I hadn't come. Am I right?"

I smiled to myself but didn't reply as I fetched an old towel for him from the scullery. He flung the cloth onto the table and swept me into his arms. "Am I right?" he said again. That time it was a whisper to my ear. His lips, cold and wet, planted a kiss on the lobe.

"Yes!" I gasped. I shuddered as the dampness leapt from his clothing into mine. He eased his embrace but briefly, lowered his head to kiss the hollow in my throat with such tenderness that I could no longer bear it.

"Stay away from me." I could scarcely speak. "You're a monster."

He let me go then, laughed as he towelled his head vigorously. He crossed the kitchen to the wood stove and bent to feed it. "Fire's out," he accused. "How's a man to get dry?"

"I've been in the tower all afternoon." The towel rub and the dampness had shaped his hair into thick curls.

"Where are your aunt and uncle?"

"They've gone to Halifax, to see a new physician for Aunt Helen's polio and to bring back Robbie."

"They won't return tonight then." There was a glint in his eye, a light of expectation. "Will you be going home to the manse?"

"No. I'll stay here again with Griff." A tug-of-war muscled into my thoughts: a jerking of the two poles of decorum and desire. Decorum finally triumphed. "And you," I said, "will not be here with me."

"I didn't suggest it," he protested. He fed kindling from the bin to the stove. "Put water on for tea, Allie. I wouldn't mind a cup."

His fingers soon curled around a pewter mug. I tried to envision them in the prim handle of a fine bone china cup. "Does your cousin not feed you?" I teased, as he devoured a second slice of dried apple cake.

He smiled as he captured the last few crumbs with his fingertips and transported them to his lips. "One piece might be enough for the average fellow," he said, "but I have a mine shaft for a stomach."

I gazed at him across the table, stretched my arm so that he could take my hand in his hand. The skin of his hand was rough and callused; it had strength and substance. He then placed his other hand atop our joined hands, and a feeling of tremendous warmth and comfort suffused me.

This was the kitchen of our own home, and we were old souls who had been together for many, many years.

I visit Alma in the hospital every day. She hasn't mentioned Alyda in my presence again, but she has told me about her clandestine relationship with Leonard Sweeney and numerous anecdotes about her years as a midwife. Even without her involvement in the mystery surrounding Alyda, she has led a rich and interesting life.

Today, I find her kneeling on the faded linoleum floor beside her bed, bare feet tucked under her buttocks, the heels taut and shiny. The tie at the back of the pale blue hospital gown has slipped open, revealing the bony shelving of her shoulder blades. Around her, on the floor, lie the scattered contents of her bedside bowl.

She glances up at me. "I can't find Leo's stone," she says, anxiety lacing her voice.

I kneel down beside her. Patches of moisture spread out like shadows beneath some of the stones. "What colour is it?"

"I don't know. I just don't know anymore." She bends forward and stretches her arm to retrieve a stone that has rolled up against the base heater. She cradles the stone in the palm of her hand and nudges it with her fingers. After a few moments of consideration, she says, "No. It can't be that one. It doesn't feel right." She continues testing the stones in this fashion, and with each failed attempt, she becomes more agitated. A tear courses down her cheek, embeds itself in the shallow trench of a wrinkle. It is soon followed by another one.

When her hand starts to shake, I select a stone from beneath the table—a flat oval one the size of a hen's egg, smooth and pale green, with one central vein of rusty orange.

"It's this one," I say. I gently pull back her fingers and place it in the palm of her hand. I'm not sure it's the one, but I'm willing to be caught in a lie. I only know that I have to do something to ease her pain.

She closes her fingers over it. "You're sure?"

"I'm sure. Leo liked stones like this. Didn't he use to skim them across the water?"

"That's right," she says. "He did."

Relief splashes across her face like the leading wave of a tidal bore.

The sun began its ascent, and a pebble grazed the frame of my bedroom window to announce Caleb's arrival. We would not have much time to spend together; Dugald Roy was overseeing the construction of a new outbuilding. I had been awake for hours, roaming the house like a ghost, thinking only of Caleb and contemplating if we could forge a future together.

He kissed me gently and held me for a long time, as if he were about to embark upon a long journey and could not bring himself to say farewell. Although he was clad in his work clothes, I received him into the front room like a gentleman caller.

The fireplace and the organ received scrutiny, but this time he went directly to my father's globe. I showed him my birthplace, the port of Southampton. He traced his finger across the Atlantic Ocean to Halifax and marvelled at the distance my family and I had travelled.

"Tell me about the voyage," he said.

I told him that I couldn't recall much, that I had spent a good part of it huddled in a deck chair, dogged with seasickness.

"You'll never want to set foot on a ship again."

"No," I replied without hesitation. "I'll bear the discomfort; the goal is always worth the effort." I trailed my fingers across the Caribbean Sea and its many islands. "See this area? Papa travelled there twice and he promised to take me one day. He described everything so vividly—palm trees waving in the winds, fruits that fall fresh and ripe into your hands, fish in shockingly bright colours in the clear waters. I still want to go there one day."

"That is what we'll do then," he said, his eyes, as always, so intense. "I've never been on a ship, Allie, and I've never travelled beyond our shores, but I swear on the day that I do, it will be in your company."

I'm falling in love with this man. How could I not? He breathes conviction.

"We'll go to Southampton first," I said. "I want to show you my birthplace and introduce you to my people."

He was speechless then, but his eyes were afire. I thought he would burst out of his skin with happiness.

We have a future. We do.

I help Alma back into bed, pull the blanket over her. Her hand still clutches Leonard's stone. I round up all the other stones and return them to the bowl. Seated again, I ask Alma, "The stone is from our shore, isn't it?"

Alma opens her fist. "Oh, yes," she says, glancing at the stone and then burying it again. "It came from down by the old pier. Leo gave it to me the day before we left for Toronto. I said I wanted something to remind me of the shore and that's what he gave me."

"It's a beautiful stone. That orange vein brings it to life."

She looks at me intently, assessing my comment. "You'd say that, of course. You're a polite, young lady. Fact is, though, that lots of folks wouldn't consider that a decent gift."

"You loved the shore and you wanted something to remind you of it. I can't think of a better present."

"You really think so? You're not just saying so to make an old lady feel better?"

I smile and place my hand briefly on the hand that is holding the stone. "I honestly think so," I say. "Leonard chose the perfect gift. He must have really loved you, Mrs. Sweeney."

"Loved me?" Alma extends her fingers slightly, stares at the stone. And then, in one swift, unexpected motion, she raises her arm and hurls the stone toward the window. It strikes the glass with a resounding *ping* and then plummets to the floor. I turn to her and find that her eyes are brimming with tears.

"He promised to stand by me," she says. "If he loved me so much, then why did he abandon me?"

I cannot respond to her question, of course, and I'm at a loss for words of any kind. I wish Mr. Sweeney were here; he would know what to say or to do.

In a few seconds, I'm relieved of deciding upon a course of action. A nurse flings aside the curtains, strides to her patient's bedside, and begins the task of diverting Alma's attention from her pain.

CHAPTER 26

Weep not for me my parents dear
I am not dead but sleeping here
As I am now you soon will be
Prepare for death to follow me

I THINK OF Ben, who has never betrayed me. And I think of how much I have hurt him.

By the time I was ready to enter Dalhousie University, Ben had already put in two years of undergrad studies in the sciences. He'd lived in residence those first two years and had found it to be a positive experience. I decided to do the same during my first year of university. Since my home was only a twenty minute walk from campus, I didn't think it was fair to ask Mom and Jack to foot the bill; I secured a summer job to help pay for the cost of residence. Ben stayed in Halifax that summer and lived with us, taking over a guest bedroom.

We both worked hard that summer, Ben on a road construction crew, and I as a waitress at a harbour front restaurant. Sometimes we worked overtime on the weekends, and I mostly worked evenings until ten or eleven o'clock. We didn't see each other very often, and I was relieved that it worked out that way. Ben was in love with me—it was evident in every glance—and I wasn't able to return that love.

One night Ben surprised me by picking me up at the restaurant. Jack usually did that, and he had no explanation for why he had taken Jack's place. It was late for Ben—he would be up again by five.

I was wide awake—I always was, coming off a shift—and he seemed a bit edgy, as if he were monitoring his store of constant energy. He'd showered and changed out of his work clothes, and tamed his hair; I was aware of the splashes of ketchup on my blouse, the mist of deep-fat fryer grease clinging to the strands of hair that swept my cheeks. I felt grimy and uncomfortable next to him.

"Let's take a walk," he said, and so we walked the streets near the harbour front. It was a cool night, after a day of rain. A faint odour of musk hung over our part of the city, of old vegetables tossed into dumpsters and sewage spiralling down and settling in the harbour. The heels of my pumps clicked on the damp grit of the sidewalks.

At one point Ben stopped in the pool of light shed by a street lamp, and I stopped too. He didn't say anything; he looked at me with such love in his eyes that I flinched, even before his hand reached out and rested lightly on my wrist. I pulled away from that grand leap of emotion in his eyes, from the hand that had pierced a boundary, and said, "God, I feel filthy. I've got to get home."

I didn't look at him, didn't see how the passion in his eyes would have been extinguished. And I did feel soiled as we walked back to the car, both of us silent now—filthy, and angry with myself for causing Ben pain and not knowing how I could make it easier for him.

It was then that I made a decision: I wouldn't go to Dalhousie for school, after all.

"My hands!" moaned Sibley. "And my wrists—they're killing me!" She extended her arms, dangled her hands, and rotated them several times. Despite her complaint, Sibley emanated a glow, the kind of glow that accompanies achievement. As a duet, we had just rehearsed for the third time Grieg's first Peer Gynt Suite, Op. 46 and we both knew that we had performed it to perfection.

"It will be the most talked-about piece at the recital," I predicted.

"Do you think there'll be a good many people in attendance?"

"Mama will be there, and Aunt Helen and Uncle Joseph. They're the ones who matter."

"And a fellow named Caleb. Will he be there?"

Sibley's words delivered the desired jolt, but she looked away immediately and could not see how stricken I was. The tip of her ear was burning.

"Tell me, Sibley. What has Noah told you?"

She recovered quickly; she met my gaze again, eyes and chin defiant. "Only that he works on Mr. Roy's farm and that you've met with him several times; that is, until Noah forbade you to do so any longer."

A reprieve—my racing mind did not need to produce an explanation. By avoiding the shore, Caleb and I had managed to conceal our more recent trysts from Noah.

"Why haven't you been open about your friendship with him?" Sibley asked.

"I was afraid that no one in the family would accept him. We are the Teasdales and he's but a farm labourer."

"Aunt Helen and Uncle Joseph aren't arrogant people."

"No, they're not, but their sense of propriety would differ from mine. I've also kept it a secret from everyone for fear that somehow word would get to Mr. Hamilton. You know that he would never sanction my friendship with him."

"Isn't he more than a friend? Isn't he your secret beau?"

"No!"

Sibley regarded me for a long time. Had I protested too strongly?

At last she said, "Noah feels that we don't know enough about this Caleb Whitelaw, and that you may have compromised yourself during your meetings with him."

I half rose from the piano bench then sat down again. "How could you allow Noah to poison your mind with such drivel? Couldn't you have come to me and asked me about Caleb directly?"

Sibley's chin tilted in defiance again. "You couldn't confide in me as your sister and your best friend? I never see you anymore, Allie. You obviously wish to spend all your time elsewhere!"

I have seldom felt more miserable and burdened with guilt. "I don't know why I didn't speak in confidence to you," I said. It's true that I may have felt disquiet regarding her tolerance of Noah, but Sibley and I have always opened our hearts to each other.

Sibley started to weep. "I'll make it up to you," I promised, wrapping my arm around her shoulder and pulling her to me.

Poor Sibley, she was disconsolate. I must spend more time with her and set things right.

One week after Alma Sweeney's discharge from hospital, Mr. Sweeney delivers an invitation to high tea at their home. I've seen Alma twice since she's come home again, but only for a short time on both occasions. I don't know if it was poor adaptation to a new setting that caused her mental decline in the hospital, but I could see immediate improvement as soon as she was home. I'm concerned, however, about taxing her in any way and ask Mr. Sweeney if he thinks she's well enough to socialize in a more formal way.

She's the one who insists, he tells me. And the student helper will make the tea and the sandwiches. Alma will simply preside.

"Could I bring Ben?" This may be a breach of etiquette, but I'm not able to stop myself. It's Ben's last day on the mountain, and I'd like him to meet Alma.

Mr. Sweeney doesn't hesitate with his response. "By all means," he says. "I'll let Mother know she can expect another guest."

Ben's leaving for Halifax tomorrow morning, moving back into my parents' home near the Dalhousie campus, where he'll continue his work on his doctorate and teach undergraduate students. And although he still has packing to do and a number of errands to run in Danton, he agrees to accompany me to high tea with Alma.

A table has been placed in the Sweeney's side yard, one of the large folding ones that you find in community halls for church suppers and other events. Three chairs have been set up with it, two on one side and one on the other. Bone china cups and saucers with a forget-me-not pattern, gold-rimmed plates, silverware, and blue linen napkins have all been laid out on white linen. The table holds two trays. One is piled high with cheese triangles and egg salad sandwiches that have been stamped into the shape of hearts by a cookie cutter; the other is laden with butter tarts, chocolate brownies, and vanilla cupcakes with a butter cream icing.

Alma has done herself up for the occasion. An antique ivory blouse with lace cuffs and a cameo at the throat. Brand-new moccasins. Her earlobes stretch beneath the weight of rectangular earrings. The bevelled green glass of the earrings mirrors the colour of her eyes.

Alma doesn't wait for an introduction to Ben. "I didn't know you had a boyfriend," she says. A lengthy appraisal of him from head to toe brings the conclusion: "He's good looking, isn't he? Aren't you the lucky girl!"

"Ben's not—"

"Come this way, young man." Alma grips Ben's arm, just above the elbow. She insists that he sit beside her at the table.

"Mr. Sweeney's not going to join us?" I ask. I take my seat, facing them.

"No, no. He's much too busy," she says, reaching for the teapot. "Owen would never take a break in the afternoon."

"Here. Let me do that for you, Mrs. Sweeney." Ben lifts the pot first, and she bestows a grateful, almost coquettish smile on him as he serves the tea.

"Besides, Owen would never have anything to eat this time of day," Alma continues. "It has to be noon time and six o'clock for him, and a steady diet of cigarettes in between." She helps herself to one of the heart-shaped sandwiches and tears away a tiny portion with her teeth. "When are you planning on getting married?" she says, addressing the question to me.

Ben jumps in before I can respond: "It's a bit early to be thinking of that, Mrs. Sweeney."

"How old are you, young man?"

"Twenty-eight."

"As good an age as any to get married. Almost too old, I'd say. Things didn't go the way I wanted in my marriage, but that doesn't mean I'm sour on the idea. I married in haste and got to repent in leisure. Now, you young people, you've probably been thinking about this for a long time. It's time to take the plunge."

"Why didn't things go the way you wanted?" I ask.

Alma doesn't seem to mind my lack of tact. "Leo wasn't happy in Toronto," she says. "He kept hopping from one job to another and he kept reminding me that it was *my* idea to go up there in the first place. And it wasn't easy raising a child, especially one that's colicky and then headstrong the way Owen was. Leo got fed up, that's what he did. One day he just didn't come home from work. Called to say that he was about to board a bus to Vancouver."

"He left you, just like that?" Ben says. "And he never came back?"

"Oh, I got a few letters and some money from him in the early years. He was wrestling a guilty conscience, I'd say, but he didn't feel guilty enough to ask me to join him out west. And then the letters stopped when I moved back here to the mountain. Even though he's still got family here in the port, I've made it my business never to find out how he fared out west. He betrayed me."

"He made a big mistake," Ben says, "leaving a woman like you."

"What did you say your name was, young man?"

"Benjamin Allenby."

"Do you live in the village? Who are your people?"

"I live on the second line. Warren and Kaye Allenby are my parents." When there is no flicker of recognition in Alma's face, he adds, "They live next door to Joshua and Rachel Montgomery."

"Josh Montgomery! Addie's husband?"

"Yes, that's right."

Ben's concern is obvious, and I too prepare myself for more on the subject of Addie. But Alma is busy examining Ben's face. "I remember your mother now. She's a nurse at the hospital, isn't she? Nice lady. You really don't look anything at all like her, young man."

And as Ben considers a response to this unexpected observation, Alma forges on. "You must be adopted," she says, assuming an air of sympathy. "There's nothing wrong with that, nothing at all." She places a reassuring hand on Ben's hand. "Sometimes someone else's child can mean more to you than your own flesh and blood."

Ben looks at me helplessly, and I shake my head with a slight movement. Correcting Alma might lead to further confusion. I change the subject by asking Alma about the origins of her gorgeous glass earrings. She smiles and settles into a story about a grandmother and a gift from a fiancé who died in an accident at the fish cannery the day before their wedding. It's a terribly sad story, but Alma relishes the telling of it and immediately invokes other reminiscences about her forebears.

Ben and I enjoy the rest of the tea, content to be a captive and appreciative audience for our hostess.

The recital was a grand success! The community hall was packed as tightly as a tin of haddies, and Sibley and I received enthusiastic applause for our note-perfect performance. As we stood upon the stage, accepting generous bouquets of tea roses, I espied a familiar face among those standing at the very back of the hall. Caleb nodded solemnly and then moved to the door to escape the crush of people.

That night, Mama presented me with Papa's brass telescope. "It's a gift for your going away," she explained. "And I know your father would be happy to see it in your hands." Sibley was delighted for me, but Noah clearly was not. I could see those little wheels in his mind, chugging to the conclusion that he *should have been the recipient of this gift—he, after all, is a* boy.

This morning I took the telescope to the shore with me when I went there to commune with Papa. How will it feel to be in Halifax, I wondered, so far away from Ile de Haute? I used the brass instrument to bring the island closer to me, but I confess to training it periodically on the edge of the bluff above Caleb's oven. Our *oven. I held out hope for his appearance, but it was not to be.*

When I returned to the house, I found that Aunt Helen had given us Martine for the day. She, Sibley and I canned beans, carrots, and pickles, and baked several peach pies and loaves of oatmeal bread. What a heavenly mélange of smells there was in our kitchen! Later, Sibley and I stitched several squares in the ring-and-dove quilt that is to be Mother's wedding gift. I sorely neglected this activity during the summer, and it felt good to take steps towards its completion.

At sunset the old pier found me shore-side again, telescope in hand. A light breeze brought welcome relief from a late summer burden of heat. Oft times, I've enjoyed my spells alone here, but this evening I found myself yearning for Caleb. I kept the telescope busy, searching the bluff in the distance, hoping that he would appear and start the descent to our cave. Again, I waited in vain.

I yearn for the world that we created exclusively for us, but I also find myself wondering why I am loath to expand it. I've promised to take him to see my family in England. Why will I not introduce him to Aunt Helen and Uncle Joseph and Sibley? Surely they would all be discreet at my urging. Sibley is right; my aunt and uncle are not self-important people. Perhaps they would not be quick to judge him, nor could they, even if they were so inclined. He is ambitious, quick-witted, and well-mannered, and he treats me with respect and tenderness.

I am doing him a great disservice. Why do I continue to exhibit such cowardice? Why am I not true to him or to myself?

"I can see why you like Alma," Ben says. "She's a grand old lady."

We're walking the upper reaches of the shore down by the ovens, a final stroll before Warren takes Ben into the city in the morning. Lucy is with us. At seven o'clock in the evening it's chilly, and banks of lowering clouds rob the land of any warmth it accumulated earlier in the day.

"I wouldn't mind being like her when I get older—having the courage to speak my mind without being overly obnoxious about it."

"You can start working on that now," he says.

I glance up to a teasing grin; it strikes me that I'm going to miss him terribly.

"Why did you play along with Alma when she assumed we were in a relationship?"

Ben laughs. "I don't think I could have convinced her otherwise. She seemed to like the idea, so I thought there was no point in disappointing her."

Will I keep the lie alive should Alma refer to it in the future? To my surprise, I find that the answer is *probably*. She's not the only one who likes the idea.

I look out to the water. The Isle of Haute is grey and desolate, swaddled in low-lying scarves of clouds. I shiver. "We never did make it over to the island," I say.

Ben removes his jacket, settles it onto my shoulders. His fingers rest on my collarbones for a moment. "Gramps is bound to know someone who can take you out there. You'll still get good weather over the next couple of months."

Do I tell him that I don't want to make that trip without him?

I like the weight of his jacket on me, the comfort of its signature scent. On an impulse I say, "I'll miss you," and then I immediately hold my breath. How will he interpret this? But he's not even looking at me; he's busy searching for a piece of driftwood to throw for Lucy.

I'm roiling inside now. I want him to know how I feel about him. I want him to grab me, shake me in justified fury! Tell me that I've been an idiot all these years!

Lucy's off in pursuit now, and he turns to me, smiles. "You can visit me whenever you want."

I grasp onto that invitation as if it's the only life buoy in a storm-tossed sea. "I know the start of the school year is always a hectic time for you, but I'm going to come down when I can."

He looks at me, the sea in his eyes adding weight and depth. "The door's always open for you," he says.

CHAPTER 27

We have laid him away in deep sadness
Yet not without hope in our breast
For again we shall join him with gladness
And enter the heavenly rest

My difficulty in letting things go—it's been a lifelong habit of mine. I've routinely dined from a stew pot of thoughts-that-should-be-avoided, and each time I've licked the spoon completely clean.

It's surprising, therefore, when Paul Haddon calls the house early one evening, and I fail to recognize his voice at first. I haven't thought of him in weeks.

"You blew it," he says. His voice has a breathless, urgent quality. "That job's gone to someone else."

I'm focused now. "I didn't want it," I say.

"Are you crazy, turning something like that down? It's right up your alley."

"I'm staying here, Paul." I enunciate each word carefully, hoping to penetrate his fog of incomprehension.

A long silence from him. I'm surprised he doesn't have an alternative strategy in place. Yes, he's arrogant, but he never leaves anything to chance. Finally, he says, "You're really going to stay there? In dueling banjos country?"

"Paul, don't—"

"Jesus, you're not serious, are you?"

When I refuse to acknowledge this question, he says, "What's keeping you there?"

"I'm still working on—"

"It can't be Ben. He was gone for the summer and he'll be heading back to school now."

Silence from me.

Paul seals it: "It *is* Ben, isn't it? It's *Ben*."

And to put an end to this misery I say, "Of course it is."

My tutoring sessions with Noah came to an end today. When I reflect upon the terms of my punishment, I admit they were easily borne. Noah proved himself to be a capable student, and the sessions gave me the opportunity to test a career in teaching. I'm sure now that this is not where my future lies. A novelist or a physician—I would be happy with either vocation. They both hold tremendous interest for me, and I'll not be deterred by the scarcity of female physicians. No doubt my professors at university will help me to decide which path to take.

"Thanks to you, I may yet get acceptance to Dalhousie," Noah said. "I've placed it at the top of my list for applications. And if I do get in, you can show me the ropes and introduce me to your friends."

My stomach curdled. Did he truly believe that I would ever admit him to my friendship circle? I sat quietly, seething, until I reminded myself that I would enjoy at least two years of freedom from him (perhaps more, if Lady Luck were kind to me).

Noah then jumped to a new point of discussion. With his never-ending ability to vex me, he said, "You've taken my advice on Whitelaw to heart."

I shook my head. He was as relentless as a terrier, jaws clamped to a rat's throat. "That was advice you dispensed?" I countered. "It sounded remarkably like a threat."

He shrugged. "It had the planned effect."

I made sure that I held his gaze. "I did not take any decisions based on your threat."

He smirked. "But you haven't met with Whitelaw. That's all that matters to me. And the vigilance, Allie; I'll stay to it until you go to Halifax."

Oh, to smack that big-headed lout on the side of his pompous face!

Paul Haddon's phone call is followed by another one, this one from Mr. Sweeney. Alma is preparing a lobster stew for supper and has invited me to come over to learn how to make it. She remembered! I've asked her a number of times if she would give me informal cooking lessons for recipes she used at the turn of the century, and now she has finally responded.

"You're two minutes late," she says, handing me an apron as I enter the kitchen. "I've already made the roux." She's wearing a blue gingham apron with a bib and oval lap piece. Mine exhibits faded herb clusters in a repeating pattern.

I open my notebook, poise my pen. "How much butter did you use and how much flour?"

Alma stares at me, perplexed. "I have no idea," she says. "I put in a couple of pats of butter, maybe a quarter cup flour. I don't think Martine ever told me how much."

"Martine d'Entremont taught you this recipe?"

"Yes, she did. My mother never really learned how to cook. She was always rushing out the door, off to deliver another baby. It's a good thing my father and I always enjoyed a good bowl of porridge." She lifts the pot an inch above the gas burner. "Now, hand me that cream," she says, in a tone of voice that reminds me of a surgeon demanding a scalpel from his OR nurse. That, too, has been prepared ahead of time, but at least it's in a Pyrex measuring cup. Two cups' worth.

"Is it heavy cream or light cream?" I ask, as she returns the pot to the burner and starts adding the cream to the roux.

"I always use light cream. Lobster's rich enough as it is. Now, get the lobster for me from the fridge, will you? It's in the big blue bowl on the bottom shelf. Owen and I boiled them and shucked them before you came over."

At least I didn't have to witness the lobsters meeting their doom. I remove a tea towel from the top of the bowl and bring the lobster meat—brilliant white and coral orange—to the counter. A fresh, appetizing scent rises from it. "They were paddling around just an hour ago," says Alma.

I steal a piece of meat from the bowl, a small piece that probably came from the claw, and enjoy it unadorned. Wait.

"Sugar," Alma says, adding about half a teaspoonful to the pot from a small, gilt-edged bowl that is likely part of a tea set. "I always add a smidgen. Gives the stew a nice lift. Now that wasn't Martine's idea; it was mine."

"Did you spend a great deal of time at Tyne Bluff? Is that how you got to know Martine and Alyda?"

"I guess you could say that," she says, stirring the cream sauce briskly to keep it smooth. "You see, I first met Allie just before she left for university, but I got to know her really well when she came back to live at the bluff. She didn't want any company at first—on account of carrying that baby, I imagine—but I was stubborn and Martine always let me in. We had an understanding, the two of us. We both thought the world of Allie and wanted the best for her."

The wooden spoon in Alma's hand circles to a slow stop. She looks pensive. I assume she's reliving a memory that she's about to share with me, but she suddenly exclaims, "Almost forgot the salt and pepper! You put them in, Rianne, and I'll tell you when to stop."

I sprinkle the spices from their small glass shakers, aware once again that I can't document any measurable ingredients. It doesn't matter; I can try to duplicate this recipe with Nan some time. The story is more important.

With a large spoon Alma now starts adding the lobster meat to the pot. "I became a good listener for Allie," she continues. "She told me all about the life that she'd had in England, when everything had been simple and she'd been happy. That's not to say her life was horrible here, even if that baby was on the way. Mrs. Helen and Dr. Joseph both treated her like gold, and Dr. Joseph even had her working in the shed to keep her mind off things."

"What was Alyda working on in this shed?" I take the spoon from Alma and start turning the pieces of lobster, coating them with the sauce.

"I guess you would call it a lab, really. It was in an old tractor shed on the property, and Dr. Joseph had started a business there, making tonics and elixirs for everything from windy spasms to whooping cough."

"Did you work in the lab, too? And what did Alyda do?"

"We both worked for Dr. Joseph, but he always made sure that

Allie had tasks that would be safe for her and the baby. Let me see—she crushed dried roots and petals in a huge granite mortar, strained certain ingredients. She even—"

Once again she pauses, and I wait anxiously, hoping that she can select another important memory for me.

It's not to be. Mr. Sweeney enters the kitchen, and I feel a sudden tremor of anxiety. I scan his face to determine if he has overhead our conversation, but it doesn't appear so. He even invites me to join him and his mother for lunch. Removing dishes from the end of the table to make room for me, he glances warily at his mother as if he's afraid she'll put a stop to this. She doesn't. Soup bowls and spoons are brought out and a fresh loaf of flaxseed bread. I'm surprised when we bow our heads at Alma's prompting to say grace. Neither Mr. Sweeney nor Alma has ever struck me as particularly devout. Perhaps it's a comforting tradition for them.

The meal is delectable. I have two bowls of the lobster stew, protesting that I can't possibly eat another bite when Alma urges me to accept a third helping. Mr. Sweeney says little throughout the meal, but he appears relaxed. And after dinner, when mother and son announce they are going to work in the garden, I join them because I'm not yet ready to leave them.

The streets of the village were almost empty today as I set out to make purchases for my new life in Halifax. Perhaps the townspeople didn't wish to risk the ire of the noon day sun.

My last stop was McCryder's Emporium. Robbie Gibson was with the proprietor at the back of the store, kneeling on the floor by a display of iron toys and a circular track. There were dozens of the tiny toys: fire engines, sulkies, phaetons, coupes, and delivery wagons. Robbie was coaxing a fire engine along the track, uttering spine-tingling sounds. When he saw me, a smile lit his face and he shouted, "Allie! Allie!" He brandished the fire engine then hugged it to his chest and said, "Mine!"

"Yes, it is, Robbie," I said. "It's a fine fire engine. And I'm glad to see you're back from Halifax and doing well."

Mr. McCryder greeted me warmly and told me of the time Papa took Robbie on the Laliah B.*, placed his captain's hat on Robbie's head, and let him take over at the helm. "It was just a year ago. Do you remember that, Robbie?"*

And as Robbie shouted, "Captain!" a shadow darkened the open door and Dugald Roy stepped into the store. He stopped when he saw me. He did not remove his cap, but it could not conceal the sidelong glance that he threw in my direction. Was he leering at me? What a loathsome creature he is!

I bade Mr. McCryder and Robbie good-bye; I could not stay in the same room with that poor excuse for humanity. As I prepared to step out of the store, I heard Mr. Roy say to Mr. McCryder, "I know every village has got to have its idiot, but do you think he should be allowed to roam free?"

As I stepped onto the veranda, my heart took another clout—there was Caleb, perched on the banister of the veranda, near one corner. "Allie!" he exclaimed, jumping down and striding to me, his eyes alight with pleasure. "I need to see you."

God in Heaven, I needed to be with him. I needed him to take me in his arms, needed him to . . . "You'll come to Halifax as soon as you can. Promise me."

He took my hand, rubbed his thumb gently across the wrist. "I can't wait 'til you're in Halifax," he said. "Meet me in the oven tomorrow, just past noon."

How could I deny him? Deny myself? I love *him.*

Tomorrow I'll meet him in the cave, and then I'll take him up the staircase and introduce him to the Teasdales of Tyne Bluff.

"One last time, Caleb, before I go to the city." I raised my hand, touched my fingers to one side of his jaw, and stroked it. "We'll meet there one last time."

Mr. Sweeney changes into a pair of ancient Hush Puppies. Alma dons a straw hat that's dented in several places. Both pull on gardening gloves so filthy that their colour scheme has been annihilated.

The Sweeneys are going to split the irises in a large bed in the back yard. Alma kneels, sweeps back a dense cluster of leaves with her forearm. Mr. Sweeney eases a spade into the earth around it, bears down a mud-stiffened shoe on its edge, and frees a large tangle of rhizomes. He hands the spade to me and kneels to prise a section from the main cluster. And as he does so, the telephone rings in the house. "Don't go anywhere," he says, wiping his hands down on his pants. I don't know if he is referring to Alma or to me.

Alma continues to kneel by the flower bed. I take up the spade. "I'll keep digging," I say.

"No, Rianne. Only Owen knows how to do that. We'll sit down and wait until he gets back."

I help Alma to her feet and guide her to an old glider that sits near the flower bed. The benches are grey and splintered; I peel back a sharp shaving of wood from one bench and seat myself opposite Alma.

"My father and I love irises too," I say. "He's arranged for stained glass inserts with an iris design to go on either side of the main door at the inn."

"Inn? What inn are you talking about?"

"The one he's building on the Whitfield property." She frowns in confusion. "Tyne Bluff," I add, and hold my breath as I wait for the response.

"Tyne Bluff. You mean where Dr. Joseph's house is?"

"Yes."

Alma nods in the direction of the iris bed. "Those are descendants of the irises at the bluff."

"They are? Where were they planted?"

"They were in the back, around a gazebo. Dr. Joseph had it built so that Mrs. Helen could enjoy the outdoors at all times. The blackflies were always thick in May and June, and of course you'd get the rainstorms or sudden squalls. It was big enough that you could sit in the centre and escape the rain flying in.

"Allie loved that gazebo. She would sit for hours in it on an old rocking chair. I remember she stitched a runner that fall. The irises were gone by then, of course, but she embroidered blue and yellow irises from memory."

And now Alma is crying, tears streaming along the creases in her cheeks. "That poor girl," she says.

I cross to the other side of the glider and wrap my arm around Alma's thin shoulders. Her body convulses in a case of the hiccups.

"What's wrong, Mother?" Mr. Sweeney crosses the lawn from the house, his leg jerking and thrusting to his hip as he increases his speed to reach us. Amid the concern in his face is an expression that clearly cries out: *What did you do to her?*

"She's fine, Mr. Sweeney. The irises just reminded her of somebody she once knew."

Alma wipes her nose with a handkerchief that's embroidered with a stylistic *A*. She looks up at her son. "Those were Allie's irises," she says. "You know that, don't you?"

Mr. Sweeney swings his head to me, scowls. "You've gone and done it again." And then, deadly precision in his voice: "Get out of here."

I jump to my feet and set the glider swinging. In my haste to step down from it, I lose my balance and almost trip into him. I stand still for a moment, fighting a wave of nausea.

Mr. Sweeney takes my hesitation as defiance.

"Get off the property," he commanded. "Now!"

Chapter 28

Just as I am without one plea
But that Thy blood was shed for me
And that Thou bidst me come to Thee
Oh lamb of God, I come

"Go back and talk to him," Ben urges.

It's almost midnight, but he's wide awake. He's a night owl, and I know his schedule: he doesn't teach a tutorial until ten tomorrow morning. I've been anxious to talk to him about what happened in Owen Sweeney's yard, but I've had to wait until now to circumvent the gossips on the mountain. They spend most of their days eavesdropping on the party lines.

"I can't go back to him," I say, "at least, not for a while. If you'd seen his face, you'd know why."

"That bad?"

An image comes to mind again—the fear in Mr. Sweeney's face, the air charged with his anger. "He was worried about Alma," I say. "He's fierce about protecting her." I pause. "I'm also wondering if he might have been looking for an excuse to stop working with me. I think it's too coincidental that this happened just as we reached the last of the journal entries."

"Why wouldn't he want to give you the rest of the history?"

"I don't know, Ben. I just get the impression that something is holding him back."

A sharp whistle at the end of the telephone line—it's swiftly muffled. He'd put the kettle on. "I'm going to sound like a broken record," he says, "but the only solution to this would be to go back to see him."

"I can't. I'm questioning our whole association now. I thought we got along well during those years I worked with him at the museum, but everything was out of balance this summer. The way he controlled the information about Alyda and the way he thought about me. He's never stopped calling me *Miss Tavener.*"

"He's from a generation that's just more formal about things like that. If you didn't like it, you could have just come right out and asked him to call you *Rianne.* He might even have been waiting for you to do that."

"I doubt that. But a friendship or the beginnings of a friendship—I think they were there. We were getting on each other's nerves at times, but I actually *like* him. And I like his mother."

"Then go back to him," Ben says, with boundless patience.

I make no promises. And a few days later, I realize that the person I need to see the most is Ben. A telephone conversation does not satisfy.

My old home in Halifax is a two-storey, ivy-covered brick house on a tree-lined street in the south end of the city. This is the house to which my mother and I moved when she married Jack. I've spent little time in it during the past eight years. When I came home for visits at Easter and Christmas, my parents and I generally headed to the mountain to spend time with Nan, Gramps, and the Allenbys.

Ben now occupies my bedroom. I sling my jacket and purse over one of the chairs in the kitchen and head to my old room to take a peek. Most of my possessions—the bedspread, books, movie posters, souvenirs of my travels with Mom and Jack—have been transferred to Gramps and Nan's place, but in some ways the room still feels like mine. My mobile of seashells, chosen at the time of Mom's wedding in the Bahamas, hangs from a hook in one corner. Just below the ceiling, stencil drawings of my favourite flowers, tiger lilies, survived recent renovations. And a pigeon, as always, is resting outside on the window ledge, the sun dappling her pearl grey back. Most of the shadow-slinging ivy leaves have already turned to deep crimson.

There's a new addition to the room, a bedside lava lamp that lazily circulates neon green globules. Ben has directed the comforter to all four corners of the bed, but I can tell that the job is a hasty one, performed for my benefit. I pull back the comforter and see the imprint of his head still on the pillow. I resist the urge to smooth it. I kneel to look under the bed. The piles of dirty clothing there make me smile. At least he's made an effort. It feels right that he's in my room and in my home.

A white blouse and a black knit tank top. A short flare skirt with a red checked design. White tights and black patent shoes. I haven't worn a Toronto outfit in almost five months.

Ben's smile of appreciation as he walks through the door vindicates my effort.

I give him a hug. In our family hugs are generally exchanged only on special occasions. That may account for the current of hesitation that runs through his body before he reciprocates. Or perhaps it is confusion.

When I step back and look at him, his smile is now tentative.

"The hug's from Mom. She asked me to give you one."

The smile expands. "How is she?"

"She's fine. Loves the people; loves what she's doing. She's gone pickerel fishing and she's even been out tracking wolves."

"What did she say about your letter and the birth stories?"

"Actually, she didn't write me." I pause. "She sent a letter to Nan and Gramps."

Ben's at the fridge, removing a bottle of Schooner beer. "She'll be in touch," he says. He points to his bottle, and I shake my head.

"No guarantees. That's Mom. I don't know why I expected something different this time around."

"Cut her some slack, Ree. She's busy. And she's probably trying to be careful about how she responds to your letter."

"Whose side are you on?"

"What?" Ben snaps off the cap of the bottle with an opener, sends me a mystified look. "I'm not taking sides."

"Can we change the subject then?"

"Sure can." He raises the bottle of beer as if he's about to pronounce a toast. "Why don't we dig into those donairs you brought along?"

There's a Lebanese deli on Spring Garden Road devoted exclusively to donairs. Its owner positions ground beef in a pita and tops it with chopped raw onions and tomatoes. So far, so good. But then there's the sauce. A combination of evaporated milk, vinegar, garlic powder, and sugar, it always makes my taste buds cringe.

"Man, this is good," says Ben. The pita, sopping with sauce and meat juices, is already falling apart in its tinfoil cradle. "So, change of subject, as requested. Any news on Mr. Sweeney?"

"I haven't gone to see him."

"No?"

"I think it's best to give him some time."

"A little apology can go a long way."

"Apology? You didn't suggest an apology the other day. Besides, *he* was the one who threw me off his property."

"He might not have handled things in the best way, but in his mind he did the right thing for his mother." He points to my donair. "Are you going to eat that?"

I attack it with a nibble on one end. "Even if Mr. Sweeney accepts an apology from me, he's not going to let me see his mother again."

"Offer him a compromise. Promise to stay away from his mother, but tell him you want to finish Alyda's story."

"He still won't want anything to do with me."

"You can prove this, can you?"

I sit in silence, herding wayward tomato pieces back into their pita fold. Must he always be so infuriatingly logical?

My reassembly completed, Ben helps himself to my donair. "Go back to Mr. Sweeney," he says. "Alyda's story deserves to be told."

I lean back in my chair, hug my arms. "You know, I came down here today because I thought you'd make things easier for me."

Ben doesn't skip a beat. "That's exactly what I've been trying to do, Ree," he says.

I do not have a comeback. Our conversation falters, gathers a bit of steam when we discuss Ben's research, but soon chugs to a halt again.

It forces me to make an early escape.

Too tightly wound to drive out of the city after my conversation with Ben, I park the Jeep near the harbour front and start walking up the hill. A shop on Blowers Street draws me to it. Two mannequins are featured in its recessed window. One is outfitted in full pirate regalia—hat with a swooping feather, black eye patch, nasty-looking sword, and a hook for a hand. The pirate is flanked by a Barbie clone, all plastic perfection and wide-eyed innocence, dressed in an elegant Victorian gown of navy serge. The bodice is trimmed with black velvet ribbon and silk appliqué lace, and the frills on the lower half of the skirt flare. Blond ringlets hang from a Gainsborough hat in silky, navy blue velvet, with tucks on the edge and a final flourish of an ostrich plume.

Victorian Barbie sets a plan in motion. Not too long ago Jack and I tossed about ideas for promoting the inn. We haven't worked out all the details yet, but once or twice a year he is going to set aside a "Victorian Days" weekend. Have friendly competitions in lawn tennis, croquet and archery, and parlour games if it's raining. It would be entertaining to exhibit the fashion of the era as I greet guests at the inn.

I open the door to the shop and almost catapult into a tiny woman. She blinks at me, eyes resentful of the admission of light. She can't be more than five feet tall, and she looks remarkably like an apple doll. Face nut brown, with wrinkles as fine and delicate as a spider's web.

She enlists my help in removing the dress from the mannequin, and in front of an antique standing mirror I try the dress on over my blouse and jeans. It's still a bit loose over my clothing, but that's a problem Nan can address.

"Try on the hat," the proprietor says, holding it out to me. She has deep dimples in her wrists.

I shake my head. Hats are something I have never enjoyed wearing. Instead, I pull up my hair and pile it high on the top of my head. It's a nice effect.

After some spirited bargaining with the apple doll, I emerge from the store with a paper package in one hand and an enormous, striped hatbox in the other.

I'm pleased with my purchases. Who knows? I may yet find a use for the extravagant hat.

Perhaps Alma will like it. Perhaps Mr. Sweeney will allow me to give it to her one day.

CHAPTER 29

My self shall slumber in the ground
Til the last trumpet shall resound
Then burst the chains without surprise
And in my Saviour's image rise

A PARCEL ARRIVES from Mom today, laden with gifts for everyone. Gramps, Warren and Ben are the recipients of porcupine quilt belts. Nan and Kaye receive mittens of tanned moosehide with beaver fur trim. My gift is a pair of Athapaskan moosehide boots with a floral design of silk embroidery and glass beads. They are exquisite; I'm not sure I'd ever dare to wear them outside.

"No letter for me?" I ask Nan.

"We got that one just a week ago."

The letter addressed to Nan and Gramps had included a conventional reference: *Give my love to Rianne.* She hadn't asked me to give Ben a hug—she's always liked him, but she's never been one for displays of physical affection. And now she still hasn't responded directly to my long letter about Alyda and the enclosures of my birth stories.

I step into the boots. They fit perfectly, but the toes of my left foot nudge an obstacle. A search uncovers a folded piece of paper in the toe of the boot. It's a short note, in Mom's handwriting: *Your father's name is Gregory Langkow. We'll have lots to talk about when I come home in November.*

Langkow. Is it pronounced Lan*coe* or Lan*cow*, as in the bovine beast? I would be happy with either one. It's a solid name. And I'll bet its bearer is a redhead.

A short note with one small offering and promises of more to come—it's not a ringing emotional endorsement, but that's never been my mother's style.

It's a good start.

Now if only I could sort things out with Mr. Sweeney.

"Don't be so twitchy," Nan says.

At least, I think that's what she just said. It's hard to be sure because she has to manoeuvre her mouth around a couple of straight pins. I stand still as she plucks one of them from her lips and slides it into a fold pinched together at my waist. She is altering the Blowers Street dress for me.

"You're making me nervous. You're going to inhale one of those pins."

"That'd be a first," Nan says, but she obliges me by removing the pin from her lips and moving the pin cushion within easier reach. "Are you sure you don't want to wear a corset?" she asks. There is a twinkle of mischief in her eye. "This dress would have been designed for one."

"Can you see me in a corset?" I obey a signal to step up on the coffee table so that she can address the hem. "Did you wear one when you were younger?"

Nan shakes her head. "I was lucky. They'd gone out of fashion by the time I hit my teens. Women had taken over the farms and gone to work in munitions factories during the war, and they just weren't practical to wear anymore. Now, your Alyda, with her upper-class English upbringing, would definitely have started wearing one before she got pregnant."

"I can't begin to imagine Alyda in a corset. In the journal entries she's really active. She's always outdoors." I recall the young woman on the edge of the bluff. Her figure had been petite and well-proportioned, but not in the distinctive shape of an hour glass.

"Then she was lucky," Nan says. "It was a barbaric custom."

There are many who would agree with Nan. Some corsets were laced so tightly that a woman could only fill the upper areas of her lungs with air. Phlegm would pool in the lower parts, instigating coughing fits in efforts to remove it. And then the pressure placed on internal organs like the stomach and intestines led to a host of digestive health problems.

Nan directs me to turn to the window. I obey, and she stands and looks at me, hands on her hips, appraising her handiwork. "I can finish this up within an hour," she says.

"There's no rush."

"When do you plan to wear it? Is it for a Halloween party?"

"No. You know I always go for the macabre stuff."

"For one of the museum fund-raisers?"

"No." This time I extend the word enough to make Nan send an enquiring glance in my direction. My face reddens.

"It would be perfect for one of those fund-raisers." Nan's voice now comes from behind.

"I won't be attending the next one." I take a deep breath. "Mr. Sweeney and I had a falling out."

Nan's face bobs back into view. "What's that supposed to mean?"

"It was my fault. I let his mother talk about Alyda and she got upset."

"That's it? That's all that happened?" She jabs a pin into the cushion. "By the liftin' I'll give that man a piece of my mind!"

"No, Nan. Please. Let me handle this on my own."

My grandmother always relishes a good showdown. She scans my face, shrugs in resignation when she sees that I truly don't want her help. And then she regards her handiwork. "So, this dress will end up in the closet with your high school prom dress and never see the light of day again?"

"No. I'll wear it for Victorian Days. Remember those theme weekends I told you about?"

"Jack was asking me for food suggestions the other day. I think I can scare up some old recipes that belonged to my mother."

"And I've already got some ideas from Alyda's scrapbook. What do you think of eels served fresh from our brook?"

Nan shudders. "I thought you were trying to *attract* people to the inn."

"We are. But we're going to have to be innovative."

Nan restores a final pin to the cushion, reaches out a hand to assist me onto the floor. "No eels," she says. "But I think we'll need to get a dress for me, too."

I'm not sure why I haven't followed Ben's advice to approach Mr. Sweeney. In many ways it makes sense to do so, but it's the magnitude of Mr. Sweeney's reaction that I can't play down. I need only recall his livid face to experience a shiver of shame along the length of my spine.

I cannot surrender my involvement in Alyda's story, however, and so it is that I find myself on Morrie Piper's path west of the graveyard, heading to cliff's edge to take the path to Caleb's oven. The path comprises a long, winding strip of hard-packed soil through a grove of spruces. It's free of stones and weeds, but one has to keep an eye to the ground because the root systems of the spruces heave to the surface every few yards.

I negotiate my way over the gnarled, half-buried extensions on the path and think of Alyda as she once travelled this path to escape the suffocating heat of a church service. I'm half-way to my destination—the point where the wooded area ends—when I raise my eyes and see the graceful folds of a dove grey dress.

Alyda! The dress is familiar, but the path curves slightly here and I see enough of her profile to positively identify her. Her hair is long to the waist again and she is walking swiftly and purposefully, as if she has an appointment to keep. An assignation with Caleb Whitelaw? I match my step to hers, but suddenly she stops on a dime and I almost collide with her. I anticipate the heat that will jump from her body into mine, but it is tension that I feel radiating from her. Fear.

A lynx crouches in the pathway, a few feet ahead of us, its maw clamped on the body of a grouse. A punctured wing fans upward and obscures half of the cat's face. One eye glares at us. Pure malevolence.

My heart careens against my ribcage. Alyda hitches her hem above her ankles and slowly starts to back up. Rooted to the pathway in fear, I make no movement of my own. Once again, I expect that she will dissolve into me, that I will feel a distinct burning sensation. Instead, she turns around—eyes alarmed, holding my gaze—and she *pushes* me. I distinctly feel the heels of her palms thrusting against my ribcage, just below the breasts. And then she dissolves into me.

I dare not look back to confirm she's no longer there. Keeping my eye on one black ear tuft of the lynx, I continue to back up until I reach a broken, wooden fence at a bend in the path. I pull out the half-rotted upper rail of the fence, which has a rusty nail twisting from one end. I clasp the wrist of the hand holding the rail with my other hand—I need to steady it.

The lynx makes a sound that vibrates low in its throat. The sound is muffled by the corpse of the bird in its muzzle, but its intent is clear to me.

This time I run.

"I saw her again, Ben. I saw Alyda."

Ben doesn't say anything. Against a backdrop of laughter I hear the rattle of ice cubes, imagine a liquid splashing into their midst.

"Are you having a party?"

"No." He sounds defensive. "I've got a few people from my Biology tutorial over."

"So, it's not a good time to talk to you."

"No. It's fine." A pause. "Go ahead."

I can tell that it's not fine, but resentment sinks its teeth into me. That he's not available to me goads me to continue. In as few words as possible I tell him about my confrontation with the lynx.

Again, there is silence from him, this time amid the *clink-clink* of cutlery and a burst of female laughter.

I jump into the void. "I think she appeared to give me a warning," I say. "To let me know that there was something dangerous up ahead."

"Lynx don't attack humans, Ree. Cougars will—they'll even stalk you. But lynx are shy."

"But I—Alyda and I ran into it when it had just made a kill. Wouldn't the lynx try to protect it?"

"Not by charging at you."

"But Alyda *pushed* me. If she didn't appear to give me a warning and help me, why do you think she was there on that path?"

The energy of the voices in the background recedes. He must be cupping the speaker end of the phone with his hand. "You wanted to see her," he says. "You *really* wanted to see her again."

Long after I've completed my conversation with Ben, I stand by the phone, my hand still resting on the receiver in its cradle.

The distance between us seems as endless as the ocean.

Chapter 30

I hope my dear thou art at rest
With saints and angels who are blessed
And in short time I hope to be
In paradise along with thee

Once a year—in September or October—Gramps slides a stepladder into the bed of Warren's old pick-up truck and drives to Ocean's Edge. Equipped with the standard tools of a graveyard kit that he was given long ago by Mr. Sweeney, he inspects my grandmother's stone cross from top to bottom and carefully removes any traces of lichen. Gramps is not as easygoing about lichen as Mr. Sweeney is. In his eyes it is a predator that must be destroyed.

No one ever accompanies Gramps on these conquests, but when I see that he's preparing the truck for this mission today, I ask him if I may come along. Still battered by my experience with Alyda and the lynx, I hope time spent with Gramps will be an antidote to its intensity, to its incomprehensibility.

Gramps hesitates long enough for me to regret that I've asked him. It's probably a special time for him, a time for reflection and communication with Addie. Since Alma's outburst about Addie's accident, I've sometimes wondered whether he does feel in any way responsible for her death.

"It's okay," I say. "I shouldn't have asked you."

"Go on. Climb in."

"Do you mind if I bring my mapping gear? I'll probably stay behind and do a section."

Gramps nods his head, and I run into the house to retrieve it.

At the graveyard, the Shasta daisies and Queen Anne's lace now defer to clusters of goldenrod. Behind Addie's grave, where the woods stretch into darkness, a solitary destroying angel stands in the middle of Morrie Piper's path. The apples on the trees display strokes of crimson. Raindrops from an early morning shower still glisten on them.

Mud speckles near the base of my grandmother's cross obscure the last line of the inscription. Gramps fills a metal pail with water from the hand pump by the tool shed and splashes it against the stone. Lightly, as if the stone is sensitive, and prone to injury. He does this two more times until the entire inscription is visible.

Next, he retrieves an old canvas tool belt from the truck and slings it around his waist; dowels and brushes have already been tucked into different pockets. Metal clangs as he eases the stepladder from the bed of the truck. He sets it up to the right of the cross so that the top tucks in just under the right arm.

"May I have one of those brushes? I ask him.

He stops, one foot on the bottom rung of the ladder; hesitates.

"I'd like to help you. Why don't I at least fill the buckets and hand the rags up to you?"

Still no word or movement from Gramps, and once again I feel uncomfortable. I've never felt this way with him before. I don't know if he doesn't trust me to do things properly, or if he's unwilling to share a ritual that he has always performed alone. "All right," he finally says.

I work quietly and efficiently at filling the bucket at the pump, soaking the flannel rags and handing them up to Gramps on the ladder. I itch to start working on the lower half of the cross, to remove the small traces of lichen that have dared to gain a foothold there, but I see that

Gramps is making good progress and I can best help him by providing a constant supply of water.

Once the cross is restored to perfection, Gramps agrees to accompany me on a visit to Alyda's grave. The paralysing stone is clean, stripped of its sponge-like quilt of lichen. A soft globe of thistledown touches down on it briefly and then continues on its journey. The plaque is gone; the epitaph is easily read. All traces of the hewn rose bushes are gone. I feel a sudden pang of loss for the extinction of the legend.

"Those rose bushes, they'll be back next year," Gramps says. "There's no killin' those root suckers; they travel for yards underneath the ground."

"Maybe we can bring the legend back to life."

"Or make up a new one." Gramps crouches by the stone, runs his hand along the side. "I'd forgotten just how huge and thick this stone is. And by crikey, lookin' at it again, I'd swear it was a resurrection stone. I saw one in a village in Sussex once, just after the war."

"What's a resurrection stone?"

His knee joints creaking in protest, Gramps borrows support from the stone as he brings himself upright again. "It's a slab they used to put on top of a grave to make things tough for body snatchers," he says. "You already know this, I'll bet, but back in Victorian times doctors would put out a call for bodies. Wanted them for medical research and they paid good money. Grave robbers would steal a corpse right out of a freshly-dug grave. It got so bad that those families with money would hire men to guard the grave or rent a resurrection stone."

I marvel at Gramps's knowledge. Resurrection stones are not something I'd come across yet in my research of the Victorian era. "But that must have been only in the bigger towns or cities," I say. "Otherwise we'd have more of these stones. Do you really think Alyda's family was concerned that her body or her baby's body might be dug up and sold?"

"No, I don't think they were worried about traditional body snatchers. But look at the size of that slab, Rianne. I'd say they didn't want anybody ever gettin' at those bodies."

The size of the slab is considerable. Today, its surface clean and its perimeter cleared of the wild roses, the gravestone reminds me of an ancient altar. Gramps's theory is an interesting one, but how could it possibly apply to young Alyda and her baby?

Only two sections of the graveyard remain to be mapped. I plan to complete them slowly, extend the amount of time to be spent on them. The typing of the inscriptions is a slow and painful process, of course, now that Ben is no longer here.

As I pull my pen and clipboard from my backpack, a feral cat emerges from a clump of goldenrod on the edge of the orchard. It is a small tortoiseshell and its mangy coat rides its ribs. I crouch down and hold out a hand to it before I realize how cruel that is—I have nothing to offer it. The cat regards the hand with disdain and slinks back into the bank of weeds again.

Perhaps the cat had its eye on the whisky jay that is perched on a drunken tablet close by. The bird bobs its tail on the crown of the marker, desecrates the stone with a generous splash of white. As I walk swiftly towards it, it squawks and takes flight.

I remove the bird's droppings with a rag dipped in Photo-Flo solution, and that is when the name *Noah Ephestus Hamilton* comes to my attention. The "Noah" and the "Ephestus" are discernible, but the "Hamilton" barely so. Different varieties of lichen have swarmed the rest of the inscription. I can't read what I assume must be the year of death, but the year of birth appears to be 1881.

If the year of birth is correct, there is a good possibility this is the grave of Alyda's stepbrother. But why is it located in a nineteenth century section of the graveyard?

I feel excitement mounting in me, the opportunity to go on the hunt again.

Mary-Anne Bell has good news for me. The newspaper archives have just reopened, and she'll go and search for copies of articles relating to the deaths of both Noah and Alyda. She hands me the Munro register, already opened to the entry for Noah Hamilton.

Noah Ephestus Hamilton
6 November 1881–27 October 1896

Dear son of the Reverend Zachariah Hamilton
and Lydia Yorke Hamilton
Who departed this life in haste
as the consequence of an accident

I could not have foreseen the fall
I did not wish to leave you all
But surely as the sun doth rise
We must surrender to surprise

Too good for earth
God called him home

No. 327 (Malcolm McAteer)
Son of parents, as noted on epitaph of gravestone; stepson of Mrs. Verity Hamilton
Brother to a female sibling who died at birth
Youngest member of the Port Carlyle Men's Christian League
Injury to the head; cause unknown

The cause of death shakes me, disturbs me almost as much as the discovery of Alyda's cause of death did. Was it a result of adolescent recklessness or folly? I think of the graceless, hulking young man from the journal entries and I wonder, too, if a lack of coordination on his part may have contributed to the accident. And then I think of Alyda's lesson to Noah in the fog-shrouded graveyard. It's not fair to make any assumptions yet.

I study Martha Munro's entries again. The traditional four-line verse is almost amusing—a whimsical meditation on the fragility of life. I'm surprised by the slight religious component in the epitaph, given that Noah was the son of a Presbyterian preacher.

"Success." Mary-Anne makes a brisk entrance with a legal-sized file folder.

The first article is a clipping from the *Port Carlyle Sentinel,* dated October 29, 1896, and written by a Charles A. Crumie. It is entitled

Mysterious Death on Old Wharf. The section of the newspaper is yellowed and slightly brittle at the crease, but every word is legible:

Our community was hard hit this week with the unusual death of one of its citizens, Noah Hamilton, son of the Reverend Mr. Zachariah Hamilton and the late Mrs. Lydia Hamilton of Halifax, and stepson of Mrs. Verity Hamilton. The deceased youth was fourteen years of age.

The corpse was discovered on the old pier west of the village at approximately four thirty in the afternoon on the twenty-seventh of October by Port Carlyle fishermen John Brodie and Theodore Andrews as they came to inspect their weir in the vicinity. It was examined by Dr. Joseph Teasdale, and he concluded that the victim died from misadventure after falling and sustaining a blow to his head on a piling of the dilapidated structure. Dr. Teasdale could not speculate as to the sequence of events that led to the fatal injury.

Deepest sympathies are extended to the grieving parents, the Reverend Mr. Zachariah Hamilton and Mrs. Verity Hamilton.

Two months. Noah died a scant two months after Alyda had given him his final tutoring session. Had he visited her at Dalhousie University? Did she return from Halifax to attend his funeral or had she already left school, certain of her pregnancy? She must have been subjected to a number of difficult and conflicting feelings over his death, and I'm sure she would have been honest and unflinching about expressing them. If only the journal hadn't ended with her departure for school in Halifax.

Next, the folder produces a copy of the *Danton Chronicle*. On the front page there is an article by reporter Lorne MacAskill, dated November 5, 1896:

Police Chief Rules No Inquest into the Death of Noah Hamilton

The Reverend Mr. Zachariah Hamilton of St. Luke's Presbyterian Church met with the constabulary of Port Carlyle on Tuesday, the third of November to petition an inquest into the recent death of his son, Noah Hamilton. The youth, who died just short of his fifteenth birthday, sustained a fatal injury to the head on the twenty-seventh day of October from an apparent fall on the old wharf. The Reverend Mr. Hamilton insists that foul play be ruled out in his death.

Police Chief Howard Lake informed the victim's father that without proof of a motive to harm the young man and in the absence of witnesses to the tragic event, an inquest would only lead to unhelpful and unnecessary speculation. The Reverend Mr. Hamilton left the offices in great distress and returned only a few minutes later to drive his fist through the window located to the right of the entrance. Dr. Joseph Teasdale was in the vicinity and could immediately attend to the unfortunate man's injury.

In view of the grief that the Reverend Mr. Hamilton is suffering in the loss of his son, no charges of damage to property will be laid against him.

I feel sorry for Reverend Hamilton. A twinge of guilt accompanies this sentiment of sympathy; Alyda vilified him in the journal entries, because he made her life even more unbearable after the loss of her father. But I can imagine how devastated the man must have been by the loss of his only child.

Mary-Anne Bell apologizes as I reach for the final article in the folder. "I'm sorry, but this is all we have on Alyda Teasdale," she says. "I couldn't find any August issues of the *Port Carlyle Sentinel* to see the results of the inquest into her drowning. I checked to make sure that issues hadn't been suspended during the summer and I also checked the September issues, but there's nothing. Unfortunately, it's not unusual for copies to go missing."

The article is found in the June 11, 1897 edition of the *Port Carlyle Sentinel* and was written by reporter C.A. Crumie:

A Tragic Death by Drowning

Once again Port Carlyle grieves the loss of one of its young citizens in the drowning death of Alyda Teasdale, daughter of the late Captain Elias Teasdale and Verity Teasdale, and stepdaughter of the Reverend Zachariah Hamilton. Less than a year ago, Noah Hamilton, son of the Reverend Mr. Hamilton, was also found dead under circumstances that remain inexplicable to this day.

Regards the latest tragedy, cannery worker Abram Pierce attests that, at approximately six o'clock in the morning of the third of June, Miss Teasdale, carrying what appeared to be a wooden cross, boarded a fishing dory belonging to Charles Raynor and then ventured out into the waters from the old pier. Mr. Pierce hailed Miss Teasdale when she was already upon the water and inquired whether she needed assistance of any kind; she assured him that she was making a short journey and would return directly. Plagued by misgivings, Mr. Pierce notified the family, and two boats and crew were launched in pursuit of the young lady. Their efforts were in vain. The empty boat was discovered near the Quaco Ledge of Isle of Haute on that day, and Miss Teasdale's remains were discovered close to the western tip of the island on the sixth of June by Mr. Ansell Woods, owner of a vessel that was delivering supplies to the lighthouse.

Shortly after recovery of the body, Dr. Robert Hall, coroner of Danton, performed a post-mortem examination and determined that the victim had died by drowning.

A formal inquest into Miss Teasdale's death will commence at two o'clock in the afternoon on the second of August in the community hall.

Once again, this is a grievous blow to the surviving parents, the Reverend and Mrs. Zachariah Hamilton, and the village offers its deepest condolences in such a strange and senseless tragedy.

"Alyda drowned." When Ben first uttered those words, an image came to mind similar to the one the young woman had formed of her father: a body floating peacefully, surrendering to the currents in the ocean. That image was soon replaced by the nightmare's version—one of Alyda struggling to stay above water by clinging to her floating tombstone. Now I envision Alyda scrambling into the dory with the burden of the cross, pausing to catch her breath, and then rowing with energy toward the island. All post-partum fatigue banished by her need to bring that cross to the island. But then the cross shifts as the boat is rocked by a wave, and Alyda, struggling to regain balance, is pitched into the ocean.

Or Alyda reaches the island, but the vessel is sucked into one of the whirlpools by Quaco Ledge.

Or—and I realize I've assumed once again Noah's role in the graveyard lesson—Alyda had no intention of coming back from Isle Haute.

No, I cannot accept the last possibility.

Chapter 31

Shed not for me the bitter tear
Nor yield the heart in sad regret
Tis but the casket slumbers here
The jem that filled it sparkles yet

The bicentennial projects keep me busy. Mr. Sweeney has not sent word that I've been dismissed from my position, and so I've continued to pursue them. Most of my waking hours now are spent taking photographs. My camera responds well to the skies of September as it captures the landmarks of the village and its surroundings. Soon I'll have more than a thousand photographs to match to the ones in the heritage collections.

The inn also occupies a good portion of my time. Its exterior is almost finished now; the construction crew is putting the siding in place. Chimney pots, the railing of the widow's walk, roof trim and gable ornaments will be added in the spring. Some of the preliminary landscaping is even in place. Birches and lilac bushes have been planted; drystone retaining walls await future flower beds.

The fall and winter months will see the completion of the interior.

Preliminary interviews will be held for some of the staff positions. Jack is particularly anxious to secure a good chef. Decisions will be made regarding paint and wallpaper, colour schemes and furnishings for the bedrooms, menus and place settings for the restaurant.

Today, Jack and I will attend an estate sale at one of the heritage Victorian homes in Bridgetown. He's decided to furnish the inn in turn-of-the-century period furniture. It will require greater planning to procure the items and may end up costing him more than modern furnishings purchased in bulk, but he has plenty of time to accomplish this over the winter.

I think of Alma, of how I would enjoy bringing her along on this outing. Since she grew up in the late Victorian period, she would have a good eye for the furnishings of the era. Mr. Sweeney, however, would veto the idea, even if we were still on good terms. I asked him just before that scene in the garden if I could take Alma to a new café in Danton. He promptly turned down the proposal. "You don't understand," he said. "People like Mother become agitated when they're taken out of their routine. New experiences are frightening to them."

"She enjoyed meeting Ben," I countered, "and she likes having me around too."

"Mother saw you and Ben in her own territory. I won't put her in a situation that might make her uncomfortable."

He was right; he knew what was best for his mother. I remember how emotionally frail Alma was during her stay in the hospital, and the marked regression that she experienced there.

Mr. Sweeney always had the last word.

Every colour in an artist's palette is on show today. The crimson, orange and golden hues of the trees and shrubs on the mountain outperform the rowdy colours of the houses that nestle into the hillside by the bay. Fall is my favourite season. I've always loved the air that coaxes the lungs to expansion, the scent of apples and baked pumpkin, the feel of newly-sharpened pencils in my hand. With the start of school and a host of other post-summer activities and events, it's as much a season of beginnings as spring is.

Bridgetown, like many of the small towns fixed to the western floor of the valley, has less than a thousand inhabitants today. Its location on the Annapolis River made it an important shipbuilding centre in Alyda's time. Among other industries, the town once counted a furniture factory, a tannery, an organ factory, a bottling plant, and a cider factory. It boasts dozens of grand homes with antique furnishings.

"How are you doing these days?" Jack asks, as we head down the mountain. "I get the feeling something's gnawing away at you."

"It's just the situation with Owen Sweeney."

"He may take a while to come around. Why don't you go to Toronto for a few days? Visit your friends before your mother gets back?"

"No, not right now."

Jack negotiates the major hairpin curve on the road before he glances over at me again. "You've almost finished the work for the graveyard and you've completed all the passages for Alyda's journal. It's a good time to take a break."

I shake my head. Everything Jack says makes sense, but I cannot abandon Alyda. She's poised to experience a life-altering event, and I must be there should the rest of her story be told.

The estate sale will take place in one of the grand Victorian houses on the main street, one that has been designated a provincial heritage property. Jack is equipped with a list of the items to be auctioned and he's particularly interested in a Victorian mantelpiece. We've arrived early to assess the goods before the sale begins, and it's obvious that others have had the same idea: cars are already lined up for blocks in either direction.

A number of the items for sale have been removed from the house and placed on the front lawn and side lawn of the property. These include several rocking chairs, dressers, a curio cabinet with open shelves, and a daybed with an ornate cover of crimson and gold pineapples. One man is working the drawers of a wardrobe as we approach, while a woman bounces on the edge of the daybed and then stretches full-length upon it. She hasn't had the decency to remove her shoes. When she finally vacates the bed, Jack pulls back the cover, applies pressure to the mattress with the palm of his hand. "This probably came from the fainting room," he says, "where the ladies went to loosen their stays."

I know from the Alyda stories that there had been a daybed in the library at Tyne Bluff; Helen Teasdale had slept there when she could no longer negotiate the stairs to the second floor. Had she also gone into the room at times to ease her breathing? Was that the original purpose of the daybed in the library? Alma might know, and I find myself battling a mounting sense of frustration that I no longer have access to her stories.

We find the executor of the estate in the kitchen of the house, seated at a folding card table. He's a short, balding man with over-sized glasses, dressed in a dark suit and tie. A faint odour of mothballs escapes him.

Jack inquires about the mantelpiece and is told that it's no longer among the items for sale. "We couldn't get it ready in time," the executor says.

My father conceals his disappointment to focus on the furnishings that are for sale. After two hours of negotiations, he is set to become the owner of the daybed, a spool-turned oak table, three rocking chairs, a solid walnut wardrobe with bevelled mirrors and brass handles, two four-poster beds, and several wash-bowl and pitcher sets in a delicate pink rosebud design.

The atmosphere in the house is stale, and as Jack pulls up a chair to complete the transactions with the executor, I escape into the backyard. It is cool and dark here, shaded by elms and a high slat-wood fence that leans in all directions. To my right, dense colonies of purple asters line the fence. To my left, is a long wooden shed, its vertical beams slippery from decay. I peer into its small window and wait for my eyes to adjust to the darkness. And when they do, I see a large and rectangular form, draped in a white sheet. The sheet has slipped from one corner to reveal a long, fluted column.

Nudging my hip against the door, I force it open and step down onto an earthen floor. With the flair of an on-stage magician, I pull the sheet down to reveal a mantelpiece—a work of fine marble, with a scallop shell like a beacon in the centre of its elegant frieze. There's no doubt in my mind it's the one that was stolen from the Whitfield house.

The estate executor resists our accusations and claims he has documents to prove the mantelpiece's provenance. Unfortunately, he cannot provide them at the moment. Jack refuses to give in. He finally threatens to call the police, and that is when the estate executor surrenders. Jack stations himself in the backyard, and I walk to a nearby hotel to call Gramps.

Gramps knows what to do. Right behind his truck, in a vehicle stocked with padded coverings and refrigerator dollies, are three of Ben's old high school friends who own a moving company in Danton. With patience and care, under the helpless watch of the executor, they remove the mantelpiece to the truck.

"Things are shaping up nicely for the Teasdale Inn," says Jack.

The recovery of the mantelpiece makes me feel restless, almost euphoric. Swept along by this sense of well-being, I finally make my way to the entrance of a trail to the bay, the vestige of a trail that leads to Alyda and Caleb's oven. The encounter with the lynx still vivid in my mind, I've taken a different route to the bluff's edge this time, through a pasture of waist-high wild grasses.

Body turned to one side, I navigate the path with caution. It is treacherous—steep-angled, and pock-marked with stones—and slick with decaying twigs and leaves. The trees that line the path release drops of water from an early afternoon shower, and more than a few of them slide down the back of my neck. Halfway down, my runners skid on a patch of loose stones, and I avoid tumbling to the bottom by grasping an exposed root at the side of the path. I lie there for a moment, catching my breath before I continue the descent, crouching and sidestepping the rest of the way.

The oven—the most westerly oven on this expanse of the shore—is located only a few feet from the foot of the pathway. I'm hesitant to carry on now, afraid that the cave won't yield any history. Thousands of high tides, waters insistent, will have long washed away any evidence of their trysts.

And yet my eyes are drawn to a row of grey stones lined up at the entrance, with more stones tumbled to either side. Surely the line of stones is too symmetrical to be a random design of nature. With the toe of my shoe I nudge the heavy, rectangular rock that is closest to me. Could this be what is left of Caleb's drystone wall? Did it resist the infinite tug of the sea?

I step into the opening, wait until my eyes adjust to the muted lighting. The cave's ceiling is generous; at its high point in the centre it clears my head by at least a foot. Drops of water slither down the walls, skirting garlands of embedded, small white stones. A shallow pool near the back feeds a stream that exits the cave and snakes around a chain of rocks to the ocean. I look in vain for two stones, positioned to serve as supports for a wooden plank.

I take yet another step and turn to face the water. Gulls keen in the distance. Alyda won't come to me here—she always dictates the terms of our encounters. But I'll try to summon an image, invoke her presence from the meetings here with Caleb long ago. I close my eyes and imagine her slipping into the entrance, breath shallow still from the effort of negotiating the rocks. And yes, she's with me now—steel-blue eyes luminous, cheeks flushed, hair wind-tangled. I feel her skin tingling, her heart thrumming with anticipation.

And Caleb . . .

I cannot invoke him.

I shake my head. As if all that's required is a collision of cells. I wait, willing myself to be patient. They met here countless times; he will come. And as I wait, a cloud steals the sunlight that forms the canvas of my closed eyelids; a shadow seals the entrance to the cave. My eyes fly open. Fear surges, pounds at the confines of my skull.

The shadow taunts me. It contracts, provides a saving glimpse of the sea in the distance. I take a deep breath and hurl myself against it, but it expands again, throws me back into the depths of the cave as if I were a rag doll. Crouched on my hands and knees, jeans soaked in the pool of water, I draw deep breaths until I am ready to stand again.

The shadow is gone. Dissolved? In retreat?

My legs burn as they carry me back to the entrance of the cave. My eyes ache in the sunlight. I raise one hand, turn it. The palm is scraped raw, dotted with infinitesimal shards of stone. Speckled with blood. The hand begins to shake, and soon every inch of my body is shaking as well.

What happened to me in the cave?

What happened to *them*?

Chapter 32

This languishing heart is at rest
Its thinking and aching is o'er
This quiet immovable breast
Is heaved by affection no more

Each day has brought some alleviation, has succeeded through the art of distance to "chip away" at the terror I experienced in that oven. But a malaise still comes over me at times—settles like the aftermath of a disturbing dream—and I know it is linked to that day.

The reconciliation with Mr. Sweeney will give me some respite.

It took place this morning, just outside of the village café. As I emerged from the restaurant with a complimentary cookie in hand, I almost collided with the old man. An awkward silence held sway between us until a seagull dispatched it with a loud squawk. The bird landed on the railing of the steps and fixed a covetous eye on my cookie.

"Miss Tavener." His fingers grazed the rim of his Greek fisherman's cap as he nodded in my direction.

I bobbed my head formally in return. "Mr. Sweeney."

And that was the extent of our conversation. He opened his mouth once, as if he were about to say more, but then snapped it shut into a thin line. Another quick nod and he stepped aside to ensure my passage down the steps.

The seagull hovered over me, casting a shadow. One bite of the cookie was enough for me. It was stale, and I'd lost all appetite for it. I tossed it over my shoulder, and the bird was rewarded for its doggedness.

I'd only gone a short distance when I heard footsteps behind me. Laboured footsteps, scraping upon gravel. I turned to face Mr. Sweeney. The cap was in his hands now.

"Mother misses you," he said. "Could you come by to see her sometime?"

Striped hatbox in hand, I make my way down the Port Carlyle Road to the Sweeney house. The front door of the museum is open as I walk by; Mr. Sweeney is seated on top of an old school desk. I step inside.

He has pulled together two desks, scarred wooden desks with built-in inkpots that form part of the schoolhouse exhibit. A shoebox lies in his lap; a slide projector sits on the other desk. He extracts a slide from the box and positions it in the tray of the projector. When I ask him if I can help, he gives me another shoe box to sort through. He's going to do a slide show for the museum's next fund-raiser and he wants me to remove all the slides that are labelled *Isle of Haute.*

"Will the fund-raiser take place at the community hall?" I ask, referring to a building in the centre of the village.

He doesn't raise his eyes to mine. "You know they always do."

I also know that Mr. Sweeney himself does not make the pitch or the presentation. He sits at the back of the room while one of his colleagues from the Danton museum takes on that role.

I glance around this room. The building that once housed a carriage collection is a spacious one, and the area we are in has sufficient room for a small-town audience. The blackboard could serve as a backdrop for the slide show, just as it is doing now. "Why don't you hold it here for a change?" I say. "People could see exactly what they are contributing to."

"No." He continues a comparison of two slides.

"If you're worried about the exhibits, we can always move some of them out of the way. Rope off areas, for example." I shift my shoebox to one hip and make gestures for my suggestions. "I'll be happy to help you out."

"No."

"If you extended the hours for this museum, opened it up more to the public and allowed school children to come through in groups, you'd get more donations."

He finally puts his box aside, regards me with exasperation. "You're like a puppy, Miss Tavener. One-note yapping. Darting and nipping at my ankles. Have you always been like this?"

A sheepish smile—it's the most I can muster for an answer.

"I've thought carefully about the way I do things," he says, picking up the box again. "Allow me that, at least."

I choose one of the school desks for myself, and we sort together quietly for about twenty minutes. Is he like me, nervous about speaking in public? And would it really be difficult for him to have large numbers in attendance here?

When he signals that he's ready to take a break, I tell him about my discovery of Noah Hamilton's grave. "One of the archivists in the Danton museum showed me articles about his death in the *Port Carlyle Sentinel*. I was shocked to find out that he'd died soon after Alyda left for school in Halifax."

"I knew you would find that piece of the puzzle once you started mapping the graveyard."

"I haven't come across the graves of Verity and Zachariah Hamilton yet. They're key players in the story."

"Ah, yes—the despised preacher and his wife. They moved to Halifax shortly after Alyda's death. Neither of them made it to a ripe old age. Verity died of pneumonia in 1903, and Reverend Hamilton lost his life in the Halifax Explosion in 1917."

"Then I wouldn't have stumbled across that puzzle piece. What if there aren't enough of them in the graveyard? The journal entries are finished. I need you to take me beyond them now. Please."

He eases down from his desk, winces as his gammy leg is slow to support him. "I'll continue to help you where I can."

"Does that mean you still don't have everything you need to pull the story together?"

"Have some patience, Miss Tavener. It's a quality that's singularly lacking in your generation."

I slip down from my desk. Collect the hatbox by sliding my fingers beneath its silver elastic band. The band bites into my flesh. "I have all the patience in the world when it comes to your mother."

He opens his mouth briefly and then compresses his lips into a thin line. His Adam's apple displaces the words that slide down his throat. "Sit down," he finally says. "I have something to tell you."

He disappears into his office for a moment, returns with Alyda's scrapbook. "Mother has been the source for these stories," he confirms, "but I'm sure you've suspected that for some time. The floodgates were opened one night about a year ago when I brought this scrapbook home. I didn't mean for her to see it. She was having a nap when I left the house, and I checked in on her as soon as I got back. I had just removed the wrappings in the mudroom when she walked in."

"She knew right away that it belonged to Alyda?"

"She did. And we sat in the living room for hours, Mother holding the book tight to her chest all the time, speaking almost as if she were in a trance at times. I scribbled notes in the margins of the newspaper that lay on the coffee-table because I didn't dare leave her to look for paper or a notebook. I didn't know if this would be my last opportunity to hear the story. As it is, there have been other occasions, but the information that she gives me is always piecemeal. I still haven't managed to pull it all together."

Mr. Sweeney fingers the pack of cigarettes in his pocket, but then abandons it. "I know you would like to interview my mother directly, but it's difficult at times for her to talk about Alyda. You saw that in the garden that day. I always wait for her to take the lead and I try to gauge her mood to see if I need to steer the conversation in a different direction."

"I'm also respectful of your mother," I say. "But she has a story to tell and she may need to tell it."

"Story? Who's got a story to tell?"

Alma poses the question as she advances into the room. She's clad in a quilted housecoat and mule slippers, and a metal barrette clings to a thin strand of hair that skims her shoulder.

Mr. Sweeney pushes back his chair. "Mother, please. You know you shouldn't leave the house without me."

"Don't get up, Owen. And don't treat me like a child. I've promised you I won't step off the property again."

She turns to me. "Did you come to look at the scrapbook? You haven't been here for a long time."

"I'm sorry," I say, rising and offering her my chair. "I've been busy helping my father at the inn." It's only a partial lie and that at least makes it palatable to me.

Alma accepts my offer, primly nods her thanks. And once I'm seated in a metal folding chair that was leaning against the file cabinet, she says to me, "Did my son ever tell you why the front cover of the scrapbook is missing?"

Mr. Sweeney stirs on the edge of his seat. "You've never told me why, Mother."

"I must have, Owen; I must have told you, but never mind. It's missing because Alyda tore it off and threw it in the fire."

Another twitch from him. "She couldn't have done that," he protests. "Even now the binding is solid. You can't just tear something like that by hand."

"Oh, but she did, Owen. She was crazed after she gave birth; childbirth can do that to you, you know. Throws some young mothers off balance. She had the strength of a crazy woman and she tore that cover clean off and flung it into the fire."

"But you stopped her from destroying the rest of the journal," I say.

"No, Rianne, I wasn't there. The doctor's wife was, and she told me what happened. She was already beside herself, Mrs. Helen was, because she hadn't managed to rescue the other journal."

Another journal? I'm shocked into silence. A sound of distress, however, escapes Mr. Sweeney's throat. "There was another one?"

"Oh yes. That scrapbook you have right there stops just before Allie got 'in the family way.' She started a new one when she went to school in Halifax. Just a journal this time, though—a smaller book, with no angels or memory scraps. And she kept writing, right up to the day she had her baby. It was maybe the one thing that kept her mind sound during the pregnancy. Anyway, she'd already thrown that second journal in the fire before Mrs. Helen could get to it."

Mr. Sweeney says, "And then Helen Teasdale hid the scrapbook in the shed."

"I imagine that's how it happened. She probably felt it would be safer outside of the house. Out of sight, out of mind. Mind you, I didn't know it was there. I should have asked Mrs. Helen later what she'd done with it. But the both of us, we just had too many other things on our minds at the time." She slides the barrette from the strand of hair and tucks it into a pocket. "And then, of course, everything went to hell in a hand basket."

I wait, scarcely able to breathe.

But Alma is not going to continue the story. "I've got to get back to my work in the kitchen," she says, walking to the door. She pauses at the doorway for a moment, then turns her head to address me over her shoulder: "You, Rianne—you come with me."

"You were too busy for an old gal like me. Well, I've been busy too." Alma pushes a stack of salmon tins to one side on the kitchen counter, makes a notation in a school scribbler. Then she hooks an arm around several stacked cans of Libby's browned beans and sweeps them to the centre of the counter.

"I've brought something for you, Mrs. Sweeney." I lift the Gainsborough hat out of its box.

Alma's eyes shine with pleasure as I place the hat on her head at a coquettish angle. She runs into her bedroom, pirouettes in front of the mirror, pleased with the effect. "The captain's wife had a hat just like this," she said. "Oh, it's not quite the same—Mrs. Teasdale's hat had two feathers and a velvet rose—but it's close enough."

"Allie's mother?"

"Yes. I saw a lady wearing it in the village one day, and my father told me she was the wife of Captain Teasdale—the one that had come back to the village from England. I saw her wearing it a couple of times when the captain was still alive, but I don't think I ever saw it again once she married the preacher man."

"Did he forbid her to wear it?"

"I can't say that he outright told her *no,* but he probably made his feelings known. He was a self-righteous old goat. Always denouncing one thing or another from the pulpit. Allie was beside herself when he banned croquet."

"Croquet? Why on earth would croquet be considered sinful?"

"Oh, you know, players would deliberately drive their balls into the bushes. It could lead to a bit of flirting—or worse." Alma sends me a wicked grin.

"Allie used to play croquet with her mother's family?"

"They had an annual tournament for years. Quite the event from the way Allie described it to me. I'd never have put up with nonsense like that from a husband!"

"What made Verity decide to marry him? She wasn't in dire financial need when the Captain died."

"That I don't know, Rianne. It was a mystery to most of the people in the village. But from what I've heard, it may have had something to do with her delicate health. Poor woman, she was always laid low by those thundering migraine headaches. They sapped all the energy out of her for days on end."

"But Alyda was almost sixteen when her father died. Sibley wasn't much younger. They must have been a big help to their mother."

Alma removes the hat and places it carefully on a peg of the clothes tree. "Don't forget," she says, "that Verity Teasdale was born into a society where a married woman had all the status. And she must have felt terribly lonely after the captain's death. She had her girls, the good doctor and Mrs. Helen, but maybe that wasn't enough for her."

"How did the Reverend Hamilton and Verity get to know each other so well in such a short period of time?"

Alma watches me in the mirror as she guides a stray lock of hair into place. "I'm not sure you can say they got to know each other well," she says. "He was the new minister in town, and she was a member of his congregation. I imagine he must have helped her through her grieving."

"They started spending more and more time together."

Alma turns around and faces me again. "And he had lost his wife."

"Perhaps it was a marriage of convenience."

"Call it what you may, but Allie never forgave her for it."

Allie never forgave her for it. This may be an assumption on Alma's part, but I'm inclined to believe that it's something she learned directly from Alyda.

It confirms that Alma and Alyda forged a close and trusting friendship.

Chapter 33

A few short years of evil past
We reach the happy shore
Where death divided friends at last
Shall meet to part no more

It's the Friday before Thanksgiving. Ben won't make it home this long weekend. He has labs to prepare for his students and mid-term exams to mark. He loves Thanksgiving, and it will be strange to have dinner without him and the clove-studded ham that is his favourite.

Ben's absence will be offset by guests who will be joining us at the table for the first time. At my suggestion, Nan and Gramps and the Allenbys have invited the Sweeneys to Thanksgiving dinner on Sunday. And they have accepted.

Owen Sweeney has also responded positively to another request. As I stand at the doorway to his home, his mother makes the final preparations for an outing to Tyne Bluff. She is smothered in a mink coat, a matching fur hat, and knitted brown mittens that look small enough for a child. It's unseasonably cold—the local weather office has even issued a snowfall warning for tonight. That's not unusual in an area where winter makes early hit-and-run appearances. "Appetizer storms," Nan calls them.

Mr. Sweeney pulls me aside. "I haven't told Mother that the house is gone," he says.

"Will she be upset?"

"I'm not sure. Just watch her carefully. You'll know what to do."

I pull open the door to the passenger side of the Jeep, but Alma swats my hand away and the door swings back into place. She opens it on her own, clambers up onto the front seat and settles herself in it.

As we reach the inn, I stop the vehicle halfway up the semi-circular driveway. Alma shakes her head as if she doubts the sight before her eyes. "It's close to the way I remember it," she says. "Change the colour of the paint to white and I'd expect the doctor and his missus to step out the front door. Somebody has spent a fortune to fix it up."

"This isn't the Teasdale house, Mrs. Sweeney. It's the inn that my father built to look just like it. As you can see, he's been true to many details of the original."

"It's not the house?" A hint of panic in her voice that soon extends to the eyes. "I thought we were going to see the house."

I place my hand on her arm. "The house isn't there anymore. My father tried everything he could to keep it, but because it was so close to where the inn was going to go, the insurance company made us tear it down."

"It's gone, then. The house is gone."

"It couldn't be salvaged. Nobody had looked after it for years."

Silence reigns. Alma removes her mittens, clasps her hands in her lap. Her bottom lip trembles. Then, she raises a hand to point to the inn through the windshield. "There's no railing on the widow's walk," she says.

"There will be. The gingerbread trim still has to go on, too. That will take place in the spring. We don't want to give those winds from the bay a head start."

"And the stained glass windows that were by the front door? The ones with the irises on them?"

"They're on order. An artist in Bridgetown is taking care of that."

More silence. Then, "Show me where the house was."

I help Alma out of the Jeep, and we walk slowly, arm in arm, to the stark lines of rocks that formed the old foundation. It's a good thing we are warmly dressed. The wind off the bay is raw and it bullies our backs.

"I thought the lilac bush would be long gone by now," Alma says.

"I did some reading up on lilacs. They can live to be over a hundred years old."

"Allie didn't get to see this bush bloom one last time before she died. In fact, it didn't bloom at all that year. We'd had a hard winter, an early spring that forced the buds, and then another cold snap. The buds just shrivelled away."

Alma removes one of her mittens and crushes some of the blossom husks between her fingers. "Did you ever find a stone under this bush?" she says. "A big grey one, about the size of a ripe watermelon? Chunk of quartzite on one end?"

"No. I've never seen one."

"Pity. That was Griff's headstone. He was buried under this bush."

"Griff! What kind of dog was he?"

"A Bullmastiff. He had a brindle coat. Always stunk to high heaven from his daily trips down to the shore, but temperament? That dog had the best disposition of any dog I've ever known."

"How did he get down to the shore?"

"The steps, of course. Dr. Joseph made sure they weren't too steep. Griff was big but he was also very agile. You know, he only died a month before Allie did. He wasn't an old dog, maybe six or seven years old. He just collapsed and died one day at the edge of the bluff. Allie was heartbroken."

I wonder where the stone is now. Griff's bones will have long disintegrated into the earth, but his tombstone must still exist somewhere. I hope it has found its way to the shore again, that the waters of the bay will embrace it for millennia to come.

Alma releases her arm from mine, turns up her collar against the wind. "Allie almost had the baby on the day that Griff died," she says. "It must have been the stress of losing him. Martine came running to the house, babbling at first in French, she was so upset. The doctor was away at a meeting in Danton, and my mother couldn't come—she'd broken her leg in a tumble into our root cellar—and so I was the one who went back with Martine to the bluff.

"Allie was lying on the fainting couch in the library, groaning in pain. Miss Helen was sitting on a stool beside her, wringing out a cloth to place on her forehead. I was scared—I remember my stomach did a mighty flip—but I felt excited too. This was going to be my first birthing, completely on my own."

"But she didn't have the baby that day?"

"No. Not that day. The pains gradually gave way that day." Alma starts to shiver despite her fur cocoon. "Take me back home, Rianne," she says. "My blood's not rich enough anymore for this kind of weather."

As we walk back to the Jeep, she stops suddenly in the middle of the field. She looks back at the foundation. I imagine that in her mind the house has risen once again. "No, she didn't have it that day," Alma says. "But it did turn out that Allie was my very first delivery."

On Friday around midnight I'm still wide awake, curled up on the couch in the front room, reading *The French Lieutenant's Woman*. The fire is burning low, but I'm too lazy to get up and replenish it. I'm warm enough nestled under two of Nan's afghan blankets that are pulled tight to my chest.

My thoughts drift to Alma and our visit to the site of the Whitfield house earlier in the day. Alma didn't describe the birth of Alyda's baby; she got visibly tired as we made our way back to the vehicle, and I didn't ask her any more questions. I now have patience and time to spare for the telling of the story. Owen Sweeney's mother can choose to serve it entirely on her terms.

An arc of light from the outside sweeps the ceiling. Who would be calling this late at night? I peer out of the window and see a car idling in the driveway, snowflakes pirouetting in its headlights. It's not long before the driver turns off the engine and climbs out of the car. He hunches into the wind and makes a run for the front door. In a long and loping gait that's unmistakeable to me. My heart tips, balances itself again.

I meet Ben at the door. Snowflakes are melting on his lashes, and he has a big grin on his face. "I thought you might still be up," he says.

It is so good to see him again, to have an opportunity to dispel the negative aura of the time I went to visit him in Halifax. "I thought you couldn't come home this weekend. You said you had a ton of work to do."

"I know. But then Rick Exner said I could borrow his car, and I thought, to hell with it, I could always bring the papers home with me. Besides, it'll be another couple of months before I get back for the Christmas holidays. I wanted to see you."

He smells of wet snow and leather and Timberline. If only I had the courage to reach up to him, cup my hands to the lines of his bearded jaw. Give warmth to his lips. *He wanted to see me.*

"You took your chances coming out in this weather."

He shrugs. "I took my time. I've been on the road for over four hours. But now that I'm here, let's go out."

"In this weather?" I tighten the blankets about my shoulders.

"Just down to the lighthouse. It'll take five minutes at the most. The roads are okay now—the plow just went by."

"It's late. Come on in, and we'll get the fire going again."

"Not until you've seen the lighthouse. The light was on when I drove by. Hot pink on all that white snow. As a girl you'll appreciate it."

"You know you're a sexist—"

"Bastard. Thank you." He parks his hands on my shoulders and turns me around. "Go get your coat and your boots."

"What if someone—"

"Leave them a note. Go."

The Port Carlyle lighthouse is typical of the lighthouses that dot this stretch of the Fundy coast—an A-line structure with white clapboard siding and a red pagoda-style roof. Ben is right; the pink light that it casts over the snow-capped boulders by the water is beautiful—intense and eerie. Beyond the light, the ocean pulses, and quietly and efficiently suffocates every snowflake that tests its waters.

A pile of old lobster traps sits beside the lighthouse entrance, stacked neatly to create a wall that is about six feet high and at least four feet deep. Ben drives behind it and parks the car. He keeps the engine running. Nobody can see us now from the main road. He turns down the radio and Deep Purple's *Smoke on the Water* recedes into a hypnotic parade of bass notes.

Ben runs his hand along the dashboard of the Buick Electra, sets a pair of fuzzy dice that's hanging from the rear view mirror swinging. The car is a 1959 but it's in good condition. "She'll be mine by Christmas," he says. "Rick's going to sell her to me for a good price."

"You'll be able to come home more often."

"That's the plan."

He reaches over the bench seat and pulls a blanket to the front. It's a Hudson's Bay point blanket, made of thick wool. I smile as he tucks it around me.

The blanket warms most of my body, but my hands continue to ache from the cold. I didn't think to bring along gloves, and even though the car has heated up nicely, it will take time to stimulate the circulation in my hands. I first blow on them and then I start rubbing them vigorously—fingers over knuckles, resistance between palms, as if I'm washing them.

Ben says, "Give me your hands."

I turn toward him, hands clasped as if in prayer. He runs his hands up and down the length of mine, briskly, efficiently. Heat catches and disseminates with the pleasing steadiness of a well-fed fire.

And then he separates my hands so that the palms face up. He blows softly, creates the lightest of summer breezes on a welcoming plain. Starts to draw light circles in the palms with the pads of his thumbs.

I can't breathe.

"Better?" he says, raising his eyes to mine.

"Bastard."

"Agreed. Just don't tell me to stop."

He draws me closer to him and begins to unbutton my coat. Soon his hand lies beneath my sweater, flat against my ribcage, close to my heart. He holds it there lightly. Is he listening to my heartbeat? Is he gauging its response?

His hand rests on my breast now. Fierce. Protective. He kisses me, parts my lips with an urgent tongue, even though he must know that I am already lost. Somehow, his hands—*our* hands—tug and guide, where it is necessary. I gasp as the cold buckle of my belt sears the skin of my abdomen.

We have chosen frenzy. Years of renunciation give way to a force that drives heat and mercy into every cell of my body.

A dizzying high. The sweet surge of peace. Ben moans and collapses beside me. His hair forms a soft wing against the curve of my cheek. Condensation from the window trickles into my hair, seeks pathways into my skull. We lie there for a long time, the heat of Ben's body feeding mine. Fueling a perfect afterglow.

It's Ben who finally raises himself first. He draws me to him, arranges the blanket across our laps. I snuggle to his side and lay my head against his shoulder.

He takes my hand, bends down to kiss each fingertip. "Warm now?" he says.

"Getting there. Keep up the good work."

He laughs, kisses the top of my head.

"The way you felt about me," I say. "When did you know?"

"The day you climbed the lookout tree for me." He takes my hand again, weaves his fingers into mine. "And you?"

"The kiss on the island." The memory evokes a familiar tightening, deep in my abdomen.

"But you turned me down."

"I was scared. You were the only friend that ever meant anything to me. I couldn't stand the thought that it mightn't work out. That I could lose you."

"God, Ree. All those years . . ."

I blink away tears. Cherish the solid warmth of his body against mine. I've never been so happy in my entire life.

"All those years ahead of us," I say.

Chapter 34

Her cabined ample spirit
It fluttered and failed for breath
Tonight it doth inherit
The vasty hall of death

Thanksgiving Sunday is here.

Saturday turned out to be a frustrating day for me. I wanted to spend time alone with Ben, but we didn't get to see much of each other. I baked pies with Nan, went grocery shopping with Kaye, and typed up notes for my book. He prepared the labs for his students and helped his father with major snow removal. We did get out together in the evening, to see *The Godfather* with a group of his friends in Danton, and they accompanied us back to Ben's house for a late party. "We'll find time before I go back," he whispered to me, more than once. My body's still humming from Friday night.

This morning Ben did some automotive tinkering with Warren; now he's back to his school work, marking mid-term exams. Nan and I assembled an apple crisp to accompany the pies at tonight's big dinner. The turkey—a twenty-pounder—has started roasting in Nan's wood-fired stove. The ham will soon join two butternut squashes in Kaye's more modern unit.

The snow is almost gone today, vanquished by rising temperatures and a powerful sun. Gramps's outside thermometer displays an agreeable sixty-two degrees.

Ben gives me a kiss when I come by his house to pick up Lucy for a run. "I've booked a room for us tonight," he says. "At that new bed and breakfast in Bridgetown."

Lucy and I head down to the ocean, to the old pier. The tide is coming in and it laps at my runners, staining the toes a dark chocolate brown. I pick up a flat stone and send it skipping onto the water. Lucy bounds into the waves, undeterred by the fact that she can't retrieve the prize in this impossible game of fetch. Her appetite is insatiable. Ten stones. Eleven. Twelve. My jeans are soon patterned with her shake-downs.

After I've thrown my last stone for Lucy, I head back up the incline and park myself on a comfortable boulder. I feel calm and happy. I listen to the susurration of the wind in the spruces up the hill. Watch the fishing weir sway in the waters. Think of the night that I'm going to spend with Ben.

And then I see them.

I leap to my feet. It's not just Alyda that I see this time. Noah, stocky legs slightly planted apart, stands in profile at the end of the wharf, facing the ocean. I simply know that it is Noah. One arm is raised as he shields his eyes from the setting sun. The wind billows his shirt like a sail.

Alyda approaches him from behind, planting each of her steps carefully on the planks of the pier. She is wearing a cape of purple, the plum colour of the lupines that line the roadsides in late spring. The wide hood, slung below the shoulders, is trimmed in black. She stops once to hook some wind-blown strands behind one ear.

Noah now appears to sense her presence and he turns around to face her. He waits. She walks faster; there seems to be a sense of urgency, now that he has seen her. She stops about two feet away from him. I can't hear what they are saying, of course, but their bodies vibrate and pierce the air around them.

Suddenly, Alyda plants both palms flat on his chest and pushes hard. Noah, seemingly solid as an oak, takes one small step back and loses his balance. It is almost comical the way his arms seek to steady him, wind-milling in unison as he tries to find a foothold. He cannot steady himself and he falls back, his head striking one of the pilings with a sickening crunch.

My heart hammers its way into my throat. I stand stock-still, swallow painfully. There is silence.

Noah lies sprawled to the piling, his head tilted at an alarming angle, his arms spread-eagled and his legs positioned together as if he has been crucified. Blood seeps from the back of his head and trickles into the slick, green algae on the base of the post. Alyda is nowhere to be seen.

Heart thundering in my chest, I turn and scramble to reach the upper level of the shore. Lucy butts my hip several times and throws me off balance, but I regain steadiness and persevere. And when I reach my goal, and when I've once again harnessed my breath, I turn and look back. The bay is calm, the golden hues of the sunset still riding its waters. A pair of loons glides by the remains of the pier. A pier bereft of anyone or anything.

"Come on, Lucy," I say. My voice is shaky. "It's time to go home."

The dog, however, streaks away from me and runs along the upper stretch of the shore, as if she needs a final burst of energy. I step onto the pathway that leads up to the road and my breath hitches in my throat. A figure is standing in the shadows of a spruce by the path. A small figure, cloaked in deep purple, its face partially obscured by a hood trimmed in black. "Alyda?" I say. I take another step forward.

And stare directly into the emerald eyes of a young and terrified Alma.

I'm not sure which one of us is more startled. But before I can utter a word or make a move, Lucy barrels into me with the speed of a cannonball and knocks me flat to the ground. Grit-splattered and winded, I raise my head and scan the pathway. Alma is no longer there.

I'm disappointed but I know what to do. I embark on the path that will take me to the Port Carlyle Road, and to the Sweeney home.

To the Alma of now.

She sits in a velvet wing chair in her parlour, two dolls tucked to either side. I think they are Caroline and Lucinda.

"Noah," I say. The dolls regard me with unblinking calm.

Alma is silent for a long time. She combs Lucinda's hair with agitated fingers. "You know," she finally says. "You know what happened to Noah."

I nod.

"You have the gift."

"I don't know if I'd call it 'a gift.' And I was so sure at first that you were Alyda."

"It's not fully formed, then," she says. "I've had it at times, but it's never fully developed with me either. I'm a bit afraid of it, I think, and I fight it. If you don't want it, you can fight it too and make it go away."

"Let's talk about the gift another time, Mrs. Sweeney. Right now I need to know why you were angry at Noah."

Alma glances down at the dolls. "I'm not sure they should hear this," she says.

"They'll understand, won't they?"

She hesitates, then brings the dolls onto her lap and anchors them to her thin chest with her forearm. "I didn't mean to kill him," she says. "I was angry and tried to give him a shove, but I never expected to move him. He was huge, that young man. He must have weighed more than two hundred pounds."

"How did he lose his balance, then?"

"There was a loose plank on the pier. He stepped back on it and it shifted, and he lost his balance."

"But you left him there! And you didn't tell anybody."

"Yes, I left him there but I made sure he was dead. You might not have seen that part, Rianne. I went back to check on him."

"And you're sure that he was dead?"

A ghost of a smile. "You young people are so sheltered from death nowadays. I'd already seen at least a dozen bodies by the time Noah died. You *know.* You just know when the spirit has left the body."

"Why did you shove him? Why were you so angry with him?"

Alma bends her head to rearrange a ribbon on the top of Caroline's head. I can't see her face but I clearly hear the voice that says, "I was sure he was the one who raped Allie."

My entire body is trembling, helpless in the onslaught of outrage.

Despite Alyda's reservations about Noah, I hadn't viewed her as the possible victim of a sexual assault. It had made sense to me to presume that Caleb was the baby's father.

I'm not sure if I'm ready to hear more of this story, but Alma is clearly prepared to take it up again. I stay seated, brace myself.

"I went down to the shore for a walk," she says. "I remember the sky—it was that sharp blue that you get in the late summer, so blue it almost hurts your eyes.

"I walked quite a ways up the shore—a lot farther along than I'd usually go— and then I saw a man rounding the bluff. He came toward me, walking quite briskly, skidding at times on the shingle. I was getting a bit nervous, but then I was able to make out who it was—Noah Hamilton. He nodded in my direction as he passed me by, but he didn't say a word to me.

"It was such a beautiful day that I decided to keep going. And when I rounded the bend, there was Allie. Standing near the entrance to the oven there, supporting herself against a big rock. She was looking out to the ocean. I don't think she saw a thing, though. Her eyes—they were loaded with pain. Revulsion. She wouldn't look at me, but something caught my eye near her feet. I looked down at the hem of her skirt and saw a long thread of scarlet spiralling into the water between the stones. And this time she moved. She looked down at the blood-stained water and she didn't even flinch. She straightened her shoulders, stood tall. She looked me in the eye and said to me, "Help me to the stairs, Alma."

"May I get you a glass of water, Mrs. Sweeney?"

Alma startles at the sound of my voice. She has been sitting quietly for several minutes, eyes not focused on anything to be found in the room. "I'm fine, young lady. Just needed a minute. I'll get on with my story now.

"I don't know exactly what happened in that cave. But about two months after that day Allie came to me. She'd already set tongues flapping, because she'd pulled out of school and had gone to live with her Aunt Helen and Uncle Joseph. She needed my help, she said, to put an end to a pregnancy. That's exactly what she said—'put an end to a pregnancy.' I don't know if it was her upper-class English upbringing, or the way she was educated, but she often spoke in a formal way."

"And?"

"I couldn't help her." A pause. "No, that's not true. I did start making some preparations. I'd watched my mother concoct potions a couple of times, and I knew the right kinds of herbs to use to flush a fetus from its mother's womb. But I'd never done it before, and in the end I chickened out. I told Allie I couldn't do it."

"So she didn't go to your mother or to anyone else. She decided to give birth to Noah's baby."

Alma shakes her head. "I don't think it was Noah's baby."

"But you told me—"

"Oh, I thought at first it was his. I was sure it was, because I'd seen him coming from the direction of the cave that day. He was spying on Allie again, but I don't think he saw the man who . . . I think Noah came too late. If he'd seen someone in the cave with Allie, he would have told me when I had it out with him on that pier. I told him straight off that he'd made Allie pregnant. If I hadn't been so stuck on him as the culprit, I might have seen genuine shock on that mug of his. He just kept saying over and over again that he hadn't touched Allie." Alma shakes her head. "I called that poor boy a liar and I shoved him."

"Caleb." Who else could it be? I start to tremble again, sick at heart from the conclusion. It doesn't make any sense at all, however. He loved her, and she loved him.

Again Alma shakes her head. "Allie agreed to meet Caleb one last time in the oven, but I don't think he ever made it there. He left for Cape Breton the next day, because he'd gotten word that his mother was deathly ill. No, I think someone else went to that oven at the time they'd agreed on, someone who'd listened in on a conversation and heard about the arrangements."

And now I know. I see Caleb and Alyda on the porch of McCryder's store on that hot summer day, Caleb entreating Alyda to see him one last time before she moved to Halifax. And someone inside that store overhearing their conversation through the open door.

My entire body is suddenly rigid with shock. I'm forced to swallow bile before I can say the man's name: *Dugald Roy.*

Chapter 35

Lo! Here I lie with my dear son
All covered with cold clay
Hoping with joy to meet our Lord
At the eternal day

Mr. Sweeney appears at the entrance to the room. He directs a solicitous glance to his mother, and Alma meets his eyes, signals with hers that she is fine.

"Dugald Roy isn't in our graveyard," I say.

Mr. Sweeney remains standing by the doorway. "He's in the United Baptist graveyard in Danton," he says. "He died one week before Alyda did."

Anger can achieve a dizzying height in a short period of time, then plunge to earth and destroy itself at an incomprehensible speed. And so it is with me. The anger within me collapses, leaves me as helpless as a jellyfish abandoned by a receding tide. "He wasn't an old man, then. How did he die?"

"He was thirty-four. He'd just imported a herd of Scottish highland cattle to his farm and he was found in their paddock."

"He was gored to death?" The image of rough justice is a pleasing one to me.

Mr. Sweeney shakes his head. "He'd been trampled by the cattle, but that occurred after his death. Dr. Teasdale examined the body and found a fatal knife wound to the heart."

"He was *murdered*?" Rough justice suddenly assumes an even finer hue. "Did they find the murderer?"

"No. The police did interrogate Caleb Whitelaw extensively, because he was the last person to see him alive. Without witnesses, a weapon, or a motive, they couldn't lay any charges."

"*Caleb.*" This time, saying the name boosts my spirits. "He came back? He came back to Alyda?"

And now Alma assumes command of the story. "On the day Dugald Roy died Caleb came to the lab while Allie and I were working there. He just stood there and watched us—that's to say, he watched Allie the whole time. That young man—he was juddering, he was so in love with that girl. But maybe he was edgy too, now that I look back on things.

"And Allie, she finished stripping the juice from a bowlful of roots and then she said to me, 'I need to go out for a bit, Alma. Will you be all right with that?' 'Of course,' I said. 'Take all the time you need.'

"She was gone maybe two hours, and I ran to meet her as soon as I saw her coming out of the maple grove. Alone. I could see she was swaying, holding onto the underside of that swollen belly of hers. I was sure she was going to drop that baby right then and there, but I got her into bed and she was all right, thank the Lord. For the time being, I guess you'd say."

I feel battered now, stranded by the tide of emotions that have swept over me. "You're telling me—"

"We cannot provide proof, Miss Tavener. And we do not know if Alyda was at the scene. But Mother and I choose to believe that Caleb Whitelaw avenged Alyda." Mr. Sweeney's lips bow upwards. "A calculated thrust to the heart killed Roy. A fitting end for the son-of-a-bitch, wouldn't you say?"

Leaves skirl in the hallway, and a stiff breeze ushers in the scent of burning wood fires as Mr. Sweeney leaves the house. Alma has asked him to gather some gourds from the garden for Nan. I pull the zipper to my jacket, prepare to leave as well. Nan and Kaye will need help with the final preparations for dinner.

"You can't go yet," Alma says. "You need to hear the rest of the story."

She appears calm and composed, and so I decide to stay. First, I fetch a glass of water for her from the kitchen and set it on the small table beside her. I settle myself on the edge of the couch again. The dolls are nowhere to be seen now. We sit quietly for a few minutes, listening to the restless leaves, to the sporadic gunfire pops of the furnace. She takes a sip from the glass of water and then she continues her story.

"Allie turned sick after she had the baby. I was afraid she had childbirth fever even though I'd done everything properly. I'd already helped my mother with so many births. And when Dr. Joseph finally arrived—you see, he'd been called away that morning to an accident at the old mill—he examined Allie and said everything was in good order. Mother and baby, a healthy son, were fine. He even said to me, 'Well done, Alma.'

"I stayed with Allie because Dr. Joseph was called away yet again and I knew something wasn't right with her. She didn't have a fever, but she *acted* as if she did. Her eyes were bright but they weren't focused, and she rambled on at times about Caleb and her dead father. She wouldn't let me put the baby to her breast, and Mrs. Helen and I became afraid for the baby too. I boiled some water and cooled it and gave it to the baby with an eye dropper, and all the while Mrs. Helen and I waited for Dr. Joseph to come back."

"And when he did?"

"He had no more luck than we had. Allie had gone crazy. She kept saying, 'They're here. The horses are here.' And when I asked her which horses, she said, 'The white ones, of course. Can't you see them, Alma?'"

Forerunners. A shiver scurries up my spine. Alyda was seeing the same forerunners of death that had appeared on the shore the night her father died.

Alma is shaking her head in memory. "She continued to ignore the baby," she says, "and while we weren't looking she slipped outside into a pouring rain, got an axe from the woodhouse, and cut down two small birch trees close to the house. She was exhausted by then and she insisted that Dr. Joseph trim the leaves and nail the trunks together in the shape of a cross. She hauled the cross right into the parlour and the next day she took a paring knife and started etching the name of her father into the horizontal bar. Dr. Joseph tried at first to take the knife away from her, but she was like a wild thing. She even pointed it straight at him and warned him away." Alma shakes her head again. "This to the uncle she loved with heart and soul."

"And the baby?"

"The poor babe, he cried non-stop. I wasn't surprised, truth be told, there was so much upheaval in that house. We were *all* at our wit's end. I bound Allie's breasts; she must have been in a lot of pain with the milk letting down, but she didn't show it. By then Dr. Joseph had gone back to the village and gotten a double-ended feeder bottle with milk from one of his other maternity patients, and the baby accepted it."

"And Alyda?"

"She woke up early the next morning, calm as a Christian martyr. There wasn't a hint of craziness in her eyes anymore. She was taking the cross to the graveyard, she told me, and she was going to talk to her father and tell him about his grandson. Then we both went over to the cradle, and she kissed the wee sleeping boy on his head and said to me, "Isn't he beautiful, Alma? He's perfect. And no one must ever blame him . . ."

Alma swallows twice, holding fingers to her throat. "I wanted to go with her," she continued, "but she said no, that Mrs. Helen might not hear the baby and I needed to be there when he woke up. She was fine again. I swear she was fine. How was I to know that she planned to take the cross to the island?"

"You couldn't know, Mrs. Sweeney. And it mightn't have been part of her original plan. At that time fishing boats were rarely tied up to the old pier anymore; almost everyone was using the new one. It could be that Alyda saw the boat from her vantage point in the graveyard and made a spur-of-the-moment decision to take the cross over to the island."

"Do you think that's what happened?" Alma sits quietly; her eyes have begun to focus on their surroundings again.

"I do. Everything may have come down to an error in judgement.

Isle of Haute seems deceptively close to the shore at times. Alyda might have thought it would be a quick and easy journey."

Alma doesn't respond but she is clearly more at ease. She sips from the glass of water, watching me over its rim.

"Tell me about the baby," I say. "He seemed to be healthy and he'd taken to the bottle. Why did he die?"

"Die?" Alma is clearly taken aback. "Who said the baby died?"

"The baby is in the graveyard, buried with Alyda." I say it gently, but emphatically. I worry that Alma is at a tipping point again.

"No. I told you, the baby took the bottle. And Dr. Joseph went back to the village for more milk."

"It states clearly on Alyda's gravestone that her baby is buried there. *And she bade her young babe join her.* It has to be her baby."

Alma's face is something to behold. Confusion gives way to enlightenment and then to a look of consummate satisfaction. "It does mention the babe, doesn't it? And I went back to the graveyard one day to see that for myself. There was such a thick fence of rose bushes around that gravestone, but I cut them all down. Yes, I did."

Alma appears spent, as if in the recounting of this event she has once again expended the energy of that night. I'm afraid that I've lost her. I give her a few minutes to compose herself and then I say gently, "The baby."

"Oh, yes. The baby." She takes a sip of water from the glass, traces a finger around its rim. "Dr. Joseph was very clever. He wrote that epitaph and he saw to it that everyone would *think* that the baby had died."

The statement is outrageous, but I can see that Alma is still with me. One foot firmly planted in the past, but the other one just as solidly placed in the present. She responds to the shock on my face by leaving her chair and joining me on the couch. She places one hand on my arm. In a soft, reassuring voice she says, "Don't worry; it was all just a ruse. I made sure that the baby stayed safe. I took it away."

I look into her eyes. "Owen," I breathe. "The baby was Owen."

Alma squeezes my wrist. She smiles.

Chapter 36

Beyond this veil of tears
There is a life above
Unmeasured by the flight of time
And all that life is love

Ben is leaning against the trunk of the old maple at the foot of the Sweeney's driveway when I emerge from the house.

"I've got to go back to the city," he says, pulling himself out of his slouch. "Rick just called, and he needs his car back tonight."

I place one cautious foot in front of the other as I descend the steps. My mind is reeling from Alma's story, still trying to assimilate other details that it learned after the revelation of Owen Sweeney's origins. "You can't even stay for Thanksgiving dinner?"

"No. I've got maybe two hours at the most."

"But I've got so much to tell you." Adrenaline surges, displaces the daze. Now I need to tell the story; he cannot deny me this.

"Let's start walking, then," he says.

Memories. Commonplace, pulse-quickening. Reinforcing, deceiving.

They often play tricks on us. In many cases, however, we are the guiding force behind memory's twists and permutations, its inclination to enhance or to diminish the importance of an event. Does it matter? No, it doesn't. Human frailty and human resilience—these qualities constitute the lifeblood of a story.

The shadows are lengthening in the graveyard when Ben and I seat ourselves on the old stone bench. All vestiges of the snow are gone. A blue jay sits in the spruce above us. For a short time it does its imitation of a rusty clothesline pulley but then it falls quiet.

"Caleb came back," Ben says, taking my hand. "That's important to you."

"It is. He came back to the mountain shortly before the baby was born. We also know that he saw Alyda in Halifax soon after she started university. She suspected then that she was pregnant and she sent him away. Alma doesn't know how much she told him at that time, because Dugald Roy had threatened her, had convinced her if she told anyone the truth he would hurt Sibley. And Alma only learned about that threat when Alyda was delirious after the birth of the baby."

"The sick—" Ben says, and he unconsciously clenches his fist around my hand until I protest. "I wondered why Joseph Teasdale didn't do anything, given his standing in the community." He massages my hand in an absent-minded manner. "His word and Alyda's word would have to have counted against Dugald Roy. It must have been tough for the doctor, sensing there was something very wrong and not being able to do anything about it."

"But Alyda finally did. She must have broken down and told Caleb the truth when he came back to the mountain that spring. It's hard to imagine her complicity in a murder, but she couldn't trust Dugald Roy and she wanted to make sure that her baby and Sibley would never be in danger."

Ben continues to stroke my hand. "There's something I don't understand," he says. "Why didn't Helen and Joseph Teasdale keep Owen? It sounds like they couldn't have a child of their own. The way you've described them, they'd have wanted to keep the son of Allie, regardless of the circumstances of his birth."

"They did. They did want him. Alma and Leonard took him up to

Ontario right after Alyda died, and Joseph Teasdale invented the baby's death so that no one could ever place a claim on the child. As soon as he was able to close down his lab business, he and Helen moved to Toronto, ostensibly to get better medical care for Helen. They couldn't take Owen right away, because they had to settle into their new home first and Helen's leg was still quite bad. Unfortunately, poor Helen got worse—she even contracted TB and was in a sanatorium for several months—and by then both she and Joseph could see that Owen had bonded with Alma. And Alma with Owen. He was two years old by then, and they couldn't stand the thought of taking him away from her."

"And that was the end of their involvement with him?"

"No. Helen died about eight years after the birth of Owen, but Joseph stayed in touch with Alma until his death sometime in the early 1930s. In fact, he sent a generous cheque to her every year at Christmas. By the way, he stayed in Toronto and became the director of the sanatorium in which Helen had been hospitalized."

"And Caleb Whitelaw? What happened to him?"

I squeeze Ben's hand. "You're going to like this part of the story. About a year after Alyda's death, Dr. Teasdale offered Caleb a job as an orderly in the sanatorium. Caleb went to Toronto, saved his money for years, and then with some financial assistance from Dr. Teasdale bought a small beef cattle farm near Guelph."

"Did he ever get married?"

"That's another interesting story. Do you remember the Teasdales' housekeeper, Martine d'Entremont? Well, she had a niece, Madeleine, and she and Sibley both went up to Toronto to study nursing. When they graduated, Dr. Teasdale got them jobs in the sanatorium. Sibley ended up marrying one of the staff doctors there, an Alexander Westcott, and Madeleine d'Entremont married a patient, a man by the name of Fred Agnew. He was a tailor in his father's business. Sibley and Madeleine both stopped working once they were married, of course."

I've been recounting the story at a great speed, mindful of the fact that we don't have much time, and I pause for a moment to catch my breath.

Ben soon makes me take it up again. "Okay," he says. "Where does Caleb come in?"

"At a Christmas dinner in the home of Dr. Teasdale in 1921. He met up with a visiting Madeleine and her three children. A *widowed* Madeleine."

"Caleb must have been—"

"Almost forty-eight at the time. He and Madeleine got married, and he became the father of those kids."

"Go on."

"That's all there is, unfortunately. Alma got all that information from Dr. Teasdale, so that story ends with his death."

"Let's get back to Mr. Sweeney, then. How long has he known that he's the son of Alyda?"

"He doesn't know." Ben glances sharply at me. "Alma has agonized about this since the day of his birth."

"I'll bet he knows."

"It all depends on what Alma's told him about his past. As far as she can remember, she's never told him that Alyda's baby survived. Without that information he can't piece everything together."

"Telling the story to you must have been a release for her." Ben tightens his arm around my shoulder. "None of us gets to go through life unscathed. Alma made a huge sacrifice, and Alyda—well, at least we know that in the last year of her life she lived with people who cared about her and who took good care of her. She was *loved.*"

I pull away from him. How can he downplay this? How can he even begin to rationalize the horror of what happened to her? But when I meet his gaze, I find that his eyes—that piercing blue of an autumn sky—are clear and honest. He believes every word he has spoken; he's not just trying to make me feel better. My heart steadies, eases itself into the comforting rhythm of comprehension. Sometimes even the living can be at peace.

Ben steals a glance at his watch. "I've got to go now," he says. "I promised Rick I'd have his car back by six."

"You go ahead." I feel drained of all energy and I know my legs will be no match for his. "I'm going to stay here."

His brow stitches in concern. "You'll be okay?"

I smile. "I'll be okay. I'm going to sit here for a while and then I'm going over to have a chat with Alyda."

He holds me then and kisses me, a prolonged kiss that is supremely satisfying. "That'll have to keep us until Christmas," he says.

I smile at him, squeeze his hand. "Oh, I think I'll find a way back into the city before then."

I watch him as he strides among the gravestones to the lichgate; it is only when he reaches it that I turn my attention to Alyda's grave. I crave to see her standing there, in the distance. Acknowledging me.

She does better than that. She's in my head again and this time she speaks to me. One word, in a whisper: *Ben.*

I return my attention to the lichgate. Ben has already gone through it. My Ben. A touchstone of all that has been good in my life.

He loves me. I need to tell him that I love him too. I jump up from the bench and I call out, "Ben! Wait!" I start running. Leaves scatter in the mayhem produced by my grinding feet.

"Ben!" I shout. My heart pounds, strengthens to the task. "Wait for me!"

Epilogue

June 3, 1973

An old Boston whaler plies an endless sea of sunlit and shimmering gems. In its wake follows an entourage of gulls—eternally hopeful. The man with his hand on the tiller is an able seaman, and he delivers our small group safely to the shores of Isle Haute.

I am the first one to leave the boat, my feet protesting their immersion in the frigid waters. Ben and Jack soon join me. Together we raise arms to receive the cross that Gramps and Mr. Sweeney slide to us across the side of the boat. It is a rough cross, fashioned from two birches, and it possesses heft in its grace and length. The bark scours my palms as I grasp it and shift it forward, away from the boat and onto the stony spit of the shore.

Gramps and Mr. Sweeney join us; Mr. Sweeney transports a shovel and my camera equipment, and Gramps joins the procession of the cross. We carry the cross inland several hundred yards to an area where patches of soil and a few resilient plants flank the shore. Jack and Ben take turns digging a hole; together we ease the cross into its new home. Groundwater rapidly displaces to the surface of the hole. Or perhaps it is saltwater from the wily, encroaching ocean beneath the island's surface. We collect rocks of all shapes and sizes and buttress the base of the cross. Somehow our choices and placements tumble into the form of a cairn.

The cross rises to nine feet. I look up at it, but the sun strikes it in such a way as to obscure part of the message on the crossbar. I shift slightly, lean my head against Ben's sun-warmed shoulder, and there it is, on the arm of the cross that is to my left: *Captain Elias Teasdale May 21, 1851–November 28, 1895.* The right arm of the cross bears the inscription: *Beloved daughter Alyda January 16, 1880–June 3, 1897.*

The birch cross lists slightly—the mast of a schooner that is heeling from the wind. It will disintegrate over time. Salt water and seashore organisms will claw into its base; the winds from the bay will show no mercy and they will deface it by stripping it of its elegant bark.

By then it will have served its purpose and another memorial will stand beside it. The son of the monument maker who created Adelaide Montgomery's tombstone is hard at work carving another cross of grey and everlasting stone with the names of the captain and his first-born daughter. He's already completed another commission, a cenotaph that will honour Captain Elias Teasdale and all the mariners and fishermen of Port Carlyle who have lost their lives at sea. It will be unveiled next week, next to the new wharf in the village, during the opening ceremony of the bicentennial celebrations.

A week after that ceremony, Ben and I will be married in St. Luke's church. The reception will take place at the Teasdale Inn, of course. Our honeymoon plans include two special visits. In our "souped-up" Buick we'll drive down to Boston first and meet redheaded Colonel Gregory Langkow for the first time. Afterwards, we'll head up to Toronto to attend the ninety-first birthday celebration of Sibley Westcott. Caleb Whitelaw died in his sleep in 1954 at the age of seventy-nine. His wife, Madeleine, died ten years later. Aside from arthritic aches and pains Sibley is healthy, and her son tells me she still has "all of her marbles." Segments of Alyda's story will continue to grow.

I mount my camera on the tripod and adjust the settings. The sun has slipped behind a bank of clouds—the lighting conditions are perfect. I'll take more than one roll of film. Alma and Sibley will have long shots and close-ups and views of every conceivable angle of the memorial and its surroundings.

Mr. Sweeney looks to the cross. A prominent vein in his temple pulses rhythmically, then quickens. Does he know he is looking at the names of his mother and his maternal grandfather? I may never know.

We all carry secrets to our graves.

And so we should.

AUTHOR'S NOTE

ISLE HAUTE. ISLE of Haute. Ile de Haute. One and the same—imposing, mysterious and real—it rises in eye's reach of at least a dozen communities strung along the Fundy Shore of Kings and Annapolis counties in Nova Scotia. The Port Carlyle of my story is a composite of these old fishing and shipbuilding villages, and Danton is a fusion of some of the larger towns that dot the floor of the Annapolis Valley.

Some historical events are mentioned in my work of fiction, or woven into it as part of the story. The sinking of the steamer *Atlantic* off the coast of Halifax occurred to huge loss of life in 1873. Accounts of the number of passengers on board and the number of fatalities vary. My figures were taken from the Nova Scotian Heritage Interpretation Park website. It is interesting to note that during the sinking of *Titanic* in 1912 a policy of "women and children first" was formally implemented.

A wedding did take place on Isle Haute on September 8, 1881. Ida Marion Card, daughter of Nelson Card, the island's lighthouse keeper, married John Wesley Patterson of Margaretsville.

Captain Joshua Slocum, who was born in the village of Mount Hanley on the North Mountain, was the first man to sail solo around the world. He travelled more than 46,000 miles in his sloop oyster boat, the *Spray*, leaving the Halifax area on July 3, 1895 and returning more than three years later to Newport, Rhode Island on June 27, 1898. He published an account of his epic voyage, *Sailing Around the World*, in 1899. Alyda makes reference to his achievement in 1896; it is, therefore, an intentional anachronism.

Finally, many readers will be familiar with the story of the notorious Ideal Maternity Home in East Chester. If you wish to know more about this chapter in Canadian history, Bette L. Cahill's book, *Butterbox Babies*, is an excellent source.

The epitaphs at the beginning of each chapter can all be found in old burial grounds of Nova Scotia, the majority of them in Kings and Annapolis counties. Alyda Teasdale's inscription is derived in part from the gravesite of Alice Murdoch, which is located in the Riverside Cemetery in Bridgetown, Annapolis County. Alice died on February 16, 1869 at the age of fifteen:

Allie here is softly sleeping
Her brief pilgrimage is o'er
But we sorrow for her only
As not lost but gone before

The *Sleep little baby sleep* epitaph can be found in the Wesleyan Methodist pioneer cemetery in Pickering, Ontario, and was transcribed in its entirety from the gravestone of Mary E, infant daughter of W./ M.A. Gimblet, who died on March 23, 1873, aged fourteen months.

The remaining epitaphs in the body of the text are pure products of my imagination or amalgams I have created after "haunting" dozens of heritage graveyards during the past two decades.

The methods that Rianne and Ben employ to clean gravestones and read their inscriptions would have been sanctioned in the 1970s. Chalk, flour, talcum powder and shaving cream have all been used in the past to highlight inscriptions, but many current experts contend that these substances can lead to the disintegration of stone. Chalk is now considered an abrasive, and flour contains yeast, which is a medium for lichen growth. Kodak Photo-Flo is still acceptable for cleaning headstones; it is a neutral detergent and will not cause the formation of stone-degrading salts and other chemicals. If you are using a different cleansing agent, ensure that it is not acidic or alkaline-based.

Wooden scrapers and soft brushes with natural bristles can be used if the stone is stable; always avoid abrasives such as steel wool (Scotchbrite, Brillo, SOS pads, etc). Water is the least aggressive cleaning agent, of course, and it is always easy to set up mirrors to supply the needed contrast for picture taking. Consult a conservationist if you are not certain how to proceed.

The heritage cemeteries of our continent are beautiful and sacred settings. If curiosity or a need for serenity leads you to them, please step softly among the tombstones and listen carefully to the spirits.

CPSIA information can be obtained at www.ICGtesting.com
Printed in the USA
LVOW130020010513

331662LV00001B/2/P

9 781475 968811